LOVE LIES WEEPING

Recent Titles by Anne Herries from Severn House

The English Civil War Series

LOVERS AND ENEMIES
LOVE LIES WEEPING

A WICKED WENCH
MILADY'S REVENGE
MY LADY, MY LOVE

Writing as Linda Sole

The Country House Series
GIVE ME TOMORROW
A BRIGHT NEW DAY

The London Series
BRIDGET
KATHY
AMY

THE TIES THAT BIND
THE BONDS THAT BREAK
THE HEARTS THAT HOLD

THE ROSE ARCH
A CORNISH ROSE
A ROSE IN WINTER

FLAME CHILD
A SONG FOR ATHENA

LOVE LIES WEEPING

Anne Herries

This first world edition published in Great Britain 2006 by
SEVERN HOUSE PUBLISHERS LTD of
9–15 High Street, Sutton, Surrey SM1 1DF.
This first world edition published in the USA 2006 by
SEVERN HOUSE PUBLISHERS INC of
595 Madison Avenue, New York, N.Y. 10022.

British Library Cataloguing in Publication Data

Herries, Anne
Love lies weeping
1. Great Britain - History - Civil War, 1642-1649 - Fiction
2. Historical fiction
3. Love stories
I. Title
823.9'14 [F]

ISBN-10 : 0-7278-6358-4 (cased)
0-7278-9167-7 (paper)
ISBN-13: 9780-7278-6358-4 (cased)

Typeset by Palimpsest Book Production Ltd.,
Polmont, Stirlingshire, Scotland.
Printed and bound in Great Britain by
MPG Books Ltd., Bodmin, Cornwall.

One

Love is a growing full or constant light; And his first minute after noon is night . . . The words of John Donne's lovely poem came to mind as Elizabeth stared out into the darkness, listening to the wind howling about the old house. In the park tall trees were bending before the force of the summer storm, but the rain had stopped and the moon had sailed out from behind the clouds, shedding its benign light over the gardens of Bellingham Hall. The moonlight called to her for she was restless, vaguely unhappy after a quarrel with her cousin Sarah earlier that afternoon.

Elizabeth had not often quarrelled with her cousin since coming to live at the Hall, for she was well aware that she lived on her uncle's charity, and in these uncertain times there was little money to spare even in this house. Her own father had been but a younger son and had carelessly married a pretty woman of no fortune. Elspeth Bellingham had died giving birth to a stillborn son five years after her daughter was born. Henry Bellingham had survived her for nine years, but he had become a hopeless drunkard and wasted what estate he had, leaving his daughter penniless when he succumbed to a fever. That had been three years previously and he had died before the country was split apart by the bloody civil war that had been raging since then.

Elizabeth shivered, trying to dismiss these disturbing thoughts. Her uncle was now her guardian, but she did not know where he was for he had left his home a week or so earlier, intending to join the King.

'I believe the war is coming to its close,' he had told his

daughter and niece before he left. 'I fear that it does not go well for His Majesty, and I must offer my sword in the battle that lies ahead. If we allow Cromwell to win now we shall be ruined, all those who have given so much for His Majesty's cause.'

Elizabeth suspected that her uncle had given more than he could truly afford for the cause. Much of the silver, which had once stood on the huge, carved buffet in the Great Hall, had gone, as had the more expensive of the family jewels. Sir Jacob Bellingham had given generously, believing that the King would win and that he would be rewarded with honours and pensions, but if the cause were lost so too would be his fortune.

It was over money that the cousins had quarrelled, for Sarah had ordered several lengths of costly silk for her new gowns, which Elizabeth believed was wasteful in their present circumstances. They seldom entertained and Sarah already had more gowns than she could possibly wear. She had told her cousin so and met with sulks and frowns.

'My father would not begrudge me a few gowns,' Sarah said. 'Just because you practice economy to the point of penny-pinching, cousin, it does not mean that I must do the same.'

'I have no choice,' Elizabeth reminded her. 'Your father has been generous in giving me a home, but I must dress myself on the small pension my maternal grandfather was able to leave me. I would not wish to be a burden to my uncle.'

'You think too much of money,' Sarah said with a curl of scorn. She was a beautiful girl with hair the colour of moon-gold and eyes that were sometimes blue sometimes green, depending on her mood. They narrowed as she looked at her younger cousin, who had brown hair and a darker complexion, becoming almost catlike as they glinted with spite. 'It does not matter what you look like for you have no prospects. Father wishes me to be well dressed, and if all goes as well as he hopes, we shall join the King in Oxford this winter. I must be dressed as befits my station for otherwise I shall not make a good marriage.'

'I think you would marry well whatever you wore,' Elizabeth said, but the words did not please her cousin and so she withdrew to the small back parlour, which was cold because there was no fire lit for her. She had spent her time reading her favourite poets for she found they gave her solace when her heart was heavy, but for some reason she was restless this night.

She looked out of the window again, feeling tempted to go outside. It could not be colder than this parlour, which struck chill on the warmest of days. Now that the storm had died down, it might be pleasant to walk. It was after all still the month of June.

Having made up her mind, she fetched her cloak from the hall and let herself out through a door at the back of the house. She could hear Sarah playing on her virginals and knew that she would not be missed for at least half an hour or so. By that time Sarah might have become bored with her own company and come in search of her cousin, but that gave Elizabeth time enough for a stroll about the gardens to ease her restlessness.

She avoided the formal parterre, heading for the rose arbour, which was her favourite place. The roses had been blooming for a week or two and the heady fragrance was wonderful, and it was far enough from the house that she could be sure that Sarah would not venture to seek her out. Her cousin avoided walking whenever she could, unless she had good reason – which usually meant that a certain gentleman had come to call. As yet Sir Jacob was unaware of the unspoken understanding between his daughter and Kit Elbury.

However, Elizabeth had seen the excitement in her cousin's eyes the last time he'd visited and guessed that they had chosen a secluded meeting-place to exchange kisses and promises, but of course she had said nothing to anyone. It was not for her to bring her cousin's behaviour to her uncle's attention. She thought he might be well pleased with the match, for though Kester Elbury had a reputation for boldness and a love of gambling and drinking, he was a staunch supporter of His Majesty and would inherit a title one day.

Just as she had suspected, it was a pleasant evening now that the sudden storm had passed and warmer than in her cheerless parlour. She found the sheltered bench that was situated at the heart of the rose arbour and sat down, breathing in the sweet perfume of roses and the other scents that had become sharper after the rain. She picked a perfect red bud and held it to her nose, enjoying its sweetness. It was very peaceful here and she often sought sanctuary from her cousin in this secret place . . .

Hearing a noise, she sighed and looked over her shoulder. Someone was nearby, which meant that her cousin had likely decided to seek her out sooner than she had expected, for the servants would not have ventured out at this hour. Most of them were afraid of the dark and the evil spirits they believed haunted the dark hours.

Elizabeth rose to her feet, looking towards the sounds of movement – footsteps and rustling. She frowned as she heard them again. They sounded odd, too heavy to be her cousin, she judged. It was like someone stumbling . . . Her ears pricked as she heard a muffled curse. Someone was definitely quite close to her and from what she'd just heard it was probably a man. She knew that a battle had been held a few leagues from Bellingham House some days earlier, and her quick mind told her that the man she could hear stumbling and cursing in the shrubbery was likely to be wounded. But was he a Royalist or a Roundhead?

Either way, she thought philosophically, if he was badly wounded he was not likely to be a danger to her and he might need help. Her conscience told her that she ought to offer it even if he were one of Cromwell's Ironsides, those fearsome troops that had inflicted defeat after defeat on the King's armies of late.

As she waited, holding her breath, she saw the man emerge

into a clear patch of garden, and the merciless moonlight told her that he had indeed suffered a terrible wound to his arm, which was hanging uselessly by his side. He lurched unsteadily towards her, his face waxen, the sleeve of his coat heavily stained with blood. Elizabeth moved to intercept him for she guessed that he was close to collapse and presented no danger to her whatever his persuasion.

'Are you badly hurt, sir?'

The man looked at her, seeming startled and for a moment afraid, as if he wondered if she would call someone and have him taken prisoner.

'I need . . .' his voice was harsh, his lips cracked and swollen. 'Water . . . just a little water, mistress, and I shall trouble you no more.'

'You are near exhausted,' Elizabeth said, venturing nearer now that she was sure he meant her no harm. 'Were you wounded in the battle?'

'At Naseby,' he said. 'They beat us . . . it was a disaster for His Majesty. I fear there is little hope for our cause now, though we shall fight on to the last.'

'You are a Royalist,' Elizabeth said and drew a sigh of relief. 'We too are loyal in this house. Will you come up to the house and allow me to treat your hurts?'

'You are kind, mistress,' he said. 'I am Rupert Saunders – Captain of His Majesty's cavalry – but I would not bring harm to you. They may search for me for I know they follow. I carry important papers for His Majesty. I must get to France – and yet my wound troubles me sorely. If I do not find rest and ease I may fail in my task and then all hope will be truly lost.'

Elizabeth moved closer to him, seeing that he was young and good to look upon. 'Let me help you, sir. I am not a skilled surgeon but I have tended my father's hurts in the past and have some experience. I may be able to help you a little, though I could not extract a ball if it has entered your shoulder.'

'It was but a sword thrust, and a mere flesh wound,'

Rupert said with a grimace. 'If you could wash the wound and bind it tightly I think I should do, mistress. Perhaps a little brandy to cleanse it . . .'

'Of course. Whatever we have is at your disposal. I know that my uncle would wish it so for he has helped other wounded cavaliers.'

'Is your uncle at home, mistress?'

'I am Elizabeth Bellingham,' she told him. 'There is only my cousin Sarah, her companion, Mistress Furnley, myself and the servants at the Hall at present, sir.'

'Are your servants loyal?' he asked. 'They will not betray you for helping me?'

'They are all loyal,' Elizabeth told him confidently, for she knew it to be true. 'Come, sir, lean on me. I fear you have lost much blood and have become weak for it.'

'You are kind, Mistress Elizabeth,' he said and smiled at her. Elizabeth's heart missed a beat as she put an arm about his waist, encouraging him to lean on her. There was something in his manner that had drawn her to him instantly. 'You will find me a heavy burden . . .'

'No heavier than my father and I have put him to bed many times.'

'Your father is not here either?'

'My father has been dead these past three years, sir.'

Rupert nodded but made no comment. In truth his arm was paining him and he was feeling light-headed from loss of blood so that he hardly knew what he said or did. He was not sure that he could have gone much further without this young woman's help.

It was a slow return to the house, and Elizabeth found him heavier to support than she had expected, but she bore up as well as she could, and, as they entered the house, she was relieved to be greeted by Mistress Furnley. The companion exclaimed in distress as she realized what was going on and hurried to assist her.

'What have we here, Elizabeth?'

'This gentleman has been hurt, Mistress Furnley,' Elizabeth

said. 'He is an acquaintance of my uncle and I am certain Sir Jacob would wish us to offer him all the assistance we can.' It was a small lie to claim acquaintance but would ensure the companion's compliance.

'Yes, of course. We must do what we can. Now then, sir, lean on me if you please. I am stronger than Elizabeth, and she is near exhausted. If you will just follow me I shall take you into the library and there we can treat your wounds.'

'Thank you, ma'am. You are kind . . .' Rupert said and stumbled, feeling faint. 'Forgive me . . .'

'He has lost a great deal of blood,' Elizabeth said. 'We must bind his wound as quickly as possible and then he should go to bed.'

'Is that wise?' Mistress Furnley raised her brows. 'The longer he stays here the more risk of discovery . . .'

'I shall leave before morning,' Rupert said. 'As soon as . . .' His words trailed off and he swayed, nearly out on his feet.

Between them, Elizabeth and Mistress Furnley managed to get him to the settle in the library. He was not able to sit upright alone, so Elizabeth held him while Mistress Furnley looked at his wound.

'I shall have to slit the sleeve of his coat,' she told Elizabeth. 'But he is much the same size as your uncle and we may furnish him with a new one before he leaves.'

'He cannot leave until he has recovered his strength,' Elizabeth said. 'If he is still unwell in the morning we must keep him here – in the priest's hole if need be.'

'I did not know of its existence,' Mistress Furnley said with a slight frown. 'It might be that we shall have to hide him for a day or so if he is unable to leave, but even to lodge him in your uncle's secret room would be dangerous. If he should be discovered . . .' It could lead to danger for them all for the penalty might be harsh.

'I am sure he would not be,' Elizabeth said. 'This house was my father's home and built by his great grandfather. They were Catholics then and when Queen Elizabeth came to the throne it was thought better to keep their religion private. They often had a priest to stay, and on several occasions it was necessary to hide him – for Sir Frederick was once accused of being involved in a popish plot against the Queen. It was not true and he escaped with payment of a heavy fine, but my father knew of the secret room and he told me.'

'Very well, Elizabeth. I must confess I should be sorry to turn such a fine gentleman away in distress. Watch over him now and I shall fetch water and bandages to bind him . . .' As she turned away, she saw that Sarah had come into the library. 'Sarah, help your cousin if you will. I shall not be long.'

'What is going on?' Sarah asked, looking at the stranger curiously. 'Who is he and how came he here?'

'His name is Rupert Saunders,' Elizabeth said. 'He tells me he was wounded at a big battle at Naseby and I found him in the garden. He asked only for water and I brought him here to bind his wounds.'

'He is quite handsome,' Sarah said, her interest aroused. 'His hair is almost red in the candlelight. Is there anything I can do?'

'Pour a little of your father's Brandywine into a glass,' Elizabeth said. 'It will do to cleanse the wound and he might like to drink a little for the pain.'

Sarah went over to the long refectory table, where a tray with wine cups and wine was always kept at the ready. She poured a generous measure into one of the cups and brought it back to them. As she did so Rupert stirred, his eyes opening. She bent over him, offering the cup, putting it to his lips.

'Drink a little of this, sir,' she said and smiled.

'An angel . . .' Rupert murmured and choked as he swallowed some of the fiery spirit. 'Have I died and gone to Heaven?'

Sarah laughed naughtily, enchanted by the compliment. 'Oh no, sir. You are at Bellingham Hall, my father's house. We are going to take care of you and make you well again.'

'Leave him to me now, Sarah,' Mistress Furnley said as she returned bearing linen and salves, and followed by a servant girl carrying a bowl and a jug filled with warm water. 'Both of you should go. Mallie and I can manage very well now.'

Sarah gave her a sulky look, but moved a few steps away from him. She knew that her companion needed to remove the gentleman's shirt and it was clearly improper for either her or Elizabeth to watch, but she was curious and she refused to leave the room. Besides, she was not so innocent that she had not seen a man without his shirt before. A secret smile touched her lips as she recalled the day she had lain in the arms of the man she loved, for that day she had all but given him her virginity, drawing back only at the last.

'We need to make up a bed for him in the chamber next to Sir Jacob's,' Elizabeth said who had also ignored the companion's advice. 'The secret room is connected to my uncle's and it will be quick and easy to move him if we should be subjected to a search.'

'No one would dare to force their way in here,' Sarah said. 'My father is the magistrate and he would have them arrested.'

Mistress Furnley gave her a speaking look but Elizabeth did not answer. She slipped from the room, knowing that Sarah found it impossible to come to terms with what had happened to them because of the war. She did not understand that her father had almost beggared himself to help the King, nor did she realize that if Cromwell's men should demand entrance they had no means of denying them.

They could only hope that water, the cleansing of his wound and a night's rest would enable the cavalier to continue his journey as he wished for Mistress Furnley was right. It would be dangerous to harbour a fugitive too long.

Rupert jerked awake as the door opened and a young woman entered bearing a tray containing a bowl of broth and a cup of wine. He was slightly disappointed to see it was the dark one, and wondered if he had imagined the blonde angel who had given him a sip of Brandywine before he fainted.

'Good afternoon, sir,' Elizabeth said and smiled. She was an attractive girl with her soft brown hair and hazel eyes, but she could not compare in looks with her cousin. 'Are you feeling any better? You woke earlier but were in such pain that Mistress Furnley gave you something to make you sleep. It was nothing harmful but only to ease your pain.'

'I feel rested,' Rupert told her. His arm was painful but he had felt pain before and this was no worse. 'I should not be here for I could bring harm to you. Every hour I stay here makes it more likely that soldiers will come to search your house.'

'If they do we shall hide you in the priest's hole,' Elizabeth said. 'It is rather small so we prefer that you stay here until you are ready to leave – but if soldiers come we shall hide you.'

'You risk much for a stranger, mistress?'

'You are one of us,' Elizabeth replied. 'My uncle has near ruined himself to help the King's cause, sir. I think he would be very angry if we turned you away and you were taken prisoner, especially as you carry important letters to France.'

'Did I tell you that?' Rupert frowned at his own carelessness. 'I must have been wandering in my wits. It is dangerous knowledge, mistress.'

'I have told no one else,' Elizabeth said. 'Indeed, I have told the servants and my cousin that they should deny all knowledge of you should you be taken. I found you and brought you here. Should I be exposed, I shall accept the blame.'

'I could not allow you to come to harm for my sake,' Rupert said and attempted to roll over. The pain from his arm made him grimace, but he managed to swing his legs over the edge of the bed. 'If you could call someone to help me dress, I shall be on my way. You have already done far too much for me.'

'Indeed, you will not, sir,' Elizabeth said. 'You will eat this good broth I have brought you and rest. If you still wish to leave – and if you can manage to ride – you shall leave tonight when it is dark. Even your enemies will not search for you at night. We must make it as hard for them to follow you as possible, so when you leave someone will accompany you for part of the way. They will be searching for one man alone, not two.'

'You speak like a general. It is a pity we did not have you on our side at Naseby,' Rupert said and laughed softly. 'I dare say you are right, Mistress Elizabeth. But I shall leave this evening, I promise you.'

'If you are strong enough I shall not try to stop you. I have no desire to cause trouble for my uncle or his people.' She gestured him back into bed and deposited the tray across his lap. 'Are you able to feed yourself or do you wish me to help you?'

'Damn it! I shall feed myself,' Rupert said. 'Fortunately, it was my left arm that was injured. I am not quite helpless.'

'I am pleased to hear it,' Elizabeth said. 'And now I shall . . .' She broke off as the door opened and her cousin entered. Sarah was wearing a gown of green silk, one of her best, her hair dressed in ringlets pinned high on her head and allowed to fall to the exquisite lace band that covered her shoulders. 'Here is my cousin, Sarah Bellingham.'

'So I did not imagine it,' Rupert said. 'The beautiful angel of my dreams is real.'

Sarah laughed, her eyes bright with amusement. The cavalier looked much better this morning. Not quite as handsome as Kit perhaps, but certainly a man to be appreciated, especially since he was not wearing a shirt and she could see his strong, muscled shoulders and chest.

'I am not an angel,' she told him. 'Merely a girl come to inquire how you do?'

'I am very much better for seeing you,' Rupert told her. 'Will you not stay with me a while and tell me about yourself?'

'I am going now,' Elizabeth warned. 'Rupert needs to rest . . .'

'I shall follow in a moment,' Sarah said, her lips pouting prettily. 'If it was proper for you to be here alone with him, what harm can there be in my sitting with Mr Saunders for a while?'

'Sir Rupert,' he said with a twinkle in his eye. 'I was knighted for services to His Majesty, Miss Bellingham.'

'Oh, do call me Sarah,' she said and came closer to the bed. 'I do not like to be called Miss Bellingham; it sounds so old.'

'Very well, Miss Sarah,' Rupert said. He looked at her keenly. She was perhaps the most beautiful girl he had ever seen and he was aware of a fierce desire to take her in his arms and kiss her . . . to do much more if it were possible and his arm did not burn like the very devil. 'I should be glad of a few moments of your time if you could spare it . . .'

Elizabeth left them alone together. It was easy to see that the cavalier was smitten by her cousin and no surprise, for few young gentlemen could resist her when she set out to charm them. Kit Elbury had not been to see them for some months now, and she had no doubt that Sarah was bored. She would enjoy a light flirtation with the cavalier, and after all he was in no condition to seduce her.

Besides, it was not for her to attempt to censure her cousin's behaviour – that must be for her companion. She would say nothing to Mistress Furnley, but if it should come to her attention she would certainly have something to say concerning Sarah's behaviour.

She did not guess that the moment she had left, Sarah had sat upon the stranger's bed and begun to flirt with him, nor that by so doing the girl had begun something that would cause them all much pain.

By that evening, Rupert was sufficiently rested to insist that he must leave them. Elizabeth had ordered that some of her uncle's clothes be given to him, also a good horse from their stables since his had gone lame a few leagues away from the Hall, which was why he had stumbled into their garden.

'I am sorry that you must leave us so soon,' Elizabeth told him as she gave him food and a flask of Brandywine for his journey. 'I wish you God speed, sir, and hope that you have a fair wind for France. Our groom, Tam Jackson, will accompany from the estate and set you on the right road.'

'You have been more than kind – all of you,' Rupert said and looked beyond her as if he hoped to see Sarah. 'Give my regards to Mistress Sarah and the good lady Furnley if you will. My arm feels much better for her ministrations, and I have no fever, which might not have been the case if she had not helped me. Perhaps one day I may return and thank you all properly.'

'We did only as much as we would for any man in such circumstances,' Elizabeth replied, but she smiled because he was attractive and a gentleman, and she liked him. Indeed, his smile set her heart racing like the wind and she wished that she might keep him for much longer. But that would be foolish and dangerous, for his sake and their own. 'God be with you, sir.'

'And with you, mistress.'

Rupert realized that he owed his recovery to her for had she not taken him in he might have fallen into a faint and died that first night. He leaned forward, kissing her impulsively on the cheek. Elizabeth blushed, her hand going to her cheek as she saw the light of laughter in his eyes.

'Farewell. I must go . . .'

Elizabeth watched him ride away with Tam, who was her own groom. She knew that Tam would lay down his life for her if need be and she had no qualms about his loyalty as they were swallowed up by the darkness. Only when she could no longer see them did she turn to go into the house.

She touched her fingertips to the place where his lips had brushed her cheek and smiled. If she were foolish she would think that her heart was lost to the cavalier who had stayed with them so briefly, but she knew that would be very silly. It was probable that she would never see him again, and if he did return one day she knew it was likely that it would be Sarah who drew him here.

Going back to her own room, Elizabeth told herself that it was but a fleeting moment in a lifetime. It was unlikely that she would ever see Sir Rupert Saunders again, and if she were sensible she would forget that he had touched her girl's heart.

The troop of Roundhead cavalry rode up to the house the next day. Their colonel, a stern-faced man, who announced himself as Sir John Bacon, asked if they had seen a fugitive in the grounds of Bellingham Hall. Mistress Furnley motioned to Elizabeth to keep behind her and then demanded to know what he meant by his accusations.

'You must know we are a household of women alone,' she said in a sharp tone, for despite her lack of fortune she was the daughter of a gentleman. 'Sir Jacob is from home on personal business, and it would be most improper for us to harbour a fugitive without his permission.'

'Indeed, ma'am,' Colonel Bacon said. His cheeks reddened as her eyes swept over him haughtily, but he stuck to his guns and demanded to be allowed to search the house. 'We have information that the fellow we seek was seen to come in this direction, and his horse was found wandering at the edge of this estate.'

'I do not care where the beast was found,' Mistress Furnley said, drawing herself up to her full height and looking down her long nose. 'Either you may take the word of a lady or you may search the house – but be warned, sir. If your men do any damage you will hear from Sir Jacob when he returns.'

Colonel Bacon looked at her warily. Sir Jacob was an important landowner, and though it was suspected that he supported the King it was not known for certain. He would clearly be well advised to go cautiously in this matter.

'If you will permit the search, it shall be conducted in a respectful manner, ma'am.'

'Then we shall not deny you,' Mistress Furnley said. 'It

will be best if only two of your men conduct the search within the house, though they may go where they please outside, and Miss Elizabeth Bellingham and I will each accompany one of your officers.'

Colonel Bacon agreed to her ultimatum, though he was well within his rights to commandeer the house itself if he believed that it belonged to a traitor or that they had been harbouring a spy.

'As you wish, ma'am. Miss Elizabeth Bellingham may accompany me and you may take my lieutenant with you. However, should we discover that you have lied to us it will go ill with you.'

'I am not in the habit of lying, sir.'

Mistress Furnley gave Elizabeth a warning look as they went their separate ways. However, they both knew that nothing remained of Rupert Saunders's brief visit, and their servants were all staunch Royalists, loyal to a man, woman and child. The Roundheads would gain nothing from them but sullen looks and stubborn silence.

Colonel Bacon lost little time in searching the house. He looked in wooden hutches, trunks and under beds, also behind curtains, but Elizabeth's serene manner was enough to tell him that he would find nothing, and within half an hour he and his men were ready to depart.

'Sir Jacob has a fine house,' he told Elizabeth as he pulled on his leather gauntlets before preparing to leave. 'I hope you ladies will forgive this intrusion, for I was merely doing my duty.' He glanced at Sarah, who had come out to join her cousin and companion on the steps of the veranda, and for a moment his jaw dropped. It was the first time he had seen her and he was struck by her beauty. 'Sir Jacob and I were slightly acquainted before the war. Perhaps afterwards . . .' He nodded his head to Mistress Furnley. 'Forgive me, ma'am.'

She inclined her head regally but gave no indication that his request for forgiveness had been granted. The three women stood together outside the house until the soldiers had disappeared from sight.

'Well, let us hope that we have seen the last of them,' Mistress Furnley said. 'They have searched the house and the outbuildings and found nothing. We must pray that they are satisfied.'

'What a horrid man,' Sarah said and shivered. 'Did you see the way he looked at me? I declare that I felt sick to my stomach for it and I pray that we shall not see that creature here again.'

'We were lucky that he did no more than look at any of us,' Elizabeth said. 'We were helpless had he decided to make us his prisoners – as he would have done if he had found evidence to place his fugitive here.'

'I am glad that he did not find anything,' Sarah said. 'I pray that Sir Rupert has gone beyond that creature.'

'He would get to the coast if he could,' Elizabeth said, 'and from there to France.'

'His father is Sir John Saunders,' Sarah informed her as they went into the house. 'They have quite a large estate I believe. Sir John has taken no part in the war. He was angry when Rupert took up for the King, but they have made up their quarrel since.' A little smile played over her lips as she remembered the time she had sat with him, laughing and teasing and being teased in return.

'Would that be the Saunders family from somewhere near St Ives in Cambridgeshire?' Mistress Furnley inquired. 'I once knew Lady Saunders. I believe the family is quite wealthy, though I had heard nothing of them for years. I think there was one son and a daughter, but of course there may be more by now.'

'Oh no, Rupert has only a sister – married to Lord Nicolas Mortimer,' Sarah said with an airy wave of her hand. 'He is his father's heir.'

'You seem to have discovered much in the short time you were with him,' her companion said, giving her a hard look.

'People tell me things,' Sarah said and smiled confidently. Sir Rupert had told her that she was beautiful and a naughty minx, and she had found his manners charming. 'I cannot help it if he liked me, can I?' She received another dark look from her companion but ignored it.

'I do wish this war would be over,' Elizabeth said. 'Too many men have died because of it . . .'

She turned away to stare out of the parlour window. Her thoughts were with Sir Rupert, for she could not help being anxious. She might never know if he had got safely to France, but she would remember him in her prayers. She wondered if his sister was worrying about him too and wished that she knew her so that she might send her word, but perhaps that might be dangerous.

She could only hope that one day she might see him again.

Lady Caroline Mortimer saw her husband ride up to the house from the upper storey windows. She gave a glad cry and ran down the stairs to meet him for it was some months since she had seen him.

'Nicolas!' she cried and was swept up into his arms as he kissed her hungrily. 'I heard of the battle and I have been on thorns until you should come home.'

'I am well as you see,' he said, looking intently into her face. 'And you, my love? Are you well – and the boy?'

'Your nephew is thriving,' she replied. 'Indeed, he grows more like your brother every day, Nicolas.' Her lovely green eyes clouded as she thought of her husband's brother, Harry, for a moment. He had died fighting for the King, and the girl he had so cruelly seduced and deserted, her cousin Mercy, had also died, giving birth to his son, whom she now cared for.

'I hope he will not be quite as Harry was,' Nicolas said, a slight frown of disapproval wrinkling his brow. The brothers had taken different sides in the conflict for they had disagreed on many things. Harry had been a gambler and a seducer, and Nicolas would never quite forgive him for the hurt he had inflicted on Caroline through her cousin. Mercy had been innocent and Harry had taken cruel advantage of her. 'Do your parents keep well, my love?'

'My father has not been so stout of late,' Caroline said looking anxious. 'Mother is well, as always – but Father . . .' She shook her head. 'I think he worries about my brother Rupert.'

Sir John Saunders had been against his son taking up for the King. He had thought His Majesty wrong to bring war to his own people, and for a time he had quarrelled with his neighbour and friend, Lord Mortimer, over it. Tragedy and sorrow had brought them together at the last, but Sir John sorely missed the man who had died in his arms so many months previously.

'I am certain that he must,' Nicolas agreed, his harsh features softening as he gazed down at her. 'I know that your brother escaped the battlefield at Naseby, Caroline. It is my understanding that he was carrying letters to France. We must pray that he got safely away, for I would not have anything happen to him despite that we fight on opposite sides.'

Caroline raised her anxious gaze to his face. 'Is this war almost done?' she asked. 'It has claimed the lives of your father and brother, Mercy too, in a way. How many more of those we love must be sacrificed to this cruel conflict?'

'Cromwell says that we have broken them this last time,' Nicolas said. 'Naseby was a heavy defeat for the King. He will retreat to Oxford if he can, but I think this time he will not be allowed to regroup his armies. Cromwell can scent victory and I believe the end will not be long in coming. Perhaps then some sense can be won from this affair. I would see the King brought to a realization of his wrongdoing, but I believe he should be restored to the throne – with limitations to his power. That is the best way forward for this country and must be the prayer of all just men.'

'I pray you are right,' Caroline said. 'And yet I fear for my brother if His Majesty is defeated . . .' Indeed, she was torn between the two sides for her husband was on one, her brother on the other.

'Those who surrender their sword will be treated with

respect,' Nicolas told her. 'This war has been bitter and many have suffered death or ruin. Men of right thinking must want an end to conflict between our people. We must do what we can to rebuild the country, to make peace. I have a little influence with Cromwell, my dearest. You may trust me to use it to buy a pardon for Rupert if need be.'

'Thank you,' Caroline said and smiled at him. She held her hand out to him. 'Come, you must take some wine and food, and then I shall take you to see your nephew. He has grown mightily since you were here . . .'

'I am eager to see him.' He smiled at his wife lovingly. As yet they had no children of their own, but he had spent little enough time at home with her for they had been married only a few months and he had been fighting for much of that time.

Caroline took his hand, drawing him through to the parlour where her parents were sitting. 'How long can you stay this time?'

'Perhaps a week,' Nicolas told her. 'But I believe the time is coming when we shall be able to keep each other company more often, my love. I would that it happens sooner than later for I weary of this conflict.'

Caroline nodded. She had been lonely without him, even though she had chosen to remain with her parents until the war was over. Yet she had known it must be so when they married, and she had accepted the bargain she had made without complaint. Nicolas was a man of conscience and he would do what he considered his duty for as long as need be.

She must wait in patience and perhaps one day he would be free to return to her and his own estate. And, if fortune smiled on them, this time she might be with child when he left her. She had her nephew Harry, and she loved him dearly, but the wish of her heart was to give her beloved husband a son and heir.

Two

Elizabeth paused on the threshold of her uncle's library. He was standing by the refectory table, a letter in his hand, his coat open, neckcloth uncharacteristically awry, and she sensed that he was deeply disturbed about something.

'Forgive me for bothering you, uncle,' she apologized as he looked at her, his brow furrowed. 'I came to return this book you were so kind as to let me borrow.' She deposited a beautiful leather-bound copy of a play by Master William Shakespeare on the table. 'I shall go at once.'

'No, no, child,' Sir Jacob said, beckoning her forward. 'You are always welcome to borrow my books, as you well know. If I frown it is not you that troubles me.'

'You are anxious, sir?'

'I have many burdens, Elizabeth. However, this news I have just received is far worse than the contemplation of my debts. I had hoped that once the war was effectively over – for we have had nothing but defeat in the two years since Naseby – His Majesty might settle with his enemies.' He sighed heavily. 'As you know, he took refuge with the Scots in May of last year, but they made him a prisoner. And on settlement of their debts, they gave him up to Parliament. I had hopes they would come to terms but it seems that the Army has become discontented and set up what they call the General Council of the Army. They have captured His Majesty and I believe that they mean to use him for their own ends, and if that be so I fear for his safety.'

It was now the spring of 1647 and many months had passed since the terrible defeat at Naseby had robbed the

King of any true hope of victory in the war, and yet they had still hoped that somehow it would all come right.

'No, uncle!' Elizabeth was shocked for she had hoped as he did, that there might be an honourable settlement, which the King could accept. 'If anything should happen to the King . . .'

'All our hopes would be at an end,' Sir Jacob said, and his hand trembled. He looked so grave, so close to despair, that Elizabeth was moved. 'Should that be the final outcome . . .' He broke off shaking his head. 'I am near ruined, niece. My only hope of salvation is for His Majesty to return to the throne. That way I might be granted recompense to enable me to save my estate.'

'I am so sorry, sir,' Elizabeth said. The winter after Naseby had been a hard one for the Royalists, and when the news came that even Montrose's army had been defeated, he had aged almost overnight. In the succeeding months she had watched him change from a strong, energetic man into a pale shadow of his former self. 'If there is anything I may do to help you, I shall not hesitate to do it.'

'I fear that soon I shall not be able to support any of us in the manner to which we are accustomed,' he said. 'I have just heard that I am to be fined for taking part in the battle of Naseby. To pay the fine I shall have to sell everything that is left to me, which is little enough. Our only hope is for Sarah to marry well, but I fear that most of our friends are in no better case. In truth I can see no escape for us.'

'I am so sorry, uncle.' His sorrow was hers for he had been kind to her and she knew what this must cost him.

'If I receive a fair offer for the house there may be enough for us to find a cottage somewhere . . .' His shoulders sagged. 'Forgive me for having brought us to this shame, Elizabeth. I do not know how we shall bear it. My family has owned this house since it was first built a hundred years ago. It will be a wrench to leave it, but I see no other way.'

'You are not at fault, sir. His Majesty demanded much of

you and you gave it. How could you know that the cause would be lost?'

'I believed in His Majesty's divine right to rule as he saw fit,' her uncle confessed. 'I gave everything in good faith – but it seems I was a blind fool. My folly hath ruined us.'

'Perhaps something will yet happen to save us,' Elizabeth said, though in her heart she did not believe it. Most of their friends would have a hard enough task to save their own estates for the fines being demanded were stringent.

'Perhaps,' Sir Jacob agreed. 'Run along now, Elizabeth. I have a letter to write. I have received an offer to buy what remains of the estate and I must see what the gentleman is prepared to pay.'

Elizabeth made him a respectful curtsey and left the library. She felt apprehensive of the future for if her uncle was reduced to poverty, how could she expect him to provide for her as well as his daughter? She would willingly have done anything he asked of her, for he had been generous enough since her father died, but she was helpless. Her small income hardly paid for her clothes and she did not know how she would live once the house was sold. It was unlikely that she would marry, and it would be difficult to find work. She had been raised as a lady and would be frowned on if she applied for a situation as a servant – and yet what else could she do?

It was just possible that she might find a post as a companion to a lady. Elizabeth had no idea how she ought to apply for such a situation, so decided she would ask Mistress Furnley. That lady had worked in the households of more than one titled person. Perhaps she could tell Elizabeth how best to go on.

'It will not be easy for you, Elizabeth,' Mistress Furnley told her when she at last managed to find her alone later that day. 'Even if you were lucky enough to secure a position, you will find it very different to the life you have led here. It is a hard life and I could not recommend it.'

'Yes, I understand that,' Elizabeth said. She had expected the older woman to discourage her, but was not daunted.

'However, I may not have a choice. If my uncle is forced to sell the estate, I cannot expect him to continue to support me.'

'No, I can see that,' Mistress Furnley replied and looked thoughtful. 'If that were to happen I should need to seek a new position myself – but I confess that I do not know if I shall find one to my liking. It was not so difficult before the war, but Sir Jacob is not the only gentleman to find himself in trouble. Most Royalist households will be much reduced in fortune.'

Elizabeth looked at her in concern. 'What will you do if you cannot find what you want?'

'I would have to go to live with my married sister for a while. Her house is small and crowded with children, and I would be required to look after them in return for my board, but at least I would have a roof over my head.'

'I am glad you have somewhere to go.'

'Do you not have any relatives that would take you in?' Mistress Furnley looked concerned for her. She had grown fond of Elizabeth who was always polite and considerate, which was not always the case with Sarah.

'No. My mother was an only child and my grandparents are dead.'

Mistress Furnley clicked her tongue. 'I shall give you the names of two ladies who might take you on, though I warn you that both have sharp tongues. I should not care to work for either of them myself, but because they can be unkind there is often a position of some sort in their households.'

Elizabeth thanked her. It was not a pleasant prospect, but she did not wish to be a burden to her uncle. She made up her mind to write to both ladies as soon as possible. To be companion to a spiteful old lady was a sorry fate, but there was nothing else she could do if her uncle could no longer support her.

'I cannot believe it!' Sarah said, coming unannounced into Elizabeth's bedchamber as she was finishing dressing some eleven days later. 'Father has just told me that he is selling the estate – this house, everything. We are to move into a tiny cottage in the village with only two bedrooms!'

'At least you will have a roof over your head,' Elizabeth said. It might not be the case for her. She had received no replies to her letters and dreaded the day she must leave her uncle's protection.

'Father says that I must share my room with you,' Sarah said in a tone of disgust. 'I told him I could not think of such a thing, but he insists there is no other way. Mistress Furnley has already given notice to leave us next week. How am I to manage in such a hovel? Oh, it is too much to ask of me.' She stared at Elizabeth, her eyes filling with tears. 'Why did Kit not come back and take me away? At least I should have a decent house to live in then.'

'You have had no word of him in all this time?'

'You know I have not,' Sarah said and gave a sob of despair. 'I think he must have been killed in the fighting for he swore to return to me as soon as he could, but he has not come. And now father tells me we are ruined and must live in a tumbledown cottage.'

Elizabeth wished that she might have offered her cousin an alternative or some hope of her lover, but until she could find a situation there was no word of comfort she could offer.

'And that isn't the worst of it,' Sarah went on, clearly too angry to need a reply. 'Do you know who is buying the estate? Do not trouble yourself to answer for you could never guess it. I do not know how Father could do this to me!'

'Your father must sell to the highest bidder, Sarah.'

'But it is that awful man who came here once. The one who insisted on searching the house after Sir Rupert had gone.'

Elizabeth stared at her in surprise. 'Can you mean Colonel Bacon?'

'Yes, that is exactly who I mean!' Sarah's eyes glinted with temper. 'How could Father do it?'

'I suppose the colonel offered a fair price.'

'That is not all,' Sarah fumed. 'The impertinence of it! He implied that he would be willing to allow my father to stay on as his dependant if I married him. Imagine that, Elizabeth! It makes my stomach turn.'

Elizabeth stared at her in horror, for she had disliked Colonel Bacon too. 'Your father would not force you to take him?'

'No, which means we must sell to him and live in a hovel,' she repeated. 'There must be others who would buy.' Sarah shuddered. 'I do not forget the way he stared at me that day – as if he had stripped away my clothes and saw me naked.'

'Sarah!' Elizabeth was shocked by her cousin's words. 'You should not say such things, dearest.'

Sarah tossed her head impatiently. 'And who is to censure me? My father has forfeited any claim to respect from me. He was such a fool! To throw away everything for a lost cause with no thought for me. What was he about, tell me that? Why should I have to suffer for his stupidity? It is unfair to me – and I have told him so.'

'You should not have spoken so unkindly to your father,' Elizabeth remonstrated. 'He suffers enough as it is . . .' The sound of a single shot from somewhere below them made her eyes widen in horror. What could it mean? 'Uncle . . .'

Elizabeth saw the stunned expression in her cousin's eyes but did not stay to comfort her. Instinct told her what she would find when she reached the library, but Mistress Furnley was there before her. She prevented Elizabeth from entering.

'My uncle. I must go to him!'

'No! It is better that you do not see, Elizabeth. There is nothing you can do for him. Sir Jacob has killed himself.'

'Oh no,' the shock made Elizabeth's voice fail and her knees felt weak. Tears pricked at her eyes, spilling over to trickle down her cheeks. 'That is terrible. I knew he was close to despair but . . .'

She cut off the words that would betray her cousin. Elizabeth had no doubt that Sarah's thoughtless accusations had driven Sir Jacob to take his life, but her pride would not let her shame her cousin before Mistress Furnley.

'What are we to do?' she asked, feeling lost and upset. 'My poor uncle.'

'A servant is with him. I shall send for the Reverend Bull and hear what he has to say. Your uncle's man of law will have to be informed. He will know what must be done.'

'Yes, of course. I shall write a note and ask Mr Simpson to call. One of the grooms may take it to his house in Kimbolten, asking him to visit us as soon as he may arrange it.'

Elizabeth was glad that she had something practical to do for her mind was reeling from the horror of what had happened. She turned to see her cousin watching her from a distance, an expression of shocked dismay on her face.

'Sarah,' she said and moved towards her, intending to comfort her.

'No! Pray do not say anything,' Sarah whispered. She turned and fled from them, leaving the house through a side-door.

'Should I go after her?' Elizabeth asked of Mistress Furnley.

'I think it best to let her come to terms with her own guilt.' She nodded as Elizabeth's eyes questioned. 'I overheard what she said to her father earlier. She is a selfish little wretch, but I believe she cared for him. She will take his death hard. It is best to leave her to herself for a while, Elizabeth. If you try to comfort her, she will turn on you in her grief.'

'Then I shall wait until she comes to me.'

Elizabeth felt the sting of tears. She had cared for her uncle, who had been a good man and had done what he thought right. It was hard to come to terms with his cruel death, and to know what the future held for them now.

'I do not like to leave you like this,' Mistress Furnley said one morning some days later. Her trunks were in the process of being brought down and loaded onto the carrier's wagon.

'Your cousin is behaving as if none of this concerns her, leaving everything to you. I feel I should stay to help you, but my sister is expecting me and if I do not go now the carrier cannot take me for another month.'

'Of course you must go,' Elizabeth said, for she knew that her cousin's companion could not afford to travel by coach. 'We have servants to look after us, and Mr Simpson says that there will be sufficient to purchase the cottage for Sarah and I to live in, and leave us a small income. We are fortunate to have so much and such good friends.'

'You are a brave, good girl,' the older woman said. 'Sarah is fortunate to have you, though I do not believe she realizes it.'

'My cousin is in shock,' Elizabeth said. 'She has scarcely left her bedroom since my uncle's . . . accident.'

They had decided to tell the Vicar that it had been an accident, which had occurred while Sir Jacob was cleaning his pistol. The Reverend Bull had looked sceptical, as well he might for the evidence pointed elsewhere, but he was a kindly man, and he had agreed that his former patron should be buried in Holy Ground to save the family more grief.

Sarah had not attended her father's funeral, pleading sickness. Elizabeth and Mistress Furnley had gone to join the other mourners, and they had invited Sir Jacob's closest friends and neighbours to return for refreshment. Many of them had been shocked, offering help with the estate, for it was not yet known that it had been sold. It would be common knowledge soon of course, as Colonel Bacon was due to take over the house in five days' time.

Mistress Furnley nodded, though clearly reluctant to abandon the girls. 'Well, I suppose you have good neighbours, and Mr Simpson will be pleased to act for you – but be careful, my dear. I did not like that man when he came here to search for Sir Rupert. He may try to take advantage of you now that you are alone. I speak of Colonel Bacon, of course.'

'It is not me he admires,' Elizabeth said frankly. 'Had he

asked for me I would have taken him for my uncle's sake, but it is Sarah he wants – and she is in no danger from him for she detests the sight of him.'

'Do not be so ready to sacrifice yourself for others,' Mistress Furnley advised with a little frown. 'You may find a man that you can love or at least respect one day. At least your cousin needs you for the moment, and you may stay with her instead of selling yourself into bondage.'

'I had no reply from either lady,' Elizabeth said and sighed. 'I dare say I was not thought suitable. Besides, I could not leave my cousin at the moment. Sarah will not face up to things and I worry for her sake.'

'Well, the ladies I told you of were far from young and may both be dead for all I know,' Mistress Furnley said with a smile. 'I see my things are stowed. I must not keep the carrier waiting. You will write to me, tell me how you go on?'

'Yes, of course,' Elizabeth promised. 'I hope we shall meet again one day. As for me, I am going to inspect the cottage Mr Simpson has purchased for us this morning. He says that it's furnished and we shall need only our personal belongings. Indeed, everything else was sold with the estate.'

Mistress Furnley nodded and went out, leaving Elizabeth alone in the parlour. She hesitated for a moment, feeling a little bereft and then went upstairs to her cousin's room, knocking at the door.

'May I come in, Sarah?'

'If you wish.' Sarah was sitting before an oak side-table brushing her lovely hair, which fell in soft waves to the small of her back. She looked at Elizabeth, her eyes still slightly red from weeping, but her expression was angry, defiant. 'It was Father's own fault. Perhaps I should not have said those things to him, but he ruined himself.'

'Yes, that is true,' Elizabeth agreed for there was no point in trying to make her cousin see the other side of it. 'However, it is done and cannot be changed. I am going to inspect the cottage, to see what needs to be repaired before we move in. I think it best if we make a start on our packing, for we shall not want to be here when the new owner arrives.'

'I cannot stand him!' She pouted sulkily. 'If Father had sold to someone else they might have allowed us to stay for a while.'

'Colonel Bacon would allow you to stay as his wife, Sarah.'

'I would rather die,' Sarah declared, her eyes flashing with temper. 'Anything would be better than that!'

'Then we must move before he comes,' Elizabeth said. 'Will you come with me to the cottage?'

'You will know what needs doing better than I,' Sarah said carelessly. She had no intention of doing anything and thought it her cousin's duty. 'But I shall call Eliza and ask her to help me make a start with my packing.'

'Very well,' Elizabeth replied. 'Well, I should . . .' She broke off as there was a knock at the door and her cousin asked the maid to enter.

'Begging your pardon, Mistress Sarah,' the girl said. 'But there is a gentleman downstairs to see you.'

Sarah looked apprehensive. 'If it is one of our neighbours come to poke his nose in – or worse Colonel Bacon – I am not well enough to leave my room.'

'It isn't the colonel, mistress – nor a neighbour.' The girl's cheeks flushed. ''Tis a fine young gentleman by the name of Sir Rupert Saunders – and he did ask for you, Mistress Sarah.'

'Sir Rupert!' Sarah threw her brush down, rising hastily to her feet. She lifted her hand mirror to look at herself, pinching her cheeks to give them colour. The news had surprised her for it was nearly two years since they had taken him in and nursed him, and she had thought he had forgotten her. 'Oh, I look a fright. What shall I do, Elizabeth?'

'You look beautiful as always, if a little tired – but he will know of Sir Jacob's death and he will understand.'

'If he has come to see me . . .' Sarah's eyes glowed suddenly. She was alive with new hope. 'It must mean he likes me, mustn't it?'

'Yes. I think he likes you very well, Sarah.'

Her cousin lifted her head, a little smile on her lips. 'Go and look at the cottage if you must,' she said. 'Perhaps we shall not need it, but it will look well to appear to accept our lot . . .'

'Sarah . . .'

Elizabeth watched as her cousin flounced out of the room. She could only guess what was in Sarah's mind, but she did not like her own thoughts. She did not believe that Sarah was in love with Sir Rupert, for she still dreamed that Kit Elbury would come back to her. It was so long now since they had heard from him that like Sarah, Elizabeth believed he must be dead or fled to France – but if he were in France he would surely have written to the girl he loved?

Perhaps Sarah truly believed he was dead. If so, she might think that her only chance of escaping the poverty she dreaded was to marry a man she liked – a man whose father was still rich enough to pay any fines that might be levied against his son.

'You look beautiful,' Rupert said, his eyes dwelling on Sarah's lovely face, noticing the shadows beneath her eyes, the grief she could not hide. 'I was so sorry to hear of your father's death. It was a tragic ending to the life of a good man.'

'My dearest father beggared himself in the King's cause,' Sarah said, gazing up at him with eyes that shimmered like green crystals. 'He was forced to sell his estate to someone – a man he must have felt his enemy. It was Colonel Bacon who came to search the house after you had left us.' She shuddered, her face pale, her eyes sending him a look of such appeal that Rupert, already half in love with her, was caught fast. 'I hate him. He has my father's estate and now he wants me. I am afraid of him. I shall never marry him, not ever! Elizabeth and I must live in a tiny cottage for it is all that we can afford – but I would rather die than give myself to that man.'

'*You* married to a canting Puritan?' Rupert was appalled

at the idea. 'That would be an abomination, Sarah. It must not happen. It shall not happen.'

'No, it shall not,' she said, stopping to pick a rose, for they had gone outside to walk in the gardens. She held it to her nose, inhaling the delicate perfume and then offered it to him. 'I must manage as best I can – though it is hardly fitting for I have no companion other than my cousin, and Elizabeth is not yet nineteen, a year my junior. I must be strong for her sake, for she has nothing, no other family. If I desert her she will be forced to seek menial work, and I would not have her sunk so low.'

'She shall not,' Rupert vowed, his heart now firmly entangled in her toils. 'You must know that I have thought of no one but you since I left here, Sarah. You have been with me day and night. I ask you now if you will wed me? Become my wife and neither you nor your cousin shall want for anything. I must pay a fine to settle with Parliament, but it is not beyond my means, and my father has a fine estate where we may stay until I find a house for you.'

'Shall we go to London?' Sarah asked, hanging her head so that he should not see the excitement in her eyes. 'Father promised that he would take me when the war was over.'

'My father has a house there that he has not used in years,' Rupert told her. 'It was let until recently, but I shall have it cleansed and made ready for you – if you can be content as my wife? You may not love me as yet, Sarah, but if devotion can bring it to pass, I shall teach you to love me as I love you.'

'How could I not love a man as kind and good as you?' Sarah asked, pleating her skirt with her fingers and looking at her toes in what she fondly believed was the way a modest girl would behave. She looked up at him then, her eyes wide, bluish green and as clear as fresh spring water. 'I have thought of you often, sir – wondered how you fared and if you got clear to France. I do not know what it is to love a man for I have no experience . . .' For a moment she remembered the day she had lain in Kit's arms, surrendering all but her virginity to his seeking mouth and hands. She had saved only that because he must ride away and she feared the consequences should she bear his child; he had taken all else – her heart, her promises of fidelity, and her innocence for she was Kit's lover in all but that final thing. 'But if you are gentle and patient with me, I shall be a good wife to you, sir.'

Rupert dropped to one knee before her, taking her hand and pressing it to his lips. 'I swear that I shall love you all my life,' he said. 'You are beautiful and innocent and I will cherish you. You shall have all that you desire – and I vow that I shall teach you to love me.'

'Already my thoughts are warm towards you,' Sarah said dimpling at him. She was beautiful in her pretty green gown, its skirt falling over a petticoat of cream and trimmed with ribbons. 'Will you not rise and kiss me on the lips, Rupert? And then we must return to the house and tell my cousin the good news. For if we are to leave here before that awful man comes, we must begin our packing at once.'

'I shall take you to my home,' Rupert said, rising and taking her hands in his. 'My parents will welcome you and we shall be married as soon as the banns can be read.'

'Oh yes,' Sarah said, gazing up at him, her eyes bright as she invited him to kiss her. As his mouth closed softly over hers, she had a picture of another man – a man with bold, laughing eyes who made her heart race with excitement, but she shut it out quickly. 'Oh, Rupert, I shall be so very happy.'

'I shall do all in my power to make you happy,' he said and looked at her adoringly for she was everything that any man could ever want.

'Are you sure this is what you want?' Elizabeth's eyes surveyed her cousin doubtfully. 'I thought you were in love with Kit Elbury?'

'That was but a childish infatuation,' Sarah seemed to dismiss her former lover with a shrug. 'Besides, he must be dead or he would have sent for me as he promised.'

'Marriage is forever,' Elizabeth warned her. 'You cannot change your mind once it is done. You must be faithful to your husband and give him love and comfort whenever he should need it.'

'You speak as if I had no idea of what marriage entails,' Sarah said with a toss of her head. 'I know that I must let him touch me intimately and whatever else he desires. It is nothing, Elizabeth. At least we shall live in comfort for he has promised you a home with us.' She smiled at her cousin, her eyes bold and imperious. 'You should be thanking me instead of raising objections. If you wanted to live in nothing more than a – a cabin and never have a pretty dress again, I did not. Rupert is handsome enough and I like him. I think it will do very well.'

'I shall say no more for it is not my affair,' Elizabeth said. She was in turmoil for on seeing Rupert again she had known that her own feelings for him had grown stronger during the past two years. Yet he loved her cousin, hardly knew that Elizabeth existed and could not imagine the pain his indifference inflicted. 'It is good of Sir Rupert to offer me a home. I shall accept for the moment, but you must not think that I shall be your dependent forever, Sarah. If the opportunity for employment occurs I shall take it.'

'You must do what you think fit,' Sarah said. In truth she did not care if her cousin left them once she was married. She had pleaded Elizabeth's case to put herself in a good light, but the younger girl had a habit of making her feel guilty, reminding her of things she would prefer to forget and so it would be easier if Elizabeth were to leave. 'But for the moment you are to come with us. Rupert is taking us to his home, which is some leagues from St Ives. We shall be married as soon as the banns are read – and then we shall go to London.'

'It is good to have you home again,' Caroline said as Nicolas came to her in the parlour of her parents' house. 'I have missed you sorely.'

His gaze went over her anxiously, noticing how drawn her face was, for he knew that she had miscarried a child a month or so after he had returned to duty some months earlier, and it had been on his mind that he had been unable to comfort her.

'Are you well now, my love?'

'My body has healed,' Caroline said, her mouth working a little as she tried to control her sadness at losing her first child. 'But I have been sorrowing and I wished you might be here with me.'

'I have wished it too,' Nicolas told her, taking her hand. 'I shall not leave you again for a while, though Cromwell has asked me to join him in London when I can. There is much to be done, for though the King is now the prisoner of the Army, there are still those that would cause trouble – pockets of resistance that must be put down. And we must labour to bring a proper settlement to this country. I know that Cromwell and others are working to put an offer to the King, and I have great hopes that we shall be able to restore him to a limited position. He must not be allowed to tear this country apart again, but England needs a leader, else they who think to rule us will squabble endlessly. Even Cromwell loses patience with them at times. I believe he too hopes for some kind of a settlement, but Charles Stuart must confess his crimes and beg pardon. If he sues for peace it may be granted.'

'I pray it may be so. We want no more war,' Caroline said. 'Rupert has sued for a pardon and been given leave to return home on payment of a fine. A messenger came only this morning: he is to be married. Her name is Sarah Bellingham, and he is bringing both her and her cousin Elizabeth to stay with us until the wedding. I understand that her father died recently and that he had beggared himself in the King's cause.'

'Rupert is to wed?' Nicolas looked thoughtful. 'It may be best if we make our home at Thornberry until I go to London. I thought that you might like to accompany me to town?'

'Oh, Nicolas, of course I would,' she said smiling up at him in relief for she had thought he meant to leave her behind once more. 'If I shall be no trouble to you?'

'How could you be a trouble to me, my dearest?' he asked, reaching out to trail loving fingers down her cheek. A little shudder of desire ran through him for he had thought of holding her in his arms on many a night, wanting her close to him in their bed. Though nearly four years married now, they had spent only weeks together.

'I am so glad that you are returned,' Caroline said. 'Rupert is expected tomorrow. We shall stay until they arrive, and then we shall go home to the manor.'

'You are welcome, Sarah,' Caroline said, embracing the girl who was to be her sister. 'I am happy to meet the lady who has captured my brother's heart, for I know Rupert. He would not wed without love.'

'Thank you, Lady Mortimer,' Sarah said, making her curtsey. 'You are most kind.'

Caroline kissed her cheek and released her, turning to look at the other girl. Elizabeth Bellingham had a serious look, her eyes slightly anxious as if she were troubled about something.

'Welcome, Mistress Elizabeth,' she said. 'I am glad to see you here.'

'Thank you, ma'am,' Elizabeth said and dipped gracefully. 'It was kind of Sir Rupert to bring me – and of you to receive us.' She turned to Caroline's mother, Lady Saunders. 'And you, ma'am. I hope I shall be no trouble to you. You must tell me if I may be of service to you in any way.'

'What a sweet child,' Lady Saunders said, smiling at her. 'I dare say I may ask you to fetch my embroidery or untangle the silks for me sometimes, for I have been used to Caroline doing it for me, and she is leaving us this afternoon.'

'My husband has come home and we must go to our own house – but it is only across the meadow. You must visit us when you have settled in,' Caroline said. 'Rupert will show you the way.' She included both young women in her invitation, but sensed at once that Sarah was not listening. She was looking about her, as if weighing up her surroundings. 'And of course we shall give a dinner for you, Sarah and Rupert.'

'A dinner . . .' Sarah's eyes were questing. 'Would it not be possible to hold a dance?'

'I hardly think it appropriate at the moment,' Nicolas said before Caroline could answer. 'Perhaps there may be some dancing for the younger folk after we have supped – but we have just come through a most dreadful war, Mistress Sarah. A dance might seem unfeeling do you not think so – especially as you are still in mourning.' He saw that her gown was a pale grey and frowned at the lack of respect. Her cousin was dressed in black, her gown more modest than Sarah's and therefore more fitting.

'My father would not have wished me to wear black for him nor to grieve too long,' Sarah replied, looking sad. 'But I did not mean to be thoughtless. It is just that we have all been sad so long and Elizabeth has never been to a ball – have you, cousin?'

'No – but I do not wish for it,' Elizabeth said and saw the flash of anger in Sarah's eyes. 'Perhaps when six months has passed – if things go well for the country and . . .' She broke off as she felt Nicolas's eyes on her, feeling a little afraid of this stern-faced man. Rupert had told her he had fought for Parliament, was close to Cromwell himself.

'Do not be afraid to speak your mind in this house,' Sir John, Caroline's father, said on seeing her discomfort. 'I did not choose to fight for either side, but I would have the country at peace again. Nicolas tells me that there are things afoot that may bring an honourable peace to this beleaguered England. We must see what develops, though I would like to see His Majesty restored if he would treat with Parliament. We must have safeguards so that this terrible tragedy can never happen again. I know that my son and Lord Mortimer are both in agreement with me.'

'Yes, of course,' Rupert said. His eyes dwelt lovingly on Sarah. 'When we are married and in London we shall give our own dance. Perhaps it is a little soon for the moment, dearest.'

'I shall do as you think best, Rupert.' Sarah smiled at him, her manner demure and all that he could desire of her. 'And now perhaps we could go to our rooms? I am a little tired from the journey.'

'Surely,' Lady Saunders said. 'Come my dear – and you too, Elizabeth – I shall take you up. I have put you next door to each other for I am sure it will be a comfort to you.'

'You are so kind, ma'am,' Sarah said. 'We shall try to be no trouble to you.'

'You will be no trouble to me or my family,' Lady Saunders said. She liked her son's choice and the cousin. The very fact that Rupert had done with fighting and come home, bringing his bride-to-be with him, was enough for his mother.

The sound of their voices died away upstairs. Nicolas frowned and looked at his brother-in-law.

'We must have a talk about things another day,' he said. 'It might be that we could help each other. If all goes well Cromwell will be a man to be reckoned with and he will need men he can trust in the shires to keep his peace. And now we must go – if you are ready, Caroline?'

'Yes, of course. I waited only to see Rupert and his betrothed,' Caroline said. She went to kiss her brother on the cheek. 'She is lovely, Rupert. I am so glad you have found someone to love – and that you have finished with the war.'

'There is no point in continuing,' Rupert told her. 'Some hotheads may make trouble, but it is over – the cause lost. Cromwell has been too clever for us. We must hope that he can restore order for there is still much unrest in the country. In some places the locals band together to fight against any soldiers who intrude in their borough, whether they be for King or Parliament. And those who should rule us cannot agree what to do next. Something must be done and if Cromwell cannot hold them I do not know any who will.'

Nicolas nodded his agreement, shook hands with his father-in-law and led Caroline out of the house to where their carriage awaited them. He handed his wife inside and climbed in beside her.

'What did you think of them?' Caroline asked. 'Sarah is very pretty, isn't she?'

'A bold piece if you ask me,' Nicolas said. 'Pretty enough I grant you – but she may be flighty. The other one seems a pleasant enough girl, but you cannot be sure on such slight acquaintance. I hope that Rupert knows his own mind on this.'

'I think Sarah is just a slightly spoiled young lady who wants some fun from life,' Caroline said, willing to be generous. 'I dare say life has been hard for them these past years, just as it has for us.'

'Life has been hard for many of our people,' Nicolas agreed. His frown softened as he looked at his wife. 'I do not mean to criticize, my love. I dare say I should find something lacking in any other woman. How could I not when I have a wife such as you? All others must fade in comparison.'

Caroline laughed softly, her hand seeking his. They had made love so sweetly the previous night, and she had found that her sorrow had lifted in his arms. She had lost a child and she longed to give her husband a son, but she was young and strong and there was plenty of time. At least she knew that there was nothing to stop her bearing a child. Next time she must take great care not to lose it.

'You are a wicked flatterer, my dearest.'

'I speak only the truth,' he said and leaned across to kiss her, his loins throbbing with desire as he felt her response. 'We have been too long apart since we were wed. I hunger for you, Caroline.'

'As I hunger for you,' she told him, a naughty light in her eyes. 'I can hardly wait for night so that we may lie together again.'

Nicolas grinned at her, seeming all at once the young lover she had crept out to meet before he went away to the wars. 'Then why should we wait?' he asked and drew her closer. 'We are master and mistress in our own home and I have no business that cannot be seen to another day.'

Three

'I hope you do not mind me calling on you unannounced,' Elizabeth said as she was shown into the parlour where Caroline was at her embroidery. 'But it was such a lovely morning and Lady Saunders asked me if I would deliver this note to you.' And if truth were known, her restlessness and the self-satisfied look in her cousin's eyes had driven her from the house. Seeing her with Rupert, knowing that he was deeply in love with her, and believing that Sarah was merely using him for her own ends, was unbearably painful for Elizabeth.

'I am delighted to see you,' Caroline said, inviting her to sit down on the settle near the large open fireplace. There was no fire that day for it was very warm and the sun came in through the open windows. 'You must stay and take some refreshment with me, Elizabeth. My husband is out somewhere on his estate. There is much in need of repair and attention, despite that my father has done his best to oversee it, for Nicolas has had little time for his own affairs these past years.'

'It must have been very hard for you with Lord Mortimer away so often?'

'Yes, indeed it was,' Caroline agreed. 'However, he is home for another week or two and then I am to accompany him to London, after Rupert and Sarah's wedding.'

'The banns are to be called this week,' Elizabeth said. She smiled despite the hurt inside for she knew she must. No one must guess how she felt for it would be seen as jealousy. 'It may seem hasty to some but your mother agrees that there is no point in wasting time. She thinks that too much time has been wasted in fighting.'

'I can only agree with her,' Caroline replied, 'though of course neither my husband nor my brother would see our point of view.' She laughed softly. 'Sarah did not wish to come with you for a walk this morning?'

'My cousin is not given to walking far if she may avoid it,' Elizabeth said. 'Besides, she was having a fitting for her wedding gown this morning. The seamstress has come especially from St Ives.'

'Ah, I see.' Caroline smiled. 'I imagine Sarah enjoys pretty things to wear, as we all do, of course.'

'Yes, Sarah has been accustomed to fine gowns.'

'And you have not?' Caroline's attention was caught by something in her voice.

'I have little enough money to provide them,' Elizabeth said. 'I have lived on my uncle's charity since my father died, though I have a tiny income left me by my grandfather.'

'I see . . .' Caroline looked thoughtful. 'You will have a new gown for the wedding?'

'I have a gown that was new last year. I shall refurbish it as best I may.'

'Oh no, that will not do,' Caroline said. 'We are much the same size. Let me have my seamstress come and fashion new gowns for both of us, Elizabeth. I have some pretty silk by me that will be enough to make up into a new gown for each of us.'

'I could not accept such a gift,' Elizabeth said, discomfited by the other's generosity. 'It is kind of you but I must not impose on you.'

'You will hurt my feelings if you refuse,' Caroline said. 'I shall not be denied. I believe that we shall be friends, Elizabeth – and you must indulge me in this. Indeed, I know that my mother and husband would support me in making this gift.'

Elizabeth's cheeks were burning. She was embarrassed to

accept and wished she had not told her kind hostess the truth, but to refuse now would seem churlish indeed.

'If you truly wish it,' she said, 'but you must tell me what I may do for you in return.'

'Be my friend,' Caroline replied simply. 'That is truly all I wish from you, Elizabeth.'

'Then I can only thank you for your kindness, Lady Mortimer.'

'You must call me Caroline. I am determined that we shall be friends. You are a sweet, pretty girl, Elizabeth, and you have become one of our family. I am sure that we shall all benefit from your company.'

Elizabeth shook her head, her cheeks warm, and yet she was pleased by Caroline's words for it seemed that she had found new friends. Perhaps Caroline would be able to help her find a new position when Sarah was wed, because she did not think she could bear to live with them then.

'Are you sure the girl did not tell you she had only an old gown to wear hoping that you would provide one for her?' Nicolas asked when Caroline told him of Elizabeth's visit.

'You misjudge her, my dearest,' Caroline remonstrated with him gently. 'I like her very much. She has lovely manners and she did not wish to take the gown. Indeed, I pressed it on her.'

'Very well,' Nicolas said and gave her an indulgent look. 'I dare say it does not matter either way, for it is merely a gown. In truth, she seemed a modest girl, unlike her cousin – but I suppose I have grown suspicious.'

'You have had reason,' Caroline said for she knew that there was always jealousy and backbiting amongst those who now flocked about Cromwell. At the beginning of the war he had been an insignificant country gentleman, but these days he was one of the most influential men in the country – perhaps the most powerful of all. Especially since the Army had revolted and become a power in its own right. 'But I would not have it sour your judgement when it comes to our friends, Nicolas.'

'Indeed, it shall not,' he said and drew her close. 'Besides, it pleases you to buy her the gown and I could never deny you anything.'

Caroline smiled as she recalled the previous night when she had lain in his arms. He had made love to her three times that night; it seemed that they could not have enough of each other after the long months of separation.

'Thank you, my dearest,' she said. 'And now I must go and speak to Cook. We have a fine ham and a side of beef for dinner this evening with a remove of neats' tongues and some plums – and I wish to make sure that everything is in hand.'

Nicolas nodded, smiling his content. Caroline was a good housewife and he had some letters to write, which would take considerable thought.

The weather had been settled now for several days, Caroline thought as she set out to walk to her parents' house. Nicolas had been called away on business but promised to be home that night, leaving her free to visit her mother and discuss the wedding.

She could smell the fresh scents of the meadow grass and the wild flowers that grew in it; it was long and dry about her skirts and rustled as she walked. She thought that it would soon be cut for the last haymaking of that year, before the harvest began in earnest.

It was at about this time of year that the fair had used to come, she remembered as she walked, thinking back to the summer before the war when she and Mercy Harris had attended to buy silks for their new gowns. She recalled that Harry Mortimer had bought them both silk neckerchiefs. He had bought one for Rowena Greenslade, the blacksmith's daughter, too.

Caroline frowned as she remembered the child she had seen in Rowena's arms a few days before all the trouble that had led to her disappearance. Had Rowena fled the wrath of the villagers who had declared her a witch – or was she dead? And what of her child? Caroline had always believed that the child must be Harry's for Nicolas had told her that his brother had seduced the blacksmith's daughter, and she herself had seen them together in Oxford during the early months of the war. Harry was almost certainly the father of two illegitimate children, Mercy's and Rowena's, but did Rowena's babe still live? He would be Harry's eldest son if he were still alive.

Her thoughts returned to the present when she saw an old woman trying to negotiate the wooden stile that led from the common ground to this fine meadow. It was clear that she was finding it difficult, and as Caroline quickened her step to offer her help, the old woman gave a cry and fell.

'Mistress, are you hurt?' Caroline asked as she hurried to where the woman lay still. As she knelt beside her, the woman opened her eyes and gave her a strange look. 'Are you in need of help? I am going to my mother's house and she will provide food for you if you are hungry.' The old woman sat up and looked at her. Something about her at that moment stirred forgotten pictures in Caroline's mind and she sought for the elusive memory. 'Forgive me – should I know you?'

'We met once,' the gypsy woman said, her lips parting in a toothless smile. 'I told you things then, mistress. You were unwed and unsure of your future – but you know it now.'

'You were the gypsy who came with that girl . . . she was killed I remember.' Carlina's death had been but one of many tragic events that had happened at that time, but it had stayed in her mind because the girl was so young.

'Aye, my poor Carlina,' Greta nodded, her wizened face lined with sorrow. 'She was my granddaughter and I loved her as none other. Her death was foretold, for she was to have brought good fortune to our people but the runes lied. Nothing but pain came from her sacrifice.'

'Did he kill her?' Caroline asked for she had oft wondered. 'Richard Woodville? It was rumoured that it might be him, but no one knew for sure. I remember that he himself was killed soon after.' By none other than Rowena it seemed and it was his death that had led to her being named a witch.

'It was to save the other one,' the old woman said answering in her own way. 'But she has betrayed us . . .' She leaned on Caroline's arm gathering what strength she had, her skinny fingers, the nails long and dirty, digging in to her flesh like the talons of a bird of prey. 'But we shall not speak of these things; they are writ and cannot be unwritten. I will tell you one thing and that is that you are to bear a child. This time you will carry it fullterm and it shall be a daughter.'

'How can you know that?' Caroline stared at her for she had not even begun to hope herself. She had missed her monthly flow by three days, but it was too soon to start hoping that her dearest wish was about to come true.

'Can you not see things yourself sometimes? Not for yourself for that is seldom given to one as young as you – but for others. Those you love?'

'Sometimes,' Caroline agreed, remembering that she had sensed pain for Rupert on a lonely moor and he had been wounded at the battle of Roundway Down. 'At least I have thought . . . but I could never be so sure.'

'I am older and I have seen much,' the gypsy said and smiled oddly. 'My time is nearly come – but you have a long life before you. Your gift will grow with you. Be sure that you use it wisely.'

'I pray that you are right and that I shall live long and happily, mistress. Will you not come to my house and let me give you something?'

'I want for nothing you have,' the old woman said. 'I am searching for a herb that grows in this meadow. It may help me live a little longer – but you have my blessing for your kindness. Not many would have bothered with such as I, mistress. Go on now and mind what I told you – it will be a safe birth and your child shall be a daughter.'

Caroline stood watching as the old woman walked on. Once before they had chanced to meet and she had been told that she would have a long and happy life but that one happiness would be denied her. She had begun to wonder if that meant she would never have a child, but now, perhaps foolishly, for it was far too soon for anyone to be sure, she had new hope.

Elizabeth had accepted the gift of the silk since Caroline had insisted on it, but she had refused the help of the seamstress for she had some skill in the art of dressmaking and time enough on her hands. It was a plausible excuse for her to remain in her room when Sarah and Rupert were both in the house. She enjoyed her needlework and she liked to read poetry when she was alone. It helped to ease the torment she felt at the prospect of her cousin's approaching wedding. She knew she must accept it and she could bear her pain when she did not have to watch them together, though she had shed many tears since coming to this house.

Rupert had been generous in offering her a home with them, but Elizabeth was not sure that she could bear to live this way for long. She must remain for the wedding and perhaps a short time afterwards, but she would use her time wisely and try to find a new position. Sarah spoke continually of going to London, and of all the pretty gowns she intended to have when she got there. Elizabeth wondered at her greed and that her future husband seemed to enjoy the prospect of indulging her, laughing when she twirled about in her latest finery for his approval.

Her father had been dead only a few weeks and yet she appeared to have not a care in the world, her pretty face alight with excitement at each new gift pressed upon her by her doting fiancé.

Perhaps she was being wicked and jealous to feel like this, Elizabeth thought. She ought not to grudge Sarah her happiness – and it was clear that Rupert was very content with his bride-to-be. Who was she to question his wisdom? Yet her heart ached for the pain she was sure her cousin would inflict whenever she did not get her own way. Sarah had cared for her father but her careless words had brought about his cruel death, how much less would she consider Rupert's feelings once she had all she wanted?

But no, it was wrong of her to harbour such thoughts. She was a jealous wicked girl and must put all such thoughts from her for they were not worthy. Elizabeth prayed for forgiveness in the darkness of the night, but nothing eased the pain that had taken root inside her.

She must forget her own hopes. Indeed, she had been foolish to harbour them these past two years. They had often sustained her in her loneliness but they were false. Her acquaintance with Rupert was slight, and she had known at the start that it was Sarah who had caught his interest, but that had not stopped her dreaming of his return. In her dreams he had seen her with new eyes, realized she loved him more than Sarah ever could, and fallen deeply in love with her. Now she was forced to face the painful reality, and it was slowly destroying her. At least, it would do so if she allowed it to eat away at her inside.

She would not become bitter and sour, Elizabeth vowed as she worked diligently on the gown she was making for her cousin's wedding. She did not think she would ever marry for she knew that she could never love anyone else as she loved Rupert, now she had really come to know him. Therefore she must find herself a position as a companion to a lady – and the best place to do that would be in London. Yet first she had to watch her cousin marry the man she herself loved, and she must do it with a smile on her lips.

And now she had done enough sewing for the moment and she would go downstairs to see what she might do to help her hostess, who had been so kind to her. The tasks she was given were small, but it pleased her to fetch and carry, and to walk to the village with Lady Saunders' messages.

Elizabeth saw Rupert coming towards her as she returned from the village after running one such errand and delivering a package to the vicarage for Lady Saunders. He was alone and seemed lost in thought, his mind far away. At first she thought that he might pass her by without noticing her, but then he stopped and doffed his hat with its curling feather. The sun shone on his dark red hair and he smiled, causing her heart to jerk and beat very fast.

'And where have you been, Mistress Elizabeth – to meet a lover I'll warrant?'

'Nay, sir,' she said and blushed. 'I have no lover. I have merely been delivering a package for your mother.'

'Ah yes, I believe she did mention something,' he said and his merry smile teased her. 'But we must find a lover for you, Elizabeth. You are too pretty and too kind to spend your life unwed.'

'You are very good, sir, but I wish you would not joke. I have no fortune and I think that perhaps I shall never marry.' And her heart was given to him, though he did not know it.

'No, that will not do,' he said, his eyes bright with amusement. 'I dare say a small dowry could be arranged if there was someone you liked.'

'No, indeed there is not,' Elizabeth said. How could he not know that she loved him? She ducked her head down and ran by him, feeling that she could not bear this a moment longer for if she were not careful she would betray herself.

'Forgive me . . .' Rupert's voice called after her. 'I did not mean to tease you . . .'

Elizabeth dared not look back. Tears were in her eyes and she cursed herself for her foolishness. How could she be breaking her heart for him when he hardly ever looked her way and when he did it was only to tease her about a lover?

But how could she expect him to notice her when he was so in love with Sarah? He thought only of his wedding day and making his beautiful bride his own. She was such a fool! He had never looked at her after he saw Sarah, and she had brought her unhappiness on herself by dreaming of something that could never be.

The day of Sarah's wedding dawned warm and fine, the sun shining from early morning. Elizabeth was up earlier than usual, because there was much to be done and she wanted to help Lady Saunders with all the extra chores that were needed to be done. So many guests were invited that every chamber in the house would be filled. Some of the guests would be lodged at Thornberry Manor, but the reception was to be held here. Because it was such a nice day, the servants would be able to set the tables out of doors, which was just as well since Elizabeth did not think they could squeeze all the guests into her hostess's parlour.

'Nicolas offered to hold the reception at the manor,' Caroline had told her, 'but my brother and father wished it held here. It is good that the weather looks set to be fair for it would have been disaster had it rained.'

After helping to inspect all the bedchambers and make sure that everything was as it should be, Elizabeth had arranged garlands of greenery and flowers for the bride so that they might lead her to church by them as was the custom. It was almost time to leave by the time she hastily changed into her own gown, which was a pale green and trimmed with ribbons of a darker shade. It became her well and a swift glance at herself in the mirror told her that she looked attractive enough.

She was one of the maidens chosen to escort Sarah to the church, the others young girls, daughters of local gentry, who giggled and laughed behind their hands, looking enviously at the lady who had captured Sir Rupert. Elizabeth heard whispering and knew that some of them had had hopes of him themselves.

She was pleased that she managed to join in their chatter and laughter, hiding her broken heart behind a smile. She had decided that she must be happy for Rupert; he at least was gaining his heart's desire, and when it came time to wish him happiness, she was able to do so with a warm smile.

'I wish you a long and happy life, sir,' she told him and was thanked with a kiss on her cheek. She turned quickly away to embrace her cousin, whispering against her ear, 'Make him happy, Sarah.'

'Of course,' Sarah said, her eyes bright with excitement. She had been showered with costly gifts from family and friends and her laughter rang out constantly throughout the reception.

Elizabeth tried not to watch her. She hated herself for her jealous thoughts, but controlled them as best she could, hiding her feelings by helping Lady Saunders to care for the guests.

'You have been busy all day,' Caroline said, coming up to her as the afternoon wore on and the guests showed no sign of leaving. 'Come, sit and talk to me. Your gown is lovely, Elizabeth. I thought you wrong to refuse the help of a seamstress, but now I see that you have skill enough of your own.'

'I have a little skill,' Elizabeth said, blushing at the compliment. 'But in truth I enjoyed making it. The material was so lovely, far nicer than any I have owned before.'

'I am glad it gave you pleasure,' Caroline said. Glancing up, she saw a gentleman approaching. 'Have you met Captain Benedict, Elizabeth? He is cousin to a friend of my mother and I believe it was she who brought him to the wedding as her escort.'

Elizabeth looked at the gentleman now joining them. He was some years her senior, older than either Sir Rupert or Lord Mortimer, though a fine, well-built gentleman. Richly dressed as befitted a Royalist gentleman, he had dark eyes and, when he smiled, seemed a man of good humour. He doffed his hat to them, revealing long, thick hair and making them an elegant leg.

'Lady Mortimer, your servant, ma'am. I trust you are well – and your husband?'

'Yes, quite well thank you, Captain Benedict,' Caroline said, and Elizabeth thought her smile a little wary. 'May I have the pleasure of introducing Mistress Elizabeth Bellingham, sir. She is Sarah's cousin and has therefore become a member of our family.'

'Honoured, mistress,' Captain Benedict said and inclined his head. He smiled at her but Elizabeth suspected he was more interested in Caroline. 'It has been a splendid occasion. I am glad that we are able to meet in happier times, Caroline.'

'I am glad that I shall not have to patch you up and send you on your way,' Caroline replied, a glimmer of humour in her eyes. 'I trust that you are well and have survived the war with no desperate hurt?'

'Any fatal wound I may have received came not from fighting my enemies,' he replied and Elizabeth noticed the flush in Caroline's cheeks. 'But the war is over is it not? We must put aside old hurts and quarrels and live in peace with each other. I have paid my fine, and since my uncle has died and left me a goodly estate, which hath no debts for he took no side in the conflict, I may settle and live my life in respectable comfort.'

'That must be the hope of all of us,' Caroline said. 'Nicolas says that the Council of the Army will make His Majesty an offer soon. If he accepts all may be well again, and sooner than we might have hoped.'

'I would not insult your husband for the world, Caroline,' Captain Benedict replied. 'But if he thinks that Charles Stuart will accept the dictates of those who sought to destroy him and all he holds dear, he is a fool. I know His Majesty as well as most, for he lets few close to him other than his family – and I believe he will reject any offer made. He believes that his right to rule comes directly from God and that those who would judge him have no jurisdiction.'

'I pray you are wrong, sir!' Elizabeth cried. 'Can the King not be brought to see that we must all bend sometimes? My uncle ruined himself in His Majesty's cause and lost his life because of it. Surely there must be an end to all this dissent? The war has gone on too long and I for one would see an end to the troubles that have brought us so low.'

Captain Benedict looked at her, his eyes thoughtful as he caught the passion in her. He had at first thought her a milk and water miss, but now he perceived that she was not what she seemed.

'If I had any influence with His Majesty I would prevail upon him to accept what is offered,' he said. 'Like you and most others in this fair land of ours I would see a settlement that all could accept – but I fear it will not happen. Charles still dreams of victory.'

Elizabeth nodded and was silent, though she could not see how the King could still cling to his hopes of victory. It was true that the past few weeks had seen him gaining popularity amongst the people, for, since the previous year, he had taken no part in the sporadic fighting that still went on up and down the country. Yet he could not truly believe that he would come to power again – could he? At least not the supreme power he had enjoyed before the war.

'Sarah and Rupert are leaving now,' Caroline said. 'Come, Elizabeth, we must go and bid them a fair journey.'

'Yes, of course.' Elizabeth followed her to where the bride and groom were in the midst of friends, who had crowded round to tease and kiss them, showering them with dried flower petals.

They were setting off on their journey to London, though they would journey only a few leagues that day to spend the night at a house that had been provided for them by friends. The guests were to be denied the privilege of the bedding ceremony, but Lady Saunders was not in favour of such customs, for in her opinion, it was an ordeal that brides had been forced to endure for too long. It was at her insistence that the custom was to be dispensed with on this occasion, for which both Rupert and Sarah had thanked her heartily.

'Have a safe journey,' Elizabeth said as she kissed her cousin's cheek. 'Be happy, Sarah.'

'Why should I be anything else?' Sarah asked with a toss of her pale ringlets. Her face was a little flushed and her eyes bright, but she looked very beautiful. 'I shall see you in a few days when you come to London with Caroline and Lord Mortimer.'

'Yes, of course,' Elizabeth said and stood back to allow others to say their farewells. Her throat was tight and she felt a sharp pain in her breast as she saw Rupert put his arm about Sarah possessively.

'You look sad,' a voice said at her elbow and she turned to find Captain Benedict at her side. 'You are not losing a cousin but gaining a family – is that not what they say?' His eyes held a merry smile as they twinkled at her.

'Yes, of course,' Elizabeth replied, but her throat felt hot. 'Excuse me, sir. I must go in and see to . . . things. The food may need to be replenished . . .'

She walked away from him, her head high. The tears were very close and she was afraid that she might weep and shame herself. It was foolish to be so upset, foolish to have allowed herself to imagine that something might happen to prevent the wedding! And very wrong of her! She was wicked to have these selfish thoughts.

Alone in her bedchamber, she allowed a few tears to fall before washing her face in cold water. She lifted her head, pride coming belatedly to her rescue. It was done now and her heart had been broken, but she must not allow anyone to guess that she loved Rupert. And she ought to go back down before her absence was noticed. Lady Saunders might need her help for with all the guests staying there was much to do. Raising her head proudly, she left her chamber and walked down the stairs. Somehow she would find a purpose in her life.

She would go to London with Caroline and Lord Mortimer for her best hope of finding some agreeable employment came from mixing with the people she would meet there in their company. But she would not make her life in her cousin's household. As soon as she could find a way of escape she would take it.

'You are so beautiful, my love. I have watched you and longed for this moment all day.' Rupert reached out to touch his wife's hair, which had been brushed until it shone and now fell beyond her shoulders in soft waves. 'You know that I love you more than my life itself? I almost fear to kiss you lest you disappear like a beautiful dream.'

'Do not be silly, Rupert,' Sarah said, feeling a flutter of alarm as she sensed the intensity of his feelings. She had not allowed herself to think of this moment, enjoying all the spoiling and pleasure of the wedding. Now at last they were alone together, and she realized that she must give herself to him – a man she scarcely knew. For a moment she wanted to recoil from his touch, to run and hide, and yet she knew that she must now meet her side of the bargain. She lifted her head, stilling her fears and the sudden rush of despair as she recalled the last time she had lain in a man's arms. She had loved Kit in her innocence, believing that he would come back to claim her – but he had not and she was this man's wife. 'You must not love me too much, Rupert, for I cannot be as perfect as you think me. I am spoiled and sometimes heedless . . .'

'Hush, my darling,' he said and reached out for her, drawing her close. 'You will always be perfect to me and I love your foolish little ways. I enjoy spoiling you.'

'Then you must not blame me if I disappoint you.'

'You could never disappoint me,' Rupert said, and then his lips were on hers, kissing her softly, tenderly, his passion held in check as he began to stroke her body with gentle, loving hands. 'You are so lovely and I have wanted you for such a long time.'

Sarah lay back on the pillows of their bed and let him have his way. He was touching her as Kit had touched her when she was a girl of barely sixteen, his hands and mouth moving over her breast, taut stomach and her thighs. She did not resist him, even when his fingers moved between her thighs, seeking out the warm hidden secret of her maidenhood. His caress was not unpleasant. She found it bearable, even though she cried out when he thrust into her and the pain was harsh, but she did not feel the singing rush of desire that she had experienced in Kit's arms.

'My sweet, lovely, innocent girl . . .' Rupert murmured against her ear. 'So beautiful . . . so sweet and good . . .' She felt the shudder run through him as he reached the climax of his pleasure.

When Rupert had done at last and lay beside her, holding her to him, Sarah felt the tears of disappointment trickling down her cheeks. She had not realized that she would feel so empty. In her ignorance she had believed that she would feel the same pleasure, the same need and wanting that she had felt when Kit loved her. He had done all that her husband had this night, except for that one last thing – and that had been painful. She had not minded all the rest, but that was an invasion of her body that she had instinctively rejected.

Rupert was sleeping now, his breathing deep and peaceful, as though he were satisfied, happy with their loving. Sarah edged away from him, feeling the soreness between her thighs and resenting it. She would not have felt thus if it had been Kit who had taken her virginity. She would have risen to his passion with an equal desire, urging him on, wanting the fulfilment they had denied themselves that last day.

She closed her eyes, forcing herself to remember Kit, to relive the wonderful feelings he had aroused in her, the longing she had felt to know all the secrets of loving. Only her fear of bearing a child while he was away at the war had held her back, but now she almost wished that she had let him take her. At least she would have experienced the pleasure that had been denied her this night.

Sarah knew the taste of bitter despair as she recalled her cousin's warning. Marriage was forever. She was tied to this man for life and she did not love him. She had believed that pretty gowns and jewels would compensate her for the lack of love, but now she realized that she had been mistaken. This emptiness inside could only grow with the passing of time – and she must submit to this thing called lovemaking whenever her husband demanded it of her.

'Oh, Kit!' Her mind called to her lost lover though she did not speak his name aloud. 'Why did you not come back to me? Why did you not send me word?'

She could not know whether Kit Elbury had lived or died, and it could make no difference to her now. She was wed to another and there was nothing she could do. She had given herself to a man she did not love for the sake of vanity, pretty gowns, a nice house and jewels.

Leaving their bed, Sarah walked softly to the window and looked out at the night. The moon was full and shed its silvery light on the gardens, somehow intensifying her loneliness. Her face was cold, her eyes bright with tears, but she knew that she must make the most of what she had. There was no going back, so she would take what she could of life. Rupert had money enough and she would buy her happiness with all the pretty trifles his fortune would allow.

After all, this intimacy that had left her feeling so cold and empty was but a fleeting thing, and Rupert doted on her. She would allow him some privileges, but there were so many excuses she could find to fob him off with a few kisses rather than the painful indignity that she had been forced to endure that night. It was easy enough to plead a headache or tiredness, and Rupert was too much the gentleman to force her. Besides, she might soon be with child and then he would surely not expect her to allow him more than kisses and a few caresses.

Sarah sighed and returned to the bed, slipping back into its warmth. She would find a way to endure what she must, and there were compensations. Soon they would be in London and they would visit the theatres, have dances and entertain their friends. She would forget the disappointment of her marriage in a whirl of pleasure and perhaps Rupert would tire of this lovemaking in time.

Elizabeth lay in her bed, sleepless, turning this way and that as she tried to stop the tormenting thoughts, but all she could see when she closed her eyes was Rupert and Sarah lying side by side in their marriage bed. She imagined him kissing, touching Sarah, caressing all the secret places of her body, and in her mind she became Sarah. She, Elizabeth, was lying beside him, responding to his touch, thrilling to the kisses that covered her willing flesh, and she felt a hot, burning urgency in the place where no man had touched her so that she whimpered with need.

The images were so real that she groaned aloud, lying on her side and pulling her night chemise tight between her legs to stop herself seeking relief from the need that overwhelmed her. Her whole body cried out with wanting as the images taunted her.

How wicked she was! It was immodest of her to think like this. Surely God would punish her? She would be struck down for having such sinful thoughts. Yet they were beyond her control. She burned for Rupert to touch her and kiss her as he was kissing her cousin. She was wracked with a hot desire that tormented her virgin body, and taunted her mind with images of paradise.

There would be no sleep for her that night. She rose from her bed and walked over to the window, looking out at the moonlit gardens. She felt so alone. It was so painful to think of Rupert and Sarah together, and yet the images continued to assault her mind. It was sinful to feel this way! No modest woman would lust after another woman's husband, but she could not help herself.

Driven to shame by her thoughts, she knelt, bending her head in prayer as she begged for release from her wicked thoughts. Yet the picture of his smiling face would not leave her and in the end she returned to bed to toss and turn once more. Tears welled up inside her, spilling over to wet her pillow.

'Oh, Rupert . . . Rupert . . .' she moaned. Why, why could he not have loved her instead of Sarah?

Four

Elizabeth craned forward to look out of the carriage window. It was early in the morning for they had set off from the inn at first light, because Lord Mortimer was in a hurry to complete their journey. She had never been to London before, and the noise from the crowded streets astounded her. There were people everywhere, and in this part of the city most of them seemed to be selling something. She caught sight of a milk maiden, a heavy yoke across her shoulders, a bucket slung from each end. Away to the right, a small market was in progress, and it was from there that much of the shouting seemed to be coming as the costers called their rival wares. Ahead of them, a wagon had shed a part of its load of wooden barrels and was impeding their progress.

Nicolas looked impatiently out of the window. Seeing the turmoil ahead, and that a fight looked imminent between some of the protagonists, he ordered his coachman to take a detour down one of the side-streets. Here the houses were closer together, the overhanging second stories so near that it looked as if people could lean out and almost touch. The gutters were overflowing with filth and as they passed one of the crowded courts that were home to large numbers of wretched hovels, the stench was almost unbearable.

'You will need to furnish yourselves with pomanders if you venture out on foot,' Nicolas warned them with a grimace as he caught the stink of a rotting carcass by the side of the road. 'It will not be so bad when we reach our lodgings, but wherever you go in the city you will encounter sights and smells you may find distasteful.'

'I did not realize it would be quite this bad,' Caroline said, holding a scented kerchief to her nose. 'Sit back and close the curtains, Elizabeth. It will not be quite so awful then.'

Elizabeth obeyed, though she was eager to see and observe for it was all new to her. She had seldom been outside her own village until she accompanied Rupert and Sarah to his home. Enclosed within the coach, the smell was less oppressive but it was warm and the rattling of the wheels over potholes in the road was uncomfortable.

It was a relief when the coach finally came to a halt and the door was opened by one of Lord Mortimer's grooms. He let down the steps, helping first Caroline and then Elizabeth to descend. She discovered that they were outside an imposing residence situated close to the river, and that the air was much sweeter here.

Since the days of the Tudors wealthy men had sought relief from the stench and ill humours of the crowded old city. This house, recently built, had a good solid structure of stone rather than the timbering so commonly used in the previous century and was part of the sprawl of new building going on. It had several good windows, and as they went inside, she noticed that the walls were panelled with a soft golden oak, an improvement that offered much comfort to the occupants. It was also of a different style to many of the houses Elizabeth had previously seen, which were mostly constructed around a central hall where the family gathered. Here, there were several parlours, which led one from the other, many of them smaller than she had been used to at her uncle's house. An entrance hall revealed a grand staircase that led up to the family rooms.

A plump-cheeked lady, who announced that she was Mistress Berkshire the housekeeper, and that she would be looking after the ladies during their stay in London, came in to the hall to greet them. Caroline had brought several maids as well as menservants with her, but they were taken to the back of the house by a separate entrance. By the time the effusive Mistress Berkshire had finished fussing round them and led the way upstairs, Elizabeth found that one of Caroline's maids had begun to unpack her trunk.

'Her ladyship said as I was to serve you now, Mistress Elizabeth,' the girl said. 'I don't know about you, mistress, but I be right glad to be out of all that noise and stink back there.' She tossed her head to indicate the bustling city they had left behind. 'If this be Londun I don't reckon much to it.'

'I must admit that it is not quite what I expected,' Elizabeth admitted with a smile. Sarah had spoken of the city in glowing terms, talking of houses and palaces and riches beyond compare. 'But we are lucky that Lord Mortimer hired such a good house for us.'

'The house be all right,' the maid replied. 'But I reckon as I'd sooner be at home. Jed says to me, "You watch out for yourself in that place, Molly. It be full of thieves and villains." That's what he do tell me and I reckon as he be right from what I see of it.' She smiled confidently and Sarah guessed that the wise Jed was her lover.

Elizabeth laughed at the girl's chatter for she liked her and she was feeling better than she had for some days. The pictures of Rupert and Sarah had faded from her dreams, and she was glad that no one could read her mind for she would have been shamed that anyone should know of her private torment.

Molly bustled about the chamber, arranging it so that Elizabeth's own things added the comforts of home, talking all the while. Elizabeth smiled inwardly. She had not expected to be given her own personal maid, and had never met her until they left Thornberry for she was of the Mortimer household, but she had soon discovered that Molly knew her business.

'Her ladyship says we shall be entertaining Lord Mortimer's friends often,' Molly informed her in her open, country manner. 'She says you'll need help to dress and that I'm to show you how to put your hair up the fashionable way.'

Elizabeth touched her hair, which she had dressed herself that morning in a neat twist at the nape of her neck. Her hair was thick and glossy but difficult to handle and she had grown accustomed to wearing it caught back so that it would not blow and tangle in the wind, as it did when she let it hang loose about her face.

'If you mean to give me ringlets they will not suit me,' Elizabeth said. 'My cousin looks very pretty with her hair done that way but I am not her.'

'You be pretty enough,' Molly replied. 'You might look prettier if you let me make a few changes, just to soften it a bit like – nothing fussy, that wouldn't suit you, but a bit fuller about the face.'

'Well, you may try if you wish this evening,' Elizabeth said and smiled at her. It was rather nice having a maid to look after her, a luxury she had not known in many years. 'And now I must see if Lady Mortimer needs me . . .'

Having tidied herself and washed off the dust of the journey, Elizabeth walked along the landing to the room she had seen Caroline enter earlier and knocked at the door. She was invited to enter and found her friend surrounded by gowns and linen that her maids were unpacking.

'You have come to rescue me from this confusion,' Caroline said and smiled at her. 'Tell me, Elizabeth, how is it that the thing one wants first when arriving at a journey's end is the thing that has been packed at the very bottom of the last trunk to be brought up?'

'I fear that question is beyond me,' Elizabeth replied and laughed. 'I came to see if I could help you. Perhaps I can find what you have lost?'

'No, no, it does not matter,' Caroline said. 'My maids will find it sooner or later. Come, my dear. I want to show you the house, and then, when we have eaten, we shall go out and explore the gardens, which I am told have a fine view of the river and the Tower . . .'

Elizabeth sensed that all was not well with her cousin as soon as she saw her. Caroline had lost no time in paying a visit to her brother's wife, and it was the day after their arrival that they were shown into Sarah's parlour. The house that belonged to Rupert's father was older and closer to Whitehall, also smaller and less comfortable than their lodgings.

'Are you well, Sarah?' Elizabeth asked as she saw slight shadows in her cousin's face. 'Is London all that you imagined?'

'London is tolerable enough,' Sarah said, her mouth screwing up in an expression that belied her words and seemed to show dissatisfaction with her life. 'I like it very well when we visit the silk merchants or the exchange, but I have been on my own some days, stuck in this poky little house while Rupert meets people. It is unfair of him and I do not believe that it is always on business that he goes out.'

'I dare say he has things to see to while you are in town, business for his father or the estate perhaps,' Elizabeth said. 'Gentlemen cannot give all their time to pleasure, Sarah.'

'It is all very well for you – you have Caroline to keep you company. I thought you were going to stay with us and help me become accustomed to living in town.'

'But of course I shall come to you if that is what you want,' Elizabeth said, puzzled by her sulky manner. 'I was not sure that you would wish me to live with you just at first.'

'I need someone to talk to,' Sarah said, and turned to Caroline as she left her brother and came to join them. 'You will not mind me having Elizabeth to live with me, will you?'

'I have a better idea,' Caroline said, giving her a warm smile. 'Rupert told me that he has had to leave you alone here and I suggested that you both come to us. Nicolas has taken a large house further out of the city. It has a splendid garden that borders on the river and we are able to sit out or stroll about and watch the birds as well as people being rowed by. Besides, it will be more comfortable for you if we all venture out to the shops together, especially when Rupert is detained on business.'

Sarah looked at her in silence for a moment and then smiled, all trace of her sullen mood gone as she pouted prettily at Rupert. 'Will you not mind if we stay with your sister, dearest?'

'I think Caroline's suggestion an excellent one,' he replied, a slightly anxious look in his eyes. 'I had not realized that Father's house was so small or so uncomfortable. I believe the house Nicolas has hired will be much more to your taste, my love.'

She held out her hand to him, gesturing to him to come and sit beside her on the settle, which he did instantly. 'You are such a kind, good husband,' she told him, sure of her power as she gazed up at him. 'Always thinking of ways to please me.'

'Your happiness is my main concern,' he replied, but Elizabeth noticed that he himself no longer seemed quite as happy as he had on his wedding day and she thought that perhaps he had suffered from Sarah's moodiness already. 'I wish only to please you, Sarah.'

'Then I shall have my things packed and join your sister tomorrow,' Sarah said. 'Rupert says we are to attend a special gathering at the house of one of his friends this evening, so I think it would be best if we remained here for that – but I shall look forward to joining you soon Caroline.'

She had ordered refreshments for her guests the moment they arrived, and now she was the perfect hostess, offering them wine and comfits, and beginning a lively conversation about a visit to the theatre.

'It was one of Master Shakespeare's comedies,' she told Elizabeth and laughed at the memory. 'I have never seen anything so amusing – but I must tell you that the heroine of the piece was a man dressed in women's clothes. It was so quaint, my dear.'

'That is surely because few decent women would take part in such activities,' Caroline said. She herself had never been to a theatre, though she had witnessed amateur productions while she was in Oxford at the homes of her kinswoman's friends. 'Did you wear a mask, Sarah? I believe it a necessary safeguard to prevent the gentlemen ogling one from the pit.'

'Oh, I started out with one,' Sarah replied with a toss of her ringlets. 'But it was not at all nice to wear and once we were seated I removed it.'

'Did it not make you feel uncomfortable to have strangers staring at you?'

'Oh, one simply ignores them,' Sarah said for she had enjoyed the looks directed at her by some of the gentlemen in the audience more than the play itself. 'Rupert was speaking of taking me again soon – why do we not make up a party and go together?'

'It may be as well to go while we still can,' Rupert said with a frown. 'I have heard that many of the theatres may soon be closed. It seems that our new rulers feel that they are an abomination and corrupt the thoughts of decent folk.'

'Oh that is too bad,' Caroline said, feeling disturbed by such news. 'Surely they cannot enforce such a ruling?'

'Not yet perhaps, but I believe they may do worse once they have the power,' Rupert told her. 'Have you not heard of these people – the Levellers they call themselves? I have attended one of their meetings and heard them speaking of the new order. They would bring us all down to base level if they could for by their doctrine no man may rise above another by reason of his birth or his own efforts – and I believe they may mean harm to His Majesty.'

'Surely not?' Caroline cried, feeling shocked. 'I do not believe that this is what Cromwell intends – does he? Nicolas does not think it I am very sure.'

'There are many factions at work at the moment,' Rupert told her. 'Some – and I believe that includes Cromwell – are for offering His Majesty some kind of limited power, but others are beginning to whisper of his trial and execution. I fear for our country if that should come to pass and we were to live under the shadow of these canting Puritans. They will squeeze all the joy from our lives if they are given the chance. I for one would feel inclined to leave England if that were so.'

'You cannot mean it?' Caroline stared at him. 'No, Rupert. I cannot believe that we shall come to such a state.'

'Oh, do not talk of such things,' Sarah said, making a face. 'It is so boring to talk of politics all the time. Rupert promised that we should have a dance when we came to London, but now he says it is not the right time . . .'

'It would be frowned upon and thought extravagant frivolity,' Rupert told her and looked frustrated, as though it was not the first time he had been called upon to explain. 'We may have to wait a few months – perhaps when we go home again, Sarah. In the country it might not be noticed so much as here.'

Sarah said nothing but her sullen look had come back again.

'Well, we shall be giving some small gatherings for our friends,' Caroline said to cover the ensuing silence. She could see that Sarah was clearly sulking and that her brother did not know how to deal with his wife's change of mood. 'Some of them will be for people that Rupert may not care to meet, but you may always go out on those evenings – and we shall invite friends that Rupert approves of on other nights and then we shall all enjoy ourselves together. I do not see why we should not have a little informal dancing, though a grand feast is out of the question, of course.'

'There you are,' Sarah said, smiling now. 'I said there was no reason why we should not have a little dance.'

'I think that Nicolas may agree with me,' Rupert said, 'but if not then I shall be delighted to be proved wrong.'

'But of course you are,' Sarah cried, teasing him now in her old way. She fluttered her lashes and pulled a face at him. 'You silly thing, Rupert. Caroline knows what is proper. I am sure she does not have to ask her husband what she may do in her own house.'

'Oh, but I do,' Caroline said. 'I did not mean to hold a proper dance, but there can be no objection to us clearing the room for an impromptu affair I think.' She saw from her brother's expression that he thought differently, but let the subject slip. She would talk to Nicolas that evening when they were alone.

'It might be frowned upon if we were to hold a grand affair,' Nicolas told her, 'but I am not yet afraid to permit some pleasure in my own house. If you wish to have dancing, my love, you may do so.'

'Do you think that Rupert is right – will these people rule our lives so strictly?'

'I have heard rumours, but I think it mostly wild talk from extremists,' Nicolas told her but looked concerned. 'There will be a power struggle and it depends who wins. If the King is sensible we may come through this, but if he refuses to listen to advice . . .' He shook his head and sighed. 'I would have wished that Rupert had not told you of his fears, Caroline. At the moment things are unsettled and all kinds of ideas are being put forward as to what kind of a land England should become in the future. I do not want to return to the old ways. I fought because I believed that Charles Stuart was a bad king. He enforced unjust taxes and I opposed them, as did more influential men than I – but I would not see his rule replaced by one that is less just.'

'Then we shall invite our closest friends to a gathering, and the dancing shall be informal,' Caroline said. 'In the meantime, Rupert tells me that he plans a visit to the theatre in the near future. I hope that you will not object, my love?'

'Playhouses are known to be licentious places,' Nicolas said with a frown. 'But provided you are well protected and go in a group, I see no harm in it.'

'Then we shall go,' Caroline said, 'for I think I should enjoy going to see a play.'

It was in fact some weeks before the proposed visit took place for Sarah took a little chill and was unwell for some days, and there were other engagements to detain them, but at last the party set out. Nicolas Mortimer refused to accompany them, but sent several of his servants to attend them on their journey.

Elizabeth was very conscious that the atmosphere in the playhouse to which Rupert had taken them was noisy and a little bawdy. She was aware that a party of gentlemen was watching them as they took their seats in the gallery and she was glad that she had chosen to wear the mask Caroline had provided for her. Sarah had worn hers until they were settled but she removed it once the performance began.

This time it was the story of Romeo and Juliet, and Elizabeth was immediately caught up in the dramatic tale of romance and tragedy. It was not until the curtain came down at the end that she became conscious of her cousin's odd behaviour. Sarah was staring fixedly at a group of young men in the pit, and one of them was gazing up at her in a way that made Elizabeth catch her breath. She recognized him instantly, knowing that he was none other than Kester Elbury, the only son of Lord William Elbury, and the man Sarah had once sworn to marry.

'Come, my dears, it is time for us to leave,' Caroline said, 'before the crowd becomes restless and trouble breaks out.' She was busy collecting her fan and tying the strings of her cloak and did not seem to notice that Sarah was apparently transfixed.

'We must go,' Elizabeth said, pulling urgently at her cousin's sleeve. 'Come, Sarah! The others are waiting . . .' She lowered her voice. 'Be careful or Rupert will notice.'

Sarah seemed to wake from her trance. She glanced at Elizabeth, understanding that her cousin had seen Kit and realized what was happening.

'Please – you will not say anything?' she whispered as they followed the others outside.

'Of course not,' Elizabeth replied. 'Why should I?'

Sarah's behaviour was merely the result of having seen Kit so suddenly, when she had believed he must be dead or fled to France. She had done nothing wrong, though she was shocked and it had clearly upset her. She had gone very pale and she was quiet as they were driven back to the house. Instead of chattering about the play as Elizabeth would have expected, she claimed a headache and retired immediately to her bedchamber, Rupert following soon after.

Elizabeth was thoughtful as she undressed that night. Was Sarah still in love with Kit? It would explain the way she had stared at him, her manner and her pallor. She had pleaded a headache but was she suffering from another ailment – one that Elizabeth understood only too well?

She could feel sympathy for her cousin, but her heart ached for Rupert. How long would it be before he realized that the wife he adored did not return his love?

Rupert left his bed and went downstairs, careful to close the bedchamber door as softly as possible. Sarah had complained of a headache and of feeling unwell again when he had tried to hold her. It was an excuse she had used all too often since their marriage, and though it pained him to think it, he believed she was averse to the lovemaking that was so delightful to him. It gave him such pleasure to hold her in his arms, to kiss and caress her, and he found it hurtful that she had shown no response to his gentle attempts to rouse her.

At first he had believed that she was shy, afraid of the things he was teaching her, but of late he had realized that she disliked being touched. He had tried to talk to her, but she had wept and begged him not to be cruel to her.

Rupert was the least demanding of men and he sincerely loved his wife. He had done his best to comfort her, to coax her into accepting his loving, but she lay unmoving, her eyes closed, frozen as ice, her face turned from him the moment he had done. This evening she had turned her back on him and complained of a terrible headache, and he believed she had been weeping into her pillow after she thought he was asleep.

Was it possible that she did not love him? Rupert felt the pain twist inside as he contemplated the future. Unless Sarah could be brought to respond to him, he must leave her to sleep alone for he would not continue to press his desires on her unwilling flesh. And yet when she smiled at him, when her eyes teased and her mouth pouted, he felt an urgent need to lie with her. How could he bear to go on like this?

What was he to do? Rupert did not feel able to confide his doubts to anyone. To speak of such private things would be a betrayal of his wife, of his love for her. And perhaps he had misjudged her. It might be that he had been too impatient, demanding too much too soon. She had been young and innocent when he'd married her and in truth they had hardly known each other. Somehow he had upset or hurt her, though he could not think what he had done. He must try to win her back to him. He had business that would keep him away from home that day, but he would find time to buy her a pretty trinket.

'This was delivered for you earlier,' Elizabeth said, handing the wax-sealed letter to her cousin. 'The maid brought it to me for it was addressed to Mistress Bellingham, but the initial is not mine.'

'You know the sender, do you not?' Sarah said, seizing the note as if she feared her cousin would withhold it. She read it swiftly, giving a little cry of distress before slipping it into the bodice of her gown.

'I thought it might be from Kit? It is his seal I think?'

'You will not tell anyone?' Sarah's eyes beseeched her.

'You must know that I would not tell tales of you.' Elizabeth gave her a worried look. 'Be careful, Sarah. You risk much if you arouse your husband's suspicions. He would be upset and angry, rightly so if he knew that you had received a letter from another man.'

'Kit has asked me to meet him. I must see him,' Sarah said, her face urgent with pleading. 'No, do not look so disapproving, cousin. I shall not do anything wrong – but I must see him just once. I must explain why I married Rupert.'

'But you ought not to be in his company alone. Only think of the consequences if you were discovered.'

'That is why I must confide in you. I must ask your help. If you are with me we may make some excuse. Say we have been shopping or merely to walk by the river.' Sarah reached out, gripping her wrist. 'Please, Elizabeth, I beg you. Help me in this.'

'Will you promise that you will see him but once?'

'Yes, yes, I promise,' Sarah cried, though in her mind she was denying her cousin. 'But I must see him. I must explain or he will think me heartless.'

'I see that this means a great deal to you,' Elizabeth said. 'When is this meeting to be?'

'This afternoon,' Sarah said. She was on fire with impatience. It had shocked her to see Kit staring up at her from the pit, but now she could not wait to see him. 'He will be waiting for us in a secluded spot near the river. We must think of some excuse – some reason why Caroline should not come with us.'

'I believe she has an appointment to see her physician this afternoon,' Elizabeth told her. 'She does not wish it known yet, but I happened to visit her in her bedchamber some days ago while she was being sick, and she told me that she is now more than two months with child.'

'That could not be better,' Sarah said, delighted by her luck. 'She may not even be aware that we have been out – and Rupert has business that will keep him from home.'

'Then we shall go to this meeting,' Elizabeth said but her heart sank as she saw the look of triumph in her cousin's eyes. What had she agreed to? She could only hope that Sarah would keep her promise.

As fortune would have it, they were able to leave the house without being seen by anyone, and, at the end of the street, found sedan chairs with porters ready to carry them the short distance to their destination.

Elizabeth's misgivings had gradually intensified, and when she saw Kit Elbury waiting for them, she knew she had been wrong to agree to this mad adventure. There was something about him – some arrogance or wildness – that she did not trust. It was in his eyes as he looked at Sarah. And when she ran to him like an eager child, Elizabeth's fear grew. She knew how reckless, how careless her cousin could be and she was apprehensive. This was wrong! So very wrong of Sarah. Would she risk her marriage for the sake of this man who had not bothered to return for her as he had promised? She had been wed barely two months and she was deceiving her husband by meeting another man.

Knowing that her company would be unwelcome, Elizabeth walked a little way behind the two as they talked and gesticulated at each other. It was clear that they were having a quarrel and she saw the anger in Kit's face, the tears on Sarah's cheeks, but could only guess at what had passed between them.

Clearly Kit had not realized she was married when he'd seen her at the theatre. If she had been pointed out to him, he had perhaps been mistaken, not understanding that she was Lady Saunders – for it might have been either Caroline or Elizabeth as far as a stranger could tell. She saw him glance her way a few times and watched as Sarah shook her head. He appeared to say something harsh for Sarah trembled and then started to weep. Elizabeth would have gone to her then, but Kit pulled Sarah roughly into his arms, holding her close. He looked at Elizabeth over her head and his expression seemed to challenge her, as if daring her to interfere.

Elizabeth was powerless. She was unable to do or say anything for she felt as if she had betrayed Rupert by agreeing to accompany Sarah on this secret tryst. She ought to have destroyed Kit's letter immediately, for she had known instinctively that it came from him.

Now she was caught in the web of deceit that she had helped to create. If she betrayed her cousin she must reveal her own part in the affair. She must wait and watch in silence and hope that her cousin would keep her word to end this now.

'You will not betray me?' Sarah asked as they returned to

the house that evening. The afternoon had vanished and it was growing late. 'We were shopping and we did not notice the time. That is what I shall say and you must agree.'

'I do not like to lie to Caroline – or Rupert.' Especially to Rupert, for whom she felt a deep sympathy. How hurt he would be if he learned of his wife's betrayal.

'You must,' Sarah said. 'If you do not I shall say that you went to meet a lover and asked me to lie for you.'

'You would not!' Elizabeth cried in horror.

'Who do you think Rupert would believe?' Sarah challenged her. 'You must help me, Elizabeth, or I shall send you away.'

'I would rather leave than help you deceive your husband!'

'If you betray me by a word or a look you will be sorry.' Sarah's eyes glittered with malice. 'Believe me, I can make your life unbearable if I choose.' She smiled oddly. 'But we should not quarrel, cousin. I have kept your secret, now you must keep mine.'

'I have no secrets.'

'Do you think I do not know that you are in love with Rupert? I have seen the way you look at him. How would you feel if I were to tell him? Would it make your flesh squirm to know that we laughed and felt sorry for you as we lay in bed together?'

'You are cruel,' Elizabeth cried, two spots of colour in her cheeks. As usual Sarah knew how to punish, how to inflict her spite in the cruellest way. 'That would be unkind and unfair.'

'Then you must do as I ask,' Sarah said, a little smile on her lips. 'Kit will leave notes for me in that old tree at the bottom of the garden – the oak that has stood there for more than a hundred years and has a little hollow in its side. If I were seen to go out early in the day it might look odd but no one will take any notice of you. You may slip out early in the morning and bring me his letters, and you may place mine there for him to collect.'

'I cannot do it,' Elizabeth said, sickened by this deceit. 'It is wrong, Sarah. You promised you would not see Kit again if I came with you this once.'

'But that was before I saw him,' Sarah said, her face pale but determined. 'He loves me still. It was not his fault that he could not come to me sooner, Elizabeth. He has been on secret missions for His Majesty – and must go away again soon, but he says we can keep in touch by our letters, until we can find a way out of this predicament.'

'A marriage is not something you can just discard like a dress you have grown tired of,' Elizabeth said. 'I warned you before you wed that it was for life.'

'Oh, you do not understand,' Sarah told her, an impetuous look in her eyes. 'I do not love Rupert and Kit wants me. I cannot bear to go on like this.'

'What do you mean?' Elizabeth was horrified. 'You cannot mean that you would leave your husband? Kit deserted you, Sarah. Where was he when you needed him? He can have no genuine excuse for not writing to you in all that time. It was Rupert who took you from the life of poverty you dreaded and gave you everything. How can you think of treating him so ill?'

'Oh, I do not know what to do,' Sarah said, her eyes troubled. As selfish as she was, she could not ignore her cousin's warning and in her heart she knew that Kit had been both careless and selfish for he surely could have found time to write to her. 'Do not look at me like that, cousin – and remember what I said or you will be sorry!'

She walked on ahead of Elizabeth, leaving her to follow in her wake. Elizabeth was anxious. What ought she to do? She wished that she might confide in someone for if Sarah was not checked she might throw away her marriage and her respectability. It was wrong to let that little voice at the back of her mind speak of the consequences of Sarah's actions. No good could come to Elizabeth through it, for Rupert would be hurt.

Elizabeth spent a restless night, unable to sleep as the worrying thoughts chased through her mind. Surely Sarah would not truly think of leaving her husband? To do so would be to cast away her good name and reputation forever. It was unthinkable! Not only for Sarah's own good, but also for the pain it would give Rupert.

She was down early for Sarah had told her she must look every morning before anyone was about to make sure there was nothing left in the hollow. She went quickly through the gardens, feeling relieved that there was so far nothing to find, and then returned to the house. As she entered through the side door that led into one of the back parlours, she saw that Nicolas Mortimer had been watching her through the window.

'You are an early riser, Mistress Bellingham?'

Elizabeth felt the colour rising in her cheeks. Was that suspicion in his eyes? Yet he could not know where she had been or for what reason.

'I did not sleep well last night, sir. I thought a walk might clear my head.'

'You have something on your mind perhaps?'

Elizabeth could not look at him as she replied, 'Nothing, sir. I may have eaten too much supper.'

'Perhaps . . .' His eyes seemed harsh and probing as he looked at her but he said nothing more, merely turning away and leaving the room.

Did Lord Mortimer dislike her? Elizabeth had never been sure of his approval, though she knew that Caroline was genuinely affectionate towards her. She suspected that Lord Mortimer was a man of high standards who expected as much of his family and friends. He would be angry, even disgusted if he learned of Sarah's secret tryst with her lover – and he would probably blame Elizabeth for accompanying her.

It was an awkward position to be in, and Elizabeth wished that she could see an easy way out of it all. She was not frightened of Sarah's threats for she was sure that Caroline would help her to find a position if she confessed the whole to her – but what of Rupert's feelings? How could she destroy his trust and love for his wife?

She could not bear the pain it must inflict on others if this sorry business were to come to light, and decided that for the moment she could do nothing. She must go on as if nothing had happened and hope that Sarah would come to her senses.

Sarah hung over the privy in her chamber as she vomited for the second time that morning. It tasted foul and she grimaced as she reached for a cup of water to rinse her mouth. She had been sick several mornings of late. What could be the matter with her?

Going back into the bedchamber she sank onto the edge of the bed. Her head was spinning and she really did feel unwell. She had used the excuse to prevent Rupert loving her so often, but this time there was no mistaking that she was ill. But she must not be ill! She had promised Kit that she would meet him again that afternoon if she could manage it, and she was determined to slip away, even if Elizabeth would not come with her.

'Is there something I can get for you, my lady?' her maid asked.

Sarah shook her head, and then got to her feet intending to leave the room and go downstairs, but as she took a step forward the room started whirling round and round and the floor came up to meet her. She heard her maid's cry of alarm, and then there was only blackness.

'I promise you there is no need for alarm,' Caroline said and smiled at her brother as he came hurrying into the parlour. 'Sarah is resting for the moment but the doctor has been and all is well – very well as it happens.'

'What do you mean?' Rupert asked. 'I was told that she had fainted and the doctor had confined her to bed for some days.'

'Because she is nearly two months with child and the doctor feels she ought to rest to ensure that she does not miscarry . . .'

'With child?' Rupert stared at her in dawning delight. 'Sarah is carrying my child. Oh, my poor love, no wonder she was always . . .' He broke off realizing that he had almost given away details that must remain private. 'How upset she must be. I must go up to her.'

'Surely she will be pleased?' Caroline said feeling puzzled by his reaction. She believed he must be pleased that he was to have a child, but he seemed more concerned with Sarah's feelings than his own. 'It is the wish of every wife to bear her husband's children, is it not?'

'Yes, of course we wish to have children,' Rupert said conscious of the puzzled expression on his sister's face. He knew that she was carrying Nicolas's child and that she was delighted at the prospect, but he was not at all sure that his wife would feel the same. 'It is a little soon that's all.'

'Yes, you have been fortunate in one way, though you might have wished for a little longer to enjoy yourselves,' Caroline said and looked thoughtful. 'Nicolas is saying that I should go home soon. Things are a little tense at the moment, because His Majesty has refused to accept the offer put to him by Cromwell and the Army Council. Nicolas feels that as I am with child I should be better in the country. Perhaps Sarah should come too? We could travel together.'

'Yes, in a week or two when she is well enough to travel,' Rupert agreed. 'I may not be able to accompany you for things are afoot that may keep me here – but I should feel easier in my mind if Sarah were with you and Mother.'

Rupert was anxious as he went up to his wife's bedchamber. What a brute he had been making so many demands on Sarah when she was already carrying his child! It was no wonder that she had complained of feeling ill so often. Well, he would be careful not to disturb her until she was feeling better, and perhaps it might do them both good to be apart for a while.

Sarah thumped the bed in frustration after Rupert had gone. She was feeling wretched and now Rupert was insisting that she return to the country to stay with his mother until their child was born. How would she see Kit if she were in the country? She would not go! She would make Rupert let her stay here.

She looked up angrily as the door opened again, this time to admit not her husband but her cousin. Elizabeth looked round the bedchamber and then brought her a sealed note.

'Is it from Kit?' she snatched it eagerly, tearing it open to read the brief lines. 'He says that if I do not meet him this afternoon he will come this evening and hope to find a note from me. You must take one for me, Elizabeth. I have to arrange a meeting.'

'But surely now that you are . . .' Elizabeth looked at her unhappily. 'You are carrying your husband's child. You cannot leave him, Sarah. It would be wicked.'

'I will not put up with all this for another seven months,' Sarah said, her eyes brimming with tears. 'I feel so ill, Elizabeth. You have no idea how miserable I am.'

'I shall take your letter for you,' Elizabeth said. 'But only if you promise me that you will give up this nonsense.'

'I promise I will do nothing for the moment,' Sarah said, 'but I love Kit and one day I shall be with him.'

Elizabeth saw the mutiny in her face and knew that for the moment she could do nothing but fetch and carry the letters her cousin insisted on giving her, though she hoped they would soon return to the country and that this deceit would be at an end. Sarah must see that she could not run off with her lover while she was carrying her husband's child.

Five

Elizabeth was sitting in the parlour with Caroline the next morning when a visitor was announced. She put her embroidery down and asked if her hostess wished to be private, but was met with a smile and a shake of her head.

'I believe this visitor comes as much to see you as me, Elizabeth.'

Elizabeth blushed and disclaimed, though she had met Captain Benedict on several occasions since they came to London, and she could not but be aware that he had been paying her some attention of late.

'Good morning, ladies,' Captain Benedict said and made them an elegant bow as he came in. He was well dressed with a froth of fine lace at his neck and a coat of black velvet. 'Such a warming sight – two beautiful ladies at their sewing. What man could wish to see a happier thing when he enters a room? Especially if it should be his own home. Lord Mortimer is a fortunate man, Caroline.'

'You speak as if you think of taking a wife yourself, sir,' Caroline said, a little challenge in her eyes. She knew that he had visited them at first for her own sake, for he had been in love with her at one time, but she suspected that he was more than a little attracted to Elizabeth and she was hoping he would make the girl an offer.

'I must confess that the idea has more appeal for me now than it once had,' he agreed genially. 'If I thought that the lady I care for would accept me I might think of making an offer quite soon.' He glanced at Elizabeth but her head was down and she was jabbing a needle rather fiercely into her embroidery, her cheeks pink.

'You cannot know unless you ask, sir,' Caroline said, giving him a wicked look for she was aware of the undercurrent between them. 'You know that my husband talks of our returning to the country in a couple of weeks?'

'I did not know that,' Captain Benedict replied. 'Perhaps I may take the liberty of calling on you at Thornberry, ma'am? I came today to tell you that I shall not be attending your dinner next week as I am needed at home.'

'Nothing serious I trust?'

'Merely a matter of business,' Captain Benedict replied. 'I have already stayed in town longer than I had intended and must see to my estate – and then I am promised to my Aunt Margaret. After I have visited her in Oxford I may have time for my own affairs.'

'Ah yes, I see,' Caroline said, reading more into this than was apparent. Margaret Farringdon was a friend of her mother's and it was on her way to this lady's house that she had first met Captain Benedict. He was very likely Margaret's heir and would no doubt wish to inform her of his intentions before making an offer of marriage. 'Then we shall expect to see you in the near future.'

'Yes, that is my hope,' Captain Benedict said. He had something in his hand. He approached Elizabeth and offered it to her. 'It is a volume of poems, Mistress Bellingham. It contains several of Master Shakespeare's sonnets but also work by others, including Edmund Spenser – of whose work I have heard you speak with praise.'

'Yes, I do admire him,' Elizabeth said. 'It is kind of you to lend it to me, sir. I shall take great care of it I assure you.'

'It was intended as a small gift, Mistress Bellingham.'

'No book such as this can be called a small gift,' Elizabeth replied with dignity. 'It is far too valuable for me to accept as a gift, but I should like to have the loan of it until we see you again.'

Captain Benedict was not too displeased with her answer, for it gave him an excellent excuse for seeing her again, and seemed to indicate that she was not averse to meeting him in the future.

'Then I must take my leave of you, ladies,' he said. 'Do not think I have forgotten you if I come not for a few months. There are things afoot that may detain us all – but I shall hope that it will be sooner rather than later.'

Caroline smiled and nodded graciously, saying nothing until the ring of his booted feet on the wooden floor had died away. She looked at Elizabeth, who had put down her embroidery in favour of the poems.

'I suspect Captain Benedict subscribed to that for your sake, Elizabeth. You might have accepted it as a gift if you wished. I am sure he will offer for you in a little while, when you have come to know each other better.'

'No! I pray you will not say so,' Elizabeth said, laying the book down immediately as if it scorched her. 'I have no wish to marry Captain Benedict.'

'Not for the moment,' Caroline agreed. 'You have met him only five or six times at most, but he is a pleasant enough man – and I believe him honest. He would make you a good husband, Elizabeth. Surely you will wish to marry one day?'

'I do not know. I have not given it much thought of yet,' Elizabeth lied. She would have married eagerly, willingly if she could have had the man she loved – the man her cousin was preparing to betray.

Sarah had lied to her cousin for she knew that Elizabeth would never consent to helping her slip away while she was supposed to be resting. But she was not going to rest in her room just because they told her she must. What did she care if she miscarried and lost her child? She did not wish to carry the babe. She had never wanted it to be conceived and it would be nothing but a nuisance.

Caroline and Elizabeth were in the front parlour when she went downstairs. She could hear them talking and thought they had a visitor for she could hear a man's voice, and it did not belong to either Lord Mortimer or Rupert.

She slipped out of the side-door and made her way through the walled garden to the grassy stretch that led down to the river. She could see Kit waiting for her just where the river bent away from the house, almost but not quite hidden behind a spreading chestnut tree, and she ran towards him, her heart racing.

Kit had seen her. He moved forward to catch her in his arms, drawing her to the other side of the tree where they would be hidden by the massive trunk. He held her pressed against it, kissing her until she could scarcely breathe. As he looked at her with a fierce light in his eyes that she took to be desire, she felt an answering chord within herself. She disliked being touched by Rupert but her body leaped with excitement when Kit kissed her.

'I thought you might bring your cousin?' he said, letting her free for a moment.

'Elizabeth would have tried to stop me if she knew.' Sarah threw herself into his arms once more and kissed him with passion. She was desperate to make the most of this meeting for she did not know when she would see him again. 'It is so awful, Kit. They have been making me stay in bed because I am with child . . .' She faltered as she saw the flash of anger in his eyes. 'No, no, do not look at me like that. It does not matter. I shall leave him as we planned . . .'

Kit moved away from her. 'This alters everything,' he said and looked annoyed. 'I told you that there are things that may take me from you, Sarah. I had thought that we could just ride where and as we pleased – but if you are carrying a child it will soon be impossible. I cannot be tied down by a woman who is in a delicate condition, not until my work for His Majesty is finished.'

'But I thought all that was over,' Sarah pouted. 'Is he not a prisoner of the Army?'

'Perhaps not for much longer,' Kit said and the wild, reckless look she loved was in his face. 'There are some of us who will fight on forever to bring His Majesty to his own again. I must be ready to go where and as he dictates – that is my first duty. Without a child you could have come with me . . .'

'How can I be rid of it? Tell me and I shall do it!'

Kit looked down into her beautiful, selfish face and reached out, lifting her chin with one finger. 'No, I'll not have the death of an innocent babe on my hands nor that of the woman I love, and it would be dangerous for both. I must leave soon on His Majesty's business – and you, my sweet, must do what your husband tells you and rest until you are delivered of the child. Then you will have done your duty and may leave him with a free conscience.'

Sarah pouted. 'But I cannot bear him to touch me – not now that I know you still love me. I would never have married him if you had written to me, told me that you would come for me when you could.'

'I wrote you letters,' Kit told her with a shrug. 'I always meant to send them – and at least one or more was sent to your home. Perhaps your cousin took them?'

'Elizabeth would not have done that,' Sarah said. 'She brought me the note you sent after you saw me at the playhouse – but it might have been my father. He thought you reckless and perhaps did not wish for you as his son-in-law.'

'It does not matter now,' Kit replied and frowned. 'This may be all the time we shall have for many months. Come, lie down with me here and let me love you. I shall carry the memory with me and you may remember it and think of me when your husband comes to your bed.'

'I shall not let him,' Sarah said, throwing herself into his arms, the excitement rising inside her as he began to kiss and caress her. She had never once felt like this when Rupert touched her, and she was panting, hot for him as he took her down on the sweet, dry grass. 'Oh, Kit . . . love me. Make me forget his touch . . .'

'You are mine,' Kit told her, stroking her face as he bent

his head to bury his face in the sweet perfume of her breasts. 'You may be his wife in law but in truth you are mine. I have thought of you always while we were apart – and this shall be the sweetest memory yet . . .'

Elizabeth was thoughtful as she went upstairs to her cousin's room. Caroline had made it plain that she expected Captain Benedict to propose to her one day, and she had once or twice thought that something of the kind might be in his mind, which is why she had been careful never to be alone with him.

It was not that she disliked him. Indeed, she found him pleasant company for he was a good-humoured man and shared many of her own tastes in reading, music and her love of the countryside. If she had never given her heart to a man who hardly knew she was alive, she thought that she could have been quite happy wed to one such as Captain Benedict.

But how could she think of marrying anyone when she loved Rupert so very much? Hardly a moment passed without her thinking of him, and of late she had begun to feel his pain rather than her own. She had noticed a certain expression in his eyes when he looked at his wife, and Elizabeth believed that he had begun to realize that Sarah did not love him as he loved her.

How much worse it would be if Sarah were to run off with her lover! She could not be the bearer of such news, it would be too shocking, too painful for him.

Going into Sarah's room, Elizabeth thought at first that her cousin was sleeping, for there was a bulge down the middle of the bed, and the covers pulled up over the pillows. Then, as she stared at it, she knew that something wasn't right. It was not the first time her cousin had arranged her bed so that she could slip out when everyone thought that she was sleeping. She took a few steps to the bed, and pulled back the covers, discovering that Sarah had padded it with bolsters and pillows to fool anyone who merely glanced in.

The servants would have tiptoed away, thinking her asleep and not wanting to disturb her.

She knew at once that Sarah had lied to her. She had pretended that she was to have met Kit the next day, when the meeting had been for that morning. And for that she had been prepared to risk the life of her unborn child!

Elizabeth was disgusted as she turned away. Next time Sarah asked her to deliver a letter for her she would refuse!

Elizabeth took the supper tray from the maid who was about to carry it up to her cousin's bedchamber.

'Please allow me to do this small thing,' she said to the girl and smiled. 'I have not seen my cousin all day . . .'

Sarah was propped up against a pile of pillows when she went in, her eyes closed and a secret smile on her lips. She opened her eyes as Elizabeth set the tray down on the little table beside the bed.

'Where is Maria? I wanted her to make my pillows comfortable. It is horrid lying here so long!'

'Then why do you not get up and join us this evening?'

'I feel unwell,' Sarah said petulantly. 'Besides, you know that I have been told to stay in bed for some days.'

'That did not stop you going out this day.'

'What are you talking about? I have been sleeping most of the day.'

'You may fool the servants but you do not deceive me, Sarah. I pulled back the covers. I know that you slipped out to meet Kit for I saw you returning from the landing at the back of the house. You are so careless, Sarah. Anyone might have seen you.'

'You wicked liar,' Sarah said, but her eyes were laughing at her cousin. 'How could you make up such stories when I have been so ill?'

'I am not the liar,' Elizabeth said, but she needed no explanation of her cousin's remarks. If she dared to step out of line, she would be the one who was branded a liar and a troublemaker.

'No, perhaps not,' Sarah said and glowered at her. 'Anyway, you need not frown so. I have told Kit that I am carrying Rupert's child and we have agreed not to see each other – at least until the babe is born.'

'Do you truly mean that?' Elizabeth asked, looking pleased. 'If that is so I am glad that you have made your decision.' Her smile faded as she looked at Sarah and saw something in her eyes. 'But what of after the child is born?'

'I do not know,' Sarah said and gave a little shrug. 'If Kit comes for me I shall leave Rupert – but he may keep the babe.'

'Oh, Sarah . . .' Elizabeth was shocked. How could her cousin talk so easily of deserting her husband and baby? It horrified her and yet at the back of her mind there was a small seed of hope. Perhaps if Rupert was left with a child to care for and no wife . . . but no, she must not allow herself such thoughts. They were wrong and wicked and she would surely be punished for it. 'I shall pray that you change your mind and make an effort to be happy with your husband and baby.'

'I care not for your prayers, cousin.' Sarah shrugged and yawned. 'I shall tell Rupert that I am well enough to travel,' she said. 'There is no reason for me to stay in town now, and at least in the country I may walk out alone and take the air.'

Had she arranged to meet Kit at Thornberry? Elizabeth was suspicious. Sarah seemed too happy, too pleased with herself. She was planning something!

Sarah came into the parlour where Elizabeth was sitting with Lady Saunders. Caroline was not with them that day. It was now more than six months since they had returned to the country and Caroline was growing tired easily for she was into her ninth month of childbearing. She never complained, though sometimes she might be seen to ease her back, but she hid her discomfort from them all, especially Nicolas. He visited from time to time, but things were difficult in the whole country and he could not spare more than a few days with his family.

It was after they had returned to Thornberry that they heard the news. King Charles had feared that the Levellers amongst the army were planning to kill him. He was in a position of trust, treated more as a troublesome guest than a prisoner by Cromwell and others. Men who had hoped to make him see what was to be gained by coming to terms with them, and because he was not closely guarded, in the November of that year he had managed to slip away from his guards at Hampton Palace. He had hoped to reach France but a storm at sea had driven the ship to seek shelter on the Isle of Wight. There, the governor had imprisoned him in Carisbrooke Castle, where he had been meeting friends and dignitaries from various factions. It was whispered that he was plotting to bring in the Scots again, and perhaps foreign mercenaries to help begin a second war.

Sarah had heard some of this from Kit, whom she had seen twice since their return to the country, though not for some months now. He had taken a passionate leave of her, vowing that he would not fail to return for her this time. She knew that he had been to France for His Majesty and that he would fight if there were to be a successful rising.

Lord Mortimer and Rupert had resolved against it. They had become close these past months, working tirelessly to bring about a settlement, but Sarah did not think they would achieve anything. She dismissed them as fools, for she believed that Kit was right when he said that one last thrust would win the war.

'The Army squabbles amongst itself,' he had told her once as she lay in his arms. 'These traitors know not what they want, one faction pulling this way, the others another. In the end they will see that there can be no peace without His Majesty.'

Sarah was not interested in politics, though she pretended to be loyal to the cause Kit believed in so passionately. She was biding her time, waiting for the moment when her body would be free of this child that grew within her. She had carried it easily enough, though she complained and wept whenever Rupert came home, determined that she would never again let him touch her intimately. How could she when she knew how it felt to lie with Kit? Rupert's loving left her cold and empty, whilst in Kit's arms she screamed in her passion and clawed his naked back.

'Have you been for a little walk?' Lady Saunders asked as she saw her daughter-in-law. Sarah still looked beautiful and when she was not sulking she could be delightful company. 'You look very well, my dear, but you must not tire yourself. You have only a month or so to wait now and then all this will be over and you will have your child. It is such a happiness to have a babe, Sarah. All this discomfort will be forgot in minutes.'

'I am sure you are right, Mama,' Sarah said and came to settle into the most comfortable chair, which had been left available for her. 'Is there any word of Caroline?'

'My daughter is feeling tired I believe,' Lady Saunders said with a smile. 'She sent word that she would not come today. As you know, she is a week or two ahead of you and should be brought to bed at any time.'

'If she feels as I do she must long for it,' Sarah said and sighed, though indeed she felt quite well apart from a backache, which had started an hour or so earlier. 'You were reading a letter just now, Elizabeth. Who was it from?'

'A lady called Margaret Farringdon,' Elizabeth said. 'I believe she is a friend of yours, Lady Saunders – and some slight relation? She writes to invite me to stay with her should I feel inclined.'

'Does she need a companion then?' Sarah asked and looked put out. She was used to thinking Elizabeth always at her beck and call. 'You cannot visit her yet. I need you here – at least until the child is born, though I would not prevent you leaving afterwards.' It might suit her better if Elizabeth were not around when Kit returned, for she knew her cousin might try to prevent her leaving her husband.

'I shall write and tell Mistress Farringdon that I may not leave until you are safely delivered of your child,' Elizabeth said. 'I had already made up my mind to do so.'

'Elizabeth has no need to seek a position as a companion,' Lady Saunders said, looking at her with approval. 'She has been of such help to me these past months that I would willingly keep her with me, and I know that Caroline is of the same mind. However, I do not think that was in Margaret's mind. I believe she has other ideas . . .' She gave Elizabeth a teasing look reminiscent of her daughter. 'Caroline has whispered in my ear, my dear, but I shall not tease you. I know you have not made up your mind.'

Elizabeth was blushing. 'As yet I have no reason to make up my mind for or against anything.'

'That can only be because you have given Captain Benedict no encouragement,' Lady Saunders said. 'He called on us a month ago and I swear he would have spoken then had you allowed it.'

'Perhaps,' Elizabeth said, knowing it was true, for Captain Benedict had kept true to his word to call on them as soon as he could, and had so far visited them twice. 'I am not sure of my feelings. I have been happy with you, ma'am, and would not wish to marry if I cannot love.'

'Love is a luxury in marriage,' Lady Saunders told her seriously. 'If it comes you are fortunate, but many marry for liking and respect, Elizabeth. Caroline was madly in love, as was my son . . .' She glanced at Sarah who was looking elsewhere, her face turned away from them, 'and dear Sarah I am sure. However, many good marriages began with a simple feeling of mutual respect.'

'I know that you are right, ma'am,' Elizabeth said for she would not dream of contradicting her kind hostess. 'However, I must take my time. I do not feel that I know Captain Benedict sufficiently well to marry him.'

'Then you must give yourself time,' Lady Saunders told her kindly. 'I would not push you into this marriage for the world, though I believe it for your own good.'

Elizabeth remained silent, bending her head over her work. Sarah however was not prepared to let it go so easily.

'You sly thing!' she cried. 'You did not tell me you had a lover!'

'I do not have a lover,' Elizabeth replied quietly. 'Captain Benedict has never attempted to kiss me, nor would I permit it. We have talked together several times now, and I do find him a pleasant companion – but as yet I have not thought further.'

'I should take him while you have the chance,' Sarah said. 'You cannot live on others' generosity forever, cousin. One day you will either have to marry or become a companion.'

Her words were accompanied by a look of dislike, and Elizabeth wondered what she had done to deserve such spite from her cousin. Although she had angered her by refusing to carry messages to Kit, she knew that Sarah had seen him since they came to the country. It was much easier for her to walk alone here than in town, and no one else thought it strange that she should go for walks that kept her from the house for more than two hours. Elizabeth knew that there was only one reason she would do so, but she had kept her silence.

'I would rather find a position as a companion if need be than marry a man I did not love,' she said and returned her cousin's gaze. This time Sarah's eyes fell first and she turned away to hide her anger.

However, as she rose from her chair, she cried out in sudden pain and clutched at herself, her face going pale. Her eyes were wild as she looked at Elizabeth and then at her mother-in-law.

'It is the baby,' she cried. 'I am sure it is the child . . .'

Lady Saunders looked at her calmly. 'I have thought you were carrying low for the past day or so,' she said. 'Do not be alarmed, my dear. Some women give birth early, and I think that is what is happening to you. It may be that the birth will be all the easier for it, Sarah.'

Sarah shook her head, bending over as the pain ripped

through her again. If this was easy she dare not think what pain other women had to endure! She gripped the older woman's arm as she came to assist her, her fingers digging into her flesh so that Lady Saunders winced.

'It hurts! It hurts so much!'

'It will only be for a little while,' Lady Saunders said soothingly. 'We shall get you to bed, Sarah, and then the doctor shall be sent for. Be a good brave girl and this will soon be over.'

Elizabeth watched in pity as Sarah writhed in agony on her pillows. She had been in labour for some hours now and yet the child did not come. Her screams were heart-rending and Elizabeth had willingly done all that she could to ease her. They had been advised to tie cloth to the bedposts so that Sarah had something to hold on to when the pains came, but they had proved useless for she would not use them. Instead she clung to Elizabeth's hand or arm, her fingers digging so deeply that it caused Elizabeth to wince. Yet she let Sarah hold on when she needed, for there was nothing else she could do.

Bathing her forehead in between the contractions, giving her warm drinks and talking to her helped a little, but when the pain struck again she was like a mad thing in her agony. She called out abuse of her husband, declaring that she hated him and that she would die before he touched her again.

'Shush, dearest,' Elizabeth warned, soothing her brow. She was glad that Rupert was not in the house to hear the things his wife was saying. He had been due to arrive that weekend, which should have been early enough to be close at hand when his child came, but Sarah's early labour had spoiled his chance, and Elizabeth was happy for it; he would have been terribly hurt had he heard her cries. 'You do not mean it, Sarah. You cannot—'

'Damn you, Elizabeth!' Sarah cried, her fingers again digging into Elizabeth's arm until she had to cry out and jerk back. 'I do mean every word. I hate Rupert and he shall never come near me again.'

'You must not say such things . . .' Elizabeth glanced round at Lady Saunders, who had just come into the room. 'She does not mean them, ma'am. It is merely the pain.'

'Yes, yes, of course.' Lady Saunders smiled. 'Sarah is not the first woman to make such a vow in childbed. I may have said something similar when Caroline was born.'

Elizabeth thanked God that the lady was so gentle and patient, for many would have condemned Sarah outright. Lady Saunders did nothing but try to soothe her desperate daughter-in-law, until a servant came to tell her the news: Caroline too was in labour and she had asked for her mother to come to her.

'This is most unfortunate,' she whispered to Elizabeth. 'I feel I must go to Caroline for she has no one but servants to tend her – do you think you can manage here until the doctor arrives?'

'Yes, I think so,' Elizabeth said. She swallowed hard. 'If the child should come before he arrives . . .'

Lady Saunders took her to one side and explained about tying the cord before cutting it. 'My housekeeper is very good at such times, my dear. I shall send her up to you so that you will not be entirely alone.'

Elizabeth thanked her and returned to her seat next to her cousin. Sarah looked at her suspiciously.

'What were you whispering about? Where has she gone?'

'Caroline has also started her labour,' Elizabeth replied. 'Lady Saunders has gone to her but her housekeeper will help me and we shall manage until the physician arrives.'

'I might have known,' Sarah said bitterly. 'I am of lesser importance than Lady Mortimer! If I die and my child with me it can matter to no one.'

'Please do not talk so wildly,' Elizabeth begged. 'Lady Saunders would not have left you in any other circumstances, but Caroline has no one of her own. I am here with you, Sarah – and we have servants to help us.'

'But you hate me,' Sarah said, tossing wildly as the pain struck her once more. 'If I die you will get your heart's desire. I know it is why you will not marry Captain Benedict. You have always wanted Rupert. And now you want me to die so that you can have him.'

'I beg you will not say such foolish things,' Elizabeth said. 'I shall not deny my feelings for Rupert but I would not have you die. Your death would cause him pain and I love him too much to be glad of something that he would find hurtful. Besides, you are my cousin and I have always cared for you.'

Sarah refused to be comforted, tossing and turning, screaming out in her pain. Her confinement lasted another hour, at which time the doctor and the babe decided to arrive at almost the same moment. Elizabeth and the housekeeper had just seen the head come through when the physician arrived in time to do all that was necessary.

He made short work of the cord and afterbirth, handing the wriggling and bloodied body of a healthy daughter to Elizabeth with a smile of triumph.

'That is the second young lady I have brought into the world this day,' he said. 'Lady Mortimer was delivered of her daughter only a few minutes ago. I rode straight here at Lady Saunders' urging immediately the babe was delivered.'

'How strange that is,' Elizabeth said. 'They are almost as twins though born to two different mothers.'

'Yes, quite strange,' the doctor replied with a smile. 'Perhaps it is a good omen for the future since both of the babies were born healthy, and the mothers have survived the ordeal and will live. Lady Mortimer's ordeal was the more severe for I had to cut her and she was a little damaged internally by the birth, but she will recover.' He beamed at Sarah. 'As for you, young lady – you have the strength of a female ox and will be running around as good as new before you know it. I think you will give your husband many fine children.'

Sarah frowned but said nothing as he went out, leaving the women to remove the soiled linen and care for mother and baby. She was exhausted and lay back with her eyes closed while she was cleansed and made comfortable. When the door closed behind the doctor and the housekeeper, who had gone out with him, she scowled.

'That man is a fool,' she said to Elizabeth. 'No one could have suffered more than I did – and I shall never bear another child for Rupert.' Inwardly she was vowing that she would bear no more children. There must be some way to avoid it. She had heard tales of potions and methods of making sure a child did not come and she would discover the secret before a man touched her again.

Elizabeth had no idea what was going through her cousin's mind. She held the baby girl in her arms, feeling entranced by her beauty, the perfect little fingers and toes, and the warmth she felt inside when the mite clenched tightly to one of her fingers.

'She is so beautiful,' she said, laying her in her mother's arms. 'But the doctor said you should feed her before you sleep if you can.'

'Feed her?' Sarah looked horrified. 'I am too tired. Take her away – feed her yourself. No, you cannot, can you? Then find a wet nurse for her – anything but do not bother me.'

She closed her eyes, clearly rejecting her duty as a mother. Elizabeth was upset by her rejection, but she knew that arrangements had already been made in case Sarah had died or been unable to feed the babe herself. A decent woman from the village, who had a child almost ready to be weaned, was waiting downstairs in case she should be needed.

Elizabeth turned from her cousin without another word. She had washed the babe and wrapped her in a soft shawl, and now she carried her downstairs to be fed by the wet nurse.

'Don't you cry my little angel,' she whispered. 'Your mother may not love you, but I love you. Your father will adore you and so will your grandparents.'

Sir John was at the bottom of the stairs to greet them. He glanced at the babe and smiled, nodding his approval.

'My wife has sent word that she will be home soon, Elizabeth, but you have done well, my dear. Rupert will be grateful to you for helping to bring his child into the world – as we all are.'

Elizabeth smiled but her throat caught with tears. If only the child in her arms was hers – hers and Rupert's. How happy she would be. She would not have refused to feed the babe. She would have delighted in holding it in her arms and thinking of Rupert's pleasure when he came home.

But he would come home to Sarah, to a wife who did not love him and would leave him as soon as she was able. Elizabeth's heart ached for him and the child who had been rejected by her mother. It was unfair that she, who had so much love to give, must stand by and watch her cousin destroy the man who loved her.

Caroline accepted her daughter with a loving smile, holding her to her breast to suckle her. She was aware of some disappointment for she had hoped for a son despite the old gypsy's prophecy. However, she could not but be delighted that she had a healthy babe and perhaps she would give her husband a son in time.

Hearing a scuffle outside her room, she looked up and smiled as Hal came running in. He was four years old now, a sturdy lad, determined and sometimes wilful, but he had such a sweet nature that they all loved him, and she had been reliably informed that he was not half the tyrant his father had been at his age.

'Mama,' Hal cried impetuously, his blue eyes bright and questing. 'They would not let me visit you. I wanted to see you and my sister, but they said you had to rest. Why do you need to rest? Are you ill?'

Caroline shook her head and smiled at him, wondering why she had felt disappointed at the birth of a daughter. In truth she already had a son, though neither she nor Nicolas had made him; he was a precious legacy handed on to them by people they cared for. Sometimes she looked for signs of her cousin Mercy Harris in Hal but he was all Harry Mortimer.

She held out her hand to him. 'Come and look at your sister, Hal. Is she not lovely?'

He clambered up on the big four-posted bed beside her, looking at the child's face, which was perfect and not at all red or ugly. Hal looked at her for several seconds, then reached out to touch her hand. She gripped him firmly and he grinned with delight as he held her little fist to his bent head.

'She's pretty,' he told Caroline. 'Is she ours? Can we keep her?'

'Yes, she is your sister,' Caroline said. In truth they were cousins but there would be time enough to explain that when the children were older and more able to understand. 'She belongs with us, but she is small and vulnerable for the moment and we must take good care of her.'

'When will she be big enough to play with me?'

'Not for a long time yet,' Caroline told him. 'She will always be your little sister and you must love her and help to protect her from harm.'

'I shall fight for her,' Hal declared stoutly. 'She is mine and I shall take care of her. When we grow up I shall marry her and keep her forever.'

Caroline laughed softly. Hal could be so full of himself at times – and at those times he was like Harry. She prayed that he would not grow up to be as selfish and demanding as his father, for Harry Mortimer had destroyed the woman he loved and caused his own father much grief.

Hal would not be like that, Caroline decided. He had Nicolas and her to help him become a good, honest man, and she would do all she could to safeguard him against the future – a future that she sometimes seemed to see as vague pictures in her mind.

A little shiver went through her. She would not allow such thoughts, such pictures into her mind at such a time. Yet even as she tried to shut them out, she was seeing Rowena Greenslade with a child in her arms – a boy child. If that child still lived he was Harry Mortimer's eldest son.

But she could not know whether the child lived or had died of some childhood disease. Nor could she be certain that Rowena's child was of Harry's getting. She believed it in her heart and at times it troubled her, but she could not know for certain.

'Where is that son of yours? Into trouble again I daresay?' Roald demanded of the woman he had taken as his own to save her being stoned as a witch. He had thought to tame her, but neither beatings nor soft words had brought her to a state of obedience and when he remembered that the child she had borne was not his he was angry. Angry that she had given him none of his own.

Rowena looked at him, resenting his power over her and his coarseness – resenting the dream she had held once and lost because of a faithless man. Harry Mortimer had wooed her with soft words and gifts, but she had not given in to him until he promised to wed her. She was a fool but she had believed he loved her.

'I do not know where be Jared,' Rowena replied with a sullen glance. 'He be wild and impossible to control – and that be your fault. 'Tis Greta and your folk that have spoiled him, sayin' as he's to be their leader one day and that he will bring them good fortune. 'Tis not I 'as put the notions into his head.'

Rowena had other ideas for her son. One day she would manage to take him and run away, back to Thornberry and the great house that belonged by rights to her son.

'You're the one that tells him he's the son of a lord,' Roald growled, looking at her angrily. He had thought her beautiful once but these days she had lost much of her appeal. He had begun to look elsewhere for there were other women ready to smile at him. 'You do him no good by it, woman. You were not wed to his father and he has no rights over that house or land. If you teach him to believe otherwise, you lay up grief for him and others.'

'It was the beginning of the war and none but me knows

the truth,' Rowena said tossing her head at him. Her black hair was greasy, straggling down her back and she had ceased to bother about her appearance, but when she looked at him that way with her black eyes, Roald felt a sudden rush of desire for her. His gaze narrowed, hot and angry as she stood there defying him, and he reached out for her, taking her wrist in his strong fingers and dragging her into the caravan though she fought him every step of the way.

Jared watched them from his vantage point in the branches of a tree nearby. He had seen countless fights between them and took little notice of their quarrels. Once as a small boy he had attempted to defend his mother and been soundly thrashed for it. He knew that Roald was not his father, for his mother had told him he was the son of Lord Harry Mortimer.

'You are his eldest son and the manor of Thornberry with all its lands belongs to you,' Rowena had told him for as long as he could remember. 'One day you must claim it for it has been stolen from you by your father's brother.'

Jared did not know where Thornberry was, for though he and his people travelled all over the country, staying away from the fighting as best they could, Roald would never take the trails that led to that place. Yet he believed his mother's stories. She had told him that there was a great house and land somewhere that belonged to him, and that one day, when he was a man, he must claim it for them. Old Greta had told him that he was the harbinger of good fortune to their people and that one day he might bring them wealth.

Jared thought that he would like to own a great house and all the land that belonged to it, because he hated the constant travelling, the hardship, and the hunger and cold that was his life here. It was hard for everyone, but Jared felt as if he did not belong among the gypsy people. The old ones made much of him, but he was expected to be wise beyond his years, to behave as the leader he would be. All Jared wanted to do was fight. He had learned to fight young because the other children were jealous of him and called him names, teasing him when the old ones were not listening. And so he fought and he learned to win. He was already taller and stronger than the others of his age, and his eyes had a determination that some thought arrogance.

Jared scrambled down the tree and went in search of Greta. She was old and she smelled awful, especially her breath, but she was kind to him and she often fed him when his mother forgot.

Six

Rupert looked at his daughter lying in her cot. Lady Saunders did not believe in swaddling bands, and so the babe was free to kick her feet as she would, and she laughed up at him. His eyes misted with tears for she was beautiful and he adored her, as he adored his wife, though she had received him with sullen looks and reproaches.

'She is lovely, Sarah,' he said. 'Thank you for my daughter.'

'She caused me too much pain for me to think her lovely,' Sarah said peevishly. She was lying in bed, propped up against a pile of pillows and determined to stay there for as long as she could. 'But I suppose she is well enough if only she would not cry so much. I would rather you had her taken to the nursery so that she does not disturb me. She makes my head ache with her noise.'

Rupert frowned. His mother had told him that the child was as good as gold, also that Sarah had refused to have anything to do with her. They had brought the crib into her bedchamber for a few hours to try and tempt her to take to the babe, but it seemed that Sarah had no maternal feeling for her daughter. Almost three weeks had passed since the birth and she had still not attempted to nurse the babe or shown any desire to hold her.

'I am sorry you are not well,' Rupert said. 'I will ask her nurse to take her away soon for I daresay she will need to be cared for – but she is beautiful. I think her a little angel. What would you like to call her?'

'I do not care,' Sarah said, annoyed by all the fuss the

child was attracting. 'You name her since you think her so perfect.'

'Very well,' he said. 'I think we should call her Angelica for she is so good and so lovely that she makes everyone who sees her love her.'

'Call her what you wish,' Sarah said, 'but have her taken away so that I can rest.'

'I had hoped you might get up for a little while today,' Rupert said. 'You know that I must leave soon. I have business that takes me back to London.'

'I am far too exhausted to get up yet,' Sarah lied for she was feeling quite well. 'The doctor said I must stay here until I feel better and I am still not well. You expect too much of me, Rupert.'

'You need not fear that I shall force myself on you. It is far too soon for resuming relations of a carnal kind and you have not been churched,' Rupert said coldly. He was angry with her for not loving her own child, and with himself for wanting her so much despite her sulking. 'I may as well leave today as you do not want me here, Sarah – but I warn you that I shall not accept this behaviour from you for much longer. You are my wife and when I return in a month's time, I shall expect you to behave as a wife.'

He strode from the room leaving Sarah to stare after him apprehensively. He had never spoken to her so harshly before and she wondered if she had pushed him too far. She was forced to stay here until Kit came for her and she must watch her tongue in future. There was more to be gained from Rupert with smiles and pouts than by sulking, and she must remember that. She had to keep him away from her bed until she could leave with Kit . . .

Elizabeth saw Rupert come down the stairs. His face was shadowed by grief and he looked close to despair. She knew that Sarah had not once shown any sign of welcoming him home, and her heart bled for him. He could not fail to be aware of his wife's coldness, both to him and the child.

'Have you been to see your daughter?' she asked, for she

knew he loved the child. 'She is beautiful, isn't she? Have you decided what to call her?'

'Yes, I shall call her Angelica,' Rupert replied. His expression softened as he looked at Elizabeth for he had been told that she had helped to bring the babe into the world and that she spent some hours in the nursery every day, giving the child the love she was denied by her mother. And his mother was full of praise for her because of all she did in the house and still room. 'She is beautiful and such a good babe – a little angel.'

'Yes, that is exactly what I thought when I first saw her,' Elizabeth said. Her heart quickened as she saw his smile. How much she loved him! She remembered the moment she had held the babe and wished that she were its mother. 'It is a beautiful name, Rupert. She will thank you for it when she is older.'

'Perhaps,' he sighed, the shadows descending once more. 'Sarah says she is feeling unwell again so I think I shall return to London earlier than I had planned. It may be that when I come again . . .'

He did not finish his sentence but Elizabeth knew what he would not say. She wanted to go to him, to put her arms about him and comfort him, but she knew she must not. He loved Sarah and he would reject her advances believing them pity, because she could never tell him that she loved him.

'Must you leave again so soon?' she asked for she loved it when he was in the house, her heart lifting with pleasure when she heard the sound of his footsteps and saw him come into a room. 'You will be missed, sir.'

'Shall I?'

There was such despair in his face then that Elizabeth dropped her guard unwittingly as she reached out to lay a hand on his arm. 'Some of us will miss you greatly, Rupert.'

For a moment Rupert gazed into her eyes and she thought that he must read her love for him there, must know that she would willingly give him all that his wife denied. Then he moved away, as if realizing that this would not do, that neither of them could afford to become involved in a dangerous situation. He was married to her cousin, and she was a young maiden and therefore innocent.

'I thank you for your sentiment, Elizabeth,' he said, forcing down the unexpected feeling of desire he had experienced when she touched him. If he was in such a sorry state he ought to seek the services of a whore rather than have unworthy thoughts of a young girl. 'But I have business that takes me away. I shall return in a month or so. It is my hope that Sarah will be recovered from the birth by then.'

Elizabeth watched as he strode away, feeling the sting of rejection. She knew that he must have sensed her feelings and he had recoiled from them; it was her fault, she ought not to have let him see so deeply into her heart. Now he would despise her for her love.

She felt deeply unhappy as she went upstairs. At least she could nurse Angelica for a while, give her love to the child who would otherwise be left mostly to the nurse who suckled her, and the servants.

'I am so bored with the country,' Sarah complained. It was spring and the weather had begun to turn fine and warm, though she seldom ventured outside these days. 'I wish we might return to London.'

'Nicolas says things are too unsettled in the country for the moment,' Caroline replied, for sporadic fighting had broken out again, though it seemed uncoordinated and Cromwell's army was in little danger from the insurgents. 'However, I think we might go to St Ives, Sarah. I have heard that there is a great fair come to that town. We may purchase silks for our new gowns and other trinkets we need. Then, perhaps, when Rupert returns he will take you back to London with him.'

Sarah stuck out her lip sullenly, for a visit to the ancient market town with her sister-in-law was not what she wanted, though it would break the tedium of her days, and she would never refuse the chance to buy silk for a new gown. She longed for the assemblies and feasts that Kit had promised her when they were in France, for he often visited the French court and was popular there.

'Well, I suppose it is something,' she agreed grudgingly. 'When shall we go?'

'I see no reason why we should not go tomorrow,' Caroline replied. 'We shall stay at an inn there overnight so that we may break our journey and make it more of an occasion.'

Sarah brightened a little for she liked company and there were bound to be lots of people at St Ives, gentlemen who would stare at her in admiration, something she never failed to enjoy.

The journey was accomplished with no mishaps, though they passed a troop of Roundhead cavalry on the road, and the sight of them made Elizabeth's heart heavy for it seemed that the country was on the brink of a second civil war.

'Do you think it is going to be as bad as last time?' Elizabeth asked of Caroline when they had reached the inn where they were to stay. They had bespoken a private parlour and were seated before the fire, about to partake of an excellent dinner. 'I pray it will not come to anything. There was too much bloodshed the last time.'

'Indeed there was,' Caroline agreed. She looked up as a gentleman entered the parlour. He was dressed in clothes that proclaimed him a Royalist of some standing, and was rather handsome with his dark hair and bold eyes. She noticed he was looking at their party intently, and frowned as she saw that Sarah was having difficulty in controlling her pleasure. 'Do you know that gentleman, sister?'

Sarah glanced at her and blushed. 'Yes, Caroline. He is an old friend – a close cousin of my father's family. I believe he wishes to speak with us.'

Kit walked over to them as she finished speaking, making an elegant leg and doffing his hat with its brave feather. 'Ladies, I beg your pardon, but I am almost certain that I know two of you – Miss Bellingham and Miss Elizabeth I believe.'

'Then you do not know that Sarah has married,' Caroline said and smiled for it was an easy mistake. 'Please, you must stay and dine with us for you have much to catch up on I dare say.'

Elizabeth could hardly keep from voicing her objections. It was outrageous of both Sarah and Kit to deceive Caroline so blatantly – but she was powerless to do anything for she could not make a scene in a public place. She watched as Kit went out of his way to charm Caroline, talking of his recent stay in France in a light-hearted way and describing some of the newer fashions and fallals that he had seen in Paris. He also managed to discover from a falsely ingenuous Sarah that she now lived at Thornberry, and was invited to visit if he was passing. He stayed for only a few minutes, apologizing for not being able to spend longer with them.

'I have urgent business,' he told Caroline. 'But I shall be passing your way in a week or two. I may call if I should not be intruding?' Having been assured by both Sarah and Caroline that they would be delighted to see him, he then took his leave.

Elizabeth made a mental note to take her cousin to task when they were alone, but she knew that she would be wasting her breath. If Sarah had grown so careless that she could meet her lover under the nose of her husband's sister, then there was no reasoning with her.

She wished fervently that she had done something more positive before it had come to this – but in truth there was very little she could do if Sarah was determined on betraying her husband. She found it difficult to smile and act as if nothing was the matter, but her pleasure in the visit was diminished. It meant that she was on edge the whole time they stayed at St Ives for she feared that her cousin might suddenly run off with her lover.

Caroline had lingered over some particularly fine silk. She was trying to decide between a deep blue and a pretty green, and she turned to ask her companions which colour they thought was the most desirable. However, Sarah and Elizabeth had walked onto a stall a little further along the street, and were deep in conversation. Indeed, they looked as if they might be arguing over something.

Caroline wondered what could have made them cross with each other, for Sarah had been on her best behaviour earlier. She knew that Elizabeth did not always approve of her cousin's sulks, but she had thought they would both be happy to visit the market, which had many excellent goods to choose from and was even bigger than she had imagined. She debated whether to order her silk or go and see what the cousins had disagreed about, but just as she was about to walk on, to the disappointment of the merchant, who had hoped she might buy both bales, she saw something that made her turn cold.

A woman was moving through the crowds of shoppers; she had a basket on her arm and was selling cheap ribbons and trinkets to any who would buy. She had a young boy with her and it was he who drew Caroline's startled gaze, for it could have been Hal. She had to look twice before she was sure it was not her nephew, but then she realized that he was taller, his hair longer and greasy, as was his companion's.

She thought that she would hardly have recognized Rowena for the blacksmith's daughter had always taken pride in her appearance, dressing in the best gowns she could afford, her hair glossy and thick. She had been beautiful then, and it was her beauty that had won her Harry Mortimer's attention. Now her hair straggled beneath a kerchief, greasy and unsightly, and her clothes were in need of a wash and of poor quality.

Suddenly, Caroline realized that this was her chance. She had thought of the child so often down the years, wishing that she knew whether he was still alive. Looking at him now, she was certain that he was Harry Mortimer's son for he was so like her own darling Hal. She moved hastily towards them, eager not to lose them in the crowd.

'Rowena! Rowena Greenslade!'

The woman stopped, looking startled, almost frightened. For a moment she stared at Caroline as if she did not remember her, and then her gaze narrowed.

'You be Mistress Saunders . . .' she muttered.

'I am Lady Mortimer now,' Caroline said, keeping her voice carefully light. 'Where did you go, Rowena? Everyone looked for you in vain. We all thought something must have happened to you? I am so glad that you are alive and that your son survived. What is his name?' She looked at the boy, feeling a surge of pity as she saw the way he was dressed, his unwashed hair and dirty hands. In that moment she longed to take him back to the manor with her, to care for him as she had cared for Harry's other son. 'How have you lived these past years?'

'What do you want to know for?' Rowena pushed the boy behind her, her face sullen, angry. Her black eyes glittered with temper. 'You leave us be. We be entitled to our lives as we please and it be no affair of yours.'

'I ask only out of concern for you and the boy. He is Harry Mortimer's son, isn't he?'

'Aye, he be the lord's son,' Rowena said and now her eyes were bright with malice. 'His true son and heir – I be Harry Mortimer's true wife.'

'I do not believe that,' Caroline said, startled by her outrageous claim. 'If he would not marry Mercy, who was I believe his true love, he would not have married you. Harry needed to marry an heiress for he was deep in debt . . .'

'You be callin' me a liar,' Rowena cried, her voice loud and angry. 'Your husband be an impostor and my son be the true lord . . .'

'If that is true you must come to the manor and bring proof of your claim,' Caroline said. 'If you were married there will be a record of it and Nicolas will seek the truth.'

'You be tryin' to trap me,' Rowena said, her gaze narrowed and suspicious. 'If I come there you'll have me taken for a witch . . .' She turned and walked off hurriedly, dragging the boy with her and disappearing into the throng of people, which closed behind her. Caroline called to her but she would not stop nor would she look back and the press of the crowd was too dense to follow.

'Is something wrong, Caroline?' Elizabeth had come to her unnoticed and was looking anxious. 'Was that gypsy woman annoying you?'

'Annoying me?' Caroline shook her head. A horrible coldness had fallen over her and she shivered. Rowena was lying. She had never been married to Harry so why was she claiming that she was his wife? Did she hope to make trouble for Nicolas? Yet she could not think that anyone would believe her? No, of course not. It was just a piece of nonsense and she would not let it upset her. 'No, she wasn't annoying me, Elizabeth. It was someone I used to know . . .' She brought her gaze back to the young woman beside her, determined not to let the dark foreboding that had fallen over her spoil the day. 'Will you help me choose some silk, my dear? I cannot decide between them and I would value your opinion.'

'Yes, of course,' Elizabeth said. 'Sarah has bought some slippers and gloves, and I think she is at the silk merchant's stall now. Perhaps we should join her?'

'Were you arguing just now?' Caroline asked.

'Oh . . . it was just some foolishness,' Elizabeth said. 'Nothing to worry about.' Nothing that she could tell Caroline for to do so would betray her cousin and that could only lead to heartache for Rupert.

Sarah could barely contain her excitement. Kit had said that he would call in a week or two when he passed their way, and she knew that he was telling her to be ready. It was almost time for her to leave with him, to leave behind the boredom and frustration of her life at the house of Rupert's parents. She would leave the child too, for Kit would not want to be bothered with another man's babe, and nor if she were truthful did she. She had no love for her daughter and spent as little time with her as she dared.

Soon now she would be free to ride away with her darling Kit and they would go to France and live a much more exciting life.

Sarah had no thought of the future beyond the excitement of escaping the life she had grown to dislike. She had not considered what it would be like to be constantly moving from one place to another, or that Kit might want to stay and fight for the King. Her dreams were all of a beautiful house in a country where the sun shone all the time. She would walk with Kit in the gardens, dance and laugh with his friends, and wear pretty clothes every day.

Because her head was filled with dreams of the life she was to lead one day she was in a sunny humour as she waited for Kit's return. She had taken to walking to the village and back most days, for the weather was good and she thought she might happen to see Kit one day soon. It was a surprise to her when she returned from her walk a few days later to find that Rupert had come home. A little shiver of apprehension went through her as she saw the hot eager light in his eyes as he came to greet her. He wanted to make love to her and she couldn't bear it. The thought of his touching her intimately made her shudder inside and she felt that she would like to run away.

'You look so well, my dearest,' he said, reaching for her hands. He moved to kiss her but she turned her face so that his lips brushed her cheek. 'I have longed to see you but work kept me in London.' And he had not wanted to return too soon for he was afraid that he might not be able to keep from her bed and he had wanted to give her sufficient time to recover from the birth. 'I have brought you something special, Sarah. Would you like your gift now or when we are alone tonight?'

'Oh, do give it to me now,' Sarah begged, her face lighting up as it always did at the mention of gifts. She was like a child in her eagerness as she took the small packet he offered, opening the silk to discover a beautiful brooch. It was a miniature of Rupert painted on ivory and surrounded by gold set with pearls and rubies, and must have been costly. 'It is very pretty . . .' She laid it aside for it was not a gift that pleased her. She did not want to wear an image of her husband. 'Thank you, Rupert.'

Rupert saw the familiar sulky expression cloud her lovely face and felt anger at her summary dismissal of a gift that had taken much thought and effort on his part. He knew that she was not at all pleased to see him, and he was suddenly filled with rage. Sarah did not love him. He had suspected it for sometime and now he was certain. Indeed, he believed that she actually disliked him. Afraid that he would give way to his anger and strike her, he turned and walked swiftly from the room. He would have done better to remain in London!

Elizabeth saw the dark, brooding expression in Rupert's eyes. He had been at home now for three days and she knew that he was both angry and unhappy. Could it be that he knew Sarah was planning to leave him for her lover? Yet that was surely impossible for he could never have seen them together.

'Have you seen Angelica this morning?' she asked, hoping to lift his mood with mention of his daughter, but he merely shook his head, his expression unremitting and cold. She had never seen him thus and wondered what was on his mind. 'She grows all the time.'

Rupert brought his gaze to Elizabeth's face. 'I am glad that you care for her, Elizabeth. I fear my wife gives her as little thought as she has for me.'

It was the first time she had heard him speak so harshly of Sarah and her heart caught. What had her cousin done to cause this?

'Have you seen Sarah this morning?' he asked. 'I have decided to return to London on the morrow and I wanted to speak to her.'

'I believe she went out for a walk half an hour or so ago,' Elizabeth said. 'I am sorry you must leave us so soon, Rupert. I had thought you were to stay for longer.'

'I was,' he replied bleakly. 'But it seems my presence makes my wife unwell. It must be better for us both if I leave.'

'Oh no, surely not . . .' Elizabeth's heart ached for him. 'She is a fool! I wish that she knew what she would throw away.'

Rupert stared at her. For a moment she saw something flicker in his eyes and her heart caught but then he turned away, leaving the parlour. She heard him speak to Caroline in the hall and then, looking through the parlour window, saw him striding away from the house. She thought that he must have decided to go in search of his wife.

Caroline came into the parlour. 'Rupert is in a fine mood this morning. He asked me if I had seen Sarah and when I said that I had not, he went off without another word.'

'I believe . . . perhaps they may have quarrelled,' Elizabeth said. 'My cousin does not always think beyond what pleases her.'

'You mean that she is selfish?' Caroline nodded thoughtfully. 'Yes, indeed she is both heedless and selfish, but Rupert must have known that when he married her. I daresay he thought it charming then but such characteristics lose their charm after marriage I believe. I am sorry if he is not happy, but he must learn to control her and not to give her her own way all the time.'

'Yes – though I am not sure if that will serve,' Elizabeth said uneasily. 'Sarah is . . .' She shook her head for it was impossible to tell Caroline that she suspected her cousin of planning to run away with her lover. 'How are you, Caroline – and your daughter?'

'We are all well at the Manor,' Caroline said. 'I have had a letter from Nicolas and he wishes us to return to London to join him when I am sufficiently recovered, which of course I am. I wondered if you would like to come with me?'

'Yes, of course I should like that very much. Sarah . . . I do not know what she will wish to do . . .'

'That is a matter for her and Rupert,' Caroline replied.

'You cannot be ruled by Sarah for the rest of your life, my dear. We must find a husband for you – someone you can like and respect.' She smiled at Elizabeth. 'That reminds me. This morning on the way here I saw that nice young man we met in St Ives. I do not think he saw me but perhaps he will call on one of us. I know you have not decided on Captain Benedict yet, Elizabeth, but perhaps you like someone else better?'

'Oh no,' Elizabeth denied instantly. 'I do not like Kit Elbury. No, not at all. I much prefer Captain Benedict.'

Caroline frowned. 'Is there something about Kit that I should know, Elizabeth? I noticed that you were very quiet the day he joined us at St. Ives, but Sarah seemed to like him very well . . .' Her gaze narrowed in suspicion. 'You did not approve, did you? Tell me, my dear – why do you dislike him so?'

'He was never my friend,' Elizabeth said. 'I do not like or approve of him, but I can tell you no more. It is not my . . .' She broke off and shook her head.

'Not your secret? Is that what you would say? Is there something more than friendship between Sarah and Kit Elbury? Please tell me, Elizabeth.'

'I cannot. Please do not ask me. I have said too much already.'

'Are you protecting Sarah?'

'It is of Rupert that I think,' Elizabeth replied. 'I fear that he may be hurt – but I cannot say more.'

'Ah yes, I see. You care for Rupert. I have observed it countless times. It is a great pity that my foolish brother did not see that you are worth twice your cousin, Elizabeth. However, I shall speak no more of that for I would not distress you for the world. I respect your decision, but I think I can guess what you will not say.'

'You will not say anything to Rupert?'

'I am not sure. I must consider what is best, Elizabeth. Naturally, I should choose my words with care, but I think my brother ought to be made aware that he may have a rival.'

'You must do as you think fit,' Elizabeth said, but she was distressed that she had inadvertently given her cousin away. 'Yet I fear it will give him much pain.'

'Perhaps better to give a little pain now than that he should suffer worse later,' Caroline said. 'And now, my dear, I must visit my mother. We shall talk again soon of the visit to London.'

'You are not angry with me for not telling you sooner?'

'It was not your place to do so, Elizabeth. Rupert must control his own wife, yet now that I know I must find some way to warn him.'

Elizabeth went up to the nursery after Caroline left her. She stood looking down at the sleeping child, her heart aching. She was afraid that a storm was brewing and it would not be long before Rupert discovered his wife's perfidy.

'What will happen to you little one?' she whispered softly, bending to touch the child's cheek. She was so beautiful and Elizabeth never ceased to wish that she were hers.

Rupert was seething with anger as he walked. He could no longer put up with this nonsense. Sarah had refused to let him near her, pretending to a headache every night. It was unreasonable and he would not put up with it. She was his wife and he had a right to expect some show of duty from her if not love. It was a bitter pill to swallow, but he had to accept that she would never love him, as he loved her. Yet surely he could expect some affection, a little kindness for all that he had given her?

He would not put up with her excuses anymore. She would do her duty this night or he . . . his thoughts were suspended as he heard laughter and voices. A man and a woman together . . . and he would swear that the woman was his wife. They were coming this way; he could hear the excitement in Sarah's voice as he drew back into a small stand of trees to his left, taking cover so that he could watch them.

The man was leading his horse. He was much Rupert's own age and build, dark haired and handsome, dressed in clothes that proclaimed him a Royalist, a cavalier of some rank. From his vantage point, Rupert studied the man's face and searched his memory . . . had their paths crossed during the war? He was not sure but he thought he might have seen him once with a party of officers about the King – one of his close aides perhaps? He did not know him to speak to nor yet his name – but Sarah did. He could see from the way that she laughed up at him that she knew the man very well.

Anger churned inside him as he clenched his fists at his sides. He was torn between rushing out at them and accusing her of betraying him and watching to see what they would do.

'When?' Sarah asked, pouting prettily up at her companion. 'When will you come for me? Please, Kit, take me away with you now. I do not want to stay here another hour.'

'I have business this afternoon,' Kit replied and laughed at her sullen face. 'No, no, do not look at me like that, my precious. I shall meet you at our special place tomorrow morning and then we shall see.'

'Promise me you will come tomorrow?' Sarah looked up at him and then gave a gurgle of laughter, avoiding him as he tried to kiss her and running on ahead so that he was forced to leave his horse and follow.

They had gone beyond Rupert's line of vision. He could not see what they did now unless he left his hiding place and revealed himself, but he could see pictures in his mind – pictures of Sarah responding to the stranger's kiss in a way she never had to his. A wounding pain struck deep into his heart, twisting inside him like the blade of a knife.

How could she behave so wantonly? The false bitch! He was consumed with such anger that he shook. His stomach heaved and he tasted the bitterness in his throat as he fought the need to vomit. She was a faithless witch, a whore who had given herself to another man. Rupert saw it all now: the reasons for her excuses, her coldness, her dislike of his touch. She did not want to lie with him because she loved someone else.

One part of him wanted to rush out and kill them both. Had he been carrying his pistol or his sword he might have done so, but he was unarmed. He could attack the man with his fists, but he was armed and would have the advantage. Besides, Rupert wanted a reckoning with his wife. He wanted Sarah alone. To kill her lover would be sweet revenge, but he wanted her to feel the pain, the despair of knowing it would happen and that she would still be wed to him – the man she despised.

Sarah kissed Kit one last time and left him. She dare not let him walk up to the house with her, for even though he had met Caroline, and she would acknowledge him as an acquaintance, it might arouse Rupert's suspicions. Sarah did not want to risk discovery now. She was so close to escaping. Kit had teased her, but in the end he had promised he would come for her the next day.

'Bring only things that have sentimental value and a change of clothes if you can manage it,' he told her. 'I am leaving for France in two days on His Majesty's business and we shall buy you all the new gowns you could wish for there. It is my intention to visit the French court and you will want to be dressed fittingly. Besides, I do not want to see you in things he bought.' There had been a flash of jealousy in his face that made her laugh. If she had doubted his love for her, she did not doubt it now.

'I shall not bring any of his family's jewels,' Sarah said. 'I have a few things my father gave me, and I can hide some things outside the house first thing in the morning when the servants are still sleepy. Later, I shall find them and come to meet you here in the woods. I shall wait at the hut we took shelter in once when it rained. You will not let me down?'

'Of course not,' Kit said. 'I was a fool to be so careless of you the first time. I shall not be so again. You are mine and we shall be together always. It matters not whether your husband gives you a divorce or not. We shall be lovers and I shall care for you forever.'

Sarah was not sure how she felt about that, but she had not argued. Rupert would surely wish to take another wife and for that he must divorce her. Then she would be free to marry Kit, and that was all she had ever wanted.

She went up to her own chamber as soon as she reached the house, and began to look through her clothes. What should she take with her? Kit had spoken of new gowns, but most of Sarah's clothes were almost new for Rupert had never left her short of money. She was deciding between a green silk gown and a deep crimson one when the door of her chamber opened. She glanced round in annoyance, prepared to tell her maid to go away, but her heart missed a beat as she saw her husband. He looked so angry!

'Rupert?' she asked, a ripple of fear going through her. Why was he looking at her that way? She knew he was a little put out because she had not let him make love to her the previous night, but he looked so very angry. She had not seen him in this mood before and it made her anxious. 'Is something wrong?'

'You dare to ask me that?' he demanded, walking towards her, his expression sending a shiver of apprehension down her spine. 'You faithless whore! I should thrash you until you beg for mercy and give you none. How long has this been going on?'

Sarah turned pale and backed away from him. What did he mean? Had he seen her with Kit? But he couldn't have done! Surely he would have accused them both if he had seen them embracing?

'I do not understand you,' she said giving a little whimper of fright. She was sick to her stomach for he was no longer the man she had led around by the nose, making him dance to her tune. 'What have I done to make you so angry with me?'

He moved closer, reaching out to seize her wrist, his fingers closing about it with a grip of iron. 'Do not dare to play the innocent with me,' he growled. 'I was a blind fool, Sarah, begging for your favours, but my eyes are open now. I know you for the false bitch you are. You were always begging me not to touch you, not to make love to you, because you had a headache – but I swear you did not refuse him. I saw you with him, looking up at him like a bitch in heat. He has had everything that you denied to me!'

'No!' Sarah tried to wrench away from him. He was hurting her and she was frightened, frightened of the monster she had aroused. She did not know this man; he was not the man she had married – nor yet the gentle husband she had taken advantage of so many times. He was a stranger and the expression in his eyes was murderous. 'You are hurting me . . .'

'I intend to hurt you,' Rupert snarled. His rage was like a red mist in his head, driving all else from his mind. 'And I intend to kill your lover – but first I shall have what you have so long denied me.'

'No, Rupert, please,' Sarah pleaded. 'Please let me go. I am sorry I married you. I should have waited for Kit. I was promised to him . . .' She gave a cry of fear as he pulled her towards the bed. 'Please don't do this. Let me go away. I shall take nothing but an old gown. Forgive me . . . please don't do this.'

'Beg all you like, whore,' Rupert muttered as he flung her to the bed, standing over her, his face like iron as he began to strip away his clothes. 'I begged you often enough. I would have given anything for a kiss freely offered, a warm loving wife to hold and love – but you would give nothing freely. In future I shall not beg, madam. You will do your duty or I shall make you.'

'Please, Rupert . . .' Tears trickled down her cheeks as he joined her on the bed. She shrank back from him, trying to wriggle away, but he took hold of her arm, forcing her to lie beside him. With his other hand, he ripped open the bodice of her gown so that her lovely breasts were revealed to his gaze. 'If you do this I shall hate you. I shall hate you for the rest of my life . . .'

'I care nothing for your hatred,' Rupert said. 'If I cannot have your love I shall take hatred above indifference. You are mine and I intend to have you whenever I please.'

'No, please do not,' she whimpered, cowering away from him like a frightened child. 'I would rather die than let you touch me! Kill me, beat me, but do not make me do that.'

'You hate me that much?' Suddenly, the pain of seeing such fear in her eyes swamped the bitter anger that had overwhelmed him. 'Tell me, what have I ever done to you that you should fear my touch so much?'

She shook her head, drawing herself into a ball, her eyes dark and fearful. 'I cannot bear you to touch me. You fill me with revulsion. Your kiss makes me sick to my stomach. If you force me I shall kill myself.'

'No!' Anger warred with disgust at his own behaviour. How had it come to this? He had almost raped his own wife! 'You must not talk so wildly. I love you. I cannot let you go to him.' He felt the sickness turn inside him as he realized that there was no hope. In his anger he had destroyed anything she had ever felt for him. 'Sarah, I beg you. It does not always have to be like this. Forgive me. I will make it up to you – anything you want.'

'I hate you,' she whispered without looking at him. 'I have never loved you and now I hate you. Go away, leave me alone. I never want to see your face again.'

Rupert looked at her for a moment longer and then turned away. He walked from the room, closing the door softly behind him.

Sarah lay where she was for some minutes after he had gone. Her tears had dried. She felt numbed, sick and frightened. She had been sure that he would rape her as he had threatened, and she was terrified that he might return and carry out his threat. How could he behave so ill to her? It was true that she had never loved Rupert and she had cheated him of his rights, but what he had done to her was far worse. He would never touch her again! She was going to leave him now before he could return!

Oh, how she hated him! Her stomach curled, the bile rising

in her throat as she thought of what he had done to her, of the pain and humiliation he had inflicted.

She rose from the bed and went to her privy where she found cold water in a pitcher and a bowl to wash herself. She could not bear the smell of him upon her skin. She left her torn gown lying on the floor where it dropped. Dressing in the crimson gown she had dithered over earlier, she gathered linen and a green gown into a bundle, and then on a spurt of defiance, she tipped all her jewels into it and tied it securely. They were payment for his treatment of her and she cared not that they belonged to his family.

She pulled a thick coverlet from the bed and another warm cloak from her coffer, and then she went to look out of her bedchamber door, looking out to make sure that no one was about. She ran swiftly down the hall and the stairs, her heart in her mouth for she was afraid that someone might see her and attempt to stop her leaving, but fortunately the servants were nowhere to be seen. Once outside the house, she began to run. She ran as fast as she could towards the woods. She must escape before anyone realized that she had gone for otherwise they would try to stop her.

She would not suffer herself to be taken back. She would not wait for Rupert to return and perhaps carry out his threat this time. There was a small hut where she and Kit had sheltered once. She would stay there for the night and in the morning she would find Kit before Rupert did and she would go with him. She would go far away from the man she hated with every fibre of her being and never think of him again.

Seven

Elizabeth had been arranging some flowers in a bowl. She was placing them on a table by the open window when she saw Rupert leave the house. He was clearly in a temper, his face like thunder. She heard him call loudly for his horse and a few minutes later he rode away. It was obvious that his mood had not improved that day, but there was little she could do about it. She considered going to see her cousin in her bedchamber for she thought that they must have quarrelled, but decided against it. To tell the truth, she was feeling a little guilty about her conversation with Caroline. Rupert was already angry. He was bound to be very hurt when he discovered Sarah's intent to leave him.

No, she would not visit Sarah, Elizabeth made up her mind. She was tired of her cousin's sharp tongue and her unkind behaviour towards her husband. She did not know how lucky she was to have such a kind and generous husband, and if Rupert had chastized her for it she had only herself to blame.

Instead of visiting her cousin, she made her way to the large room at the top of the house that was the nursery. It was warm because the walls were panelled in a dark wood that kept out the draughts, and there was a small fire burning even though the day had been warm.

'Mistress Elizabeth,' the nurse greeted her with a smile. 'You have come to see Angelica. She has been very good today and she is ready for a little spoiling. Would you care to hold her?'

'Yes please,' Elizabeth said. She welcomed the babe into

her arms, smiling down at her and talking to her in the silly, loving way that women will to young babes. Angelica gurgled and blew bubbles, seeming to listen to every word that Elizabeth said to her. 'You are so beautiful, my darling.' She sang a lullaby to the child as she held her, wishing with all her heart, as always, that the child were hers.

Why, oh why, could Rupert not have loved her instead of Sarah? She would never have given him cause to scowl or ride away from his home as if the devil were after him.

Rupert rode hard for some time, his thoughts too painful to be borne. What had he been thinking of? It was a despicable thing that he had done – to threaten his own wife. His anger had made him cruel and uncaring and he must have hurt her as he threw her down on the bed. Sarah would hate him now, and perhaps he deserved it. A part of him wanted to return and beg her pardon once more, but his pride would not let him. He had loved her so desperately and she had betrayed him with another man.

The pain twisted and turned inside him, making him want to scream in his agony. How could he bear the knowledge that she had preferred another man to love her? Was he such a brute?

Rupert had never indulged in such rough sport. He knew that some of his friends were at times cruel to the women they lay with, especially if they had taken too much strong drink – but he had never hurt even the meanest trollop. The memory of the way he had threatened Sarah turned like a maggot in his brain. It was a terrible thing he had done and he could never forgive himself – so where was the point in begging for her forgiveness?

'I must have been mad . . .' he muttered as he saw the lights of the inn ahead. 'I was out of my mind with jealousy . . . forgive me, Sarah. I beg you, forgive me.'

But he knew that she would not forgive him. His marriage was at an end and he had only himself to blame. Even now he was torn between remorse and anger, and he knew that his salvation that night lay only in drinking until he could forget.

'Have you seen Sarah?' Lady Saunders asked when they gathered to eat supper that evening. 'I went to her room earlier but there was no reply when I knocked. I thought she must have come down, but she does not appear to be in the house. Surely she would not stay out this late?'

'I have not seen her since she went for a walk this morning, though I thought she had returned. I know that Rupert was looking for her and afterwards rode off.' Elizabeth frowned and hesitated. 'He seemed a little out of sorts. I think he was very angry.'

Lady Saunders looked upset. 'Do you think they might have quarrelled? Is that why Sarah would not answer me?'

Elizabeth felt a cold shiver down her spine as she wondered if Sarah had run away. God forbid that her thoughts proved true. 'Would you like me to go up and ask her to come down, ma'am?'

'I think I should feel easier in my mind if you spoke to her, Elizabeth. I know she is given to moods, but she hath a good appetite and does not normally go without her meals.'

'I shall go up at once,' Elizabeth said. 'At least I can set your mind at rest. I am sure she must be in her bedchamber.'

Elizabeth went quickly up the stairs. She knocked at Sarah's door but there was no reply so she opened it and went in. She saw that one of the maids had the gown Sarah had been wearing earlier in her arms and was looking at it anxiously.

'Is something the matter, Mary?'

'It's this gown, Mistress Elizabeth. I found it on the floor of Mistress Sarah's privy. It has been badly torn and I do not think it will mend.'

Elizabeth examined the torn material and shook her head. 'I think it is ruined, though you might make something of it for yourself if you used the undamaged part. I am sure that your mistress will not want it again.' She frowned and fingered the gown thoughtfully. How had it come to be torn like that? 'Is my cousin here, Mary?'

'No, Mistress Elizabeth,' the girl replied. 'I have been tidying her room for she had been looking through her clothes earlier and left some things lying about.'

'Did she not call you to help her change her gown?'

Mary shook her head. 'She must have managed alone.'

'That is unlike her, is it not?'

'Yes . . .' Mary hesitated. 'I think she may have gone . . .'

'Gone?' A chill ran down Elizabeth's spine. 'Why do you say that?'

'Because there are two gowns missing, some linen, two cloaks and . . . her jewels. I found the box lying on the floor when I came in, mistress. I thought she must have taken them out to try them on with her gowns. She sometimes does that – but then she leaves the ones she does not wear lying on the coffer or strewn on her bed . . .'

'Show me her jewel casket,' Elizabeth said. The girl handed it to her and Elizabeth opened it; there was nothing left but the miniature that Rupert had recently given Sarah. 'Where did you find this?'

'It was lying on the floor just there,' Mary said and looked a little frightened. 'I swear that it was empty when I found it, Mistress Elizabeth. I have not taken anything.'

'I did not suspect you of it,' Elizabeth said. 'Put the gown on the bed for now. You may return here and finish your work later. I want you to come down and tell your story to Lady Saunders if you please.'

'Shall I be turned off, mistress?' The girl was understandably nervous for the matter of the missing jewels was serious.

'You have done nothing wrong,' Elizabeth reassured her. 'But I am anxious about my cousin. I think a search may need to be made but I want to place the facts before Lady Saunders and hear what she thinks of this.'

When they returned to the dining-parlour, it was to find that Sir John had joined his wife and was drinking a glass of wine. He frowned as he saw that Elizabeth was followed into the parlour by his daughter-in-law's serving woman.

'What is this?' he asked a little testily for he was ready for his supper. 'Lady Saunders tells me that Sarah is sulking in her room again. What has she to say for herself?'

'Nothing, sir, for she is not there,' Elizabeth said. 'I am sorry to have to inform you that Sarah has disappeared.'

'Disappeared?' Lady Saunders cried in alarm. 'What can have happened to her?'

'Are you sure she did not go out with Rupert?' Sir John asked.

'I saw Rupert ride away alone earlier,' Elizabeth said. 'Mary – tell Sir John what you found when you went into your mistress's chamber.'

The girl spoke haltingly, but her story did not falter. She stood with her hands before her, but she looked at Sir John and answered his questions without fear.

'Very well, you may go,' he said after he had heard her out. He waited until the door closed after her, and then looked at his wife. 'Have you any idea why Sarah would leave without saying a word to anyone?'

'No, of course not,' Lady Saunders said and looked shocked. 'I know Angelica is in the nursery for I looked in on her before I came down. If Sarah has gone she has not taken the child.' She turned to Elizabeth, clearly in some distress. 'Do you have any idea where she would go, my dear – or why?'

'Forgive me, I fear that this will grieve both you and Sir John,' Elizabeth said. 'I do not know for certain but I think that she and Rupert quarrelled. He was very angry with her this morning and he went looking for her. I believe they may have quarrelled when he returned for I saw him ride away from the house and he seemed angry.'

'That is ridiculous,' Sir John said. 'A wife does not run off just because there has been a disagreement with her husband. It happens all the time and the world would be upside down if every girl took it into her head to run off after an argument. There must be something more . . .' His gaze narrowed as he looked at Elizabeth. 'You know what it is, do you not?'

Elizabeth hesitated, unwilling to speak but knowing that she must. 'Forgive me. I cannot be sure. If I should falsely accuse Sarah . . .'

Sir John swore loudly. 'Do you tell me that she has a lover – that she has left her husband for another man?'

Elizabeth swallowed hard. 'I cannot say for certain. It may be so. I know that she . . .' She quailed before the look in his eyes.

'And you have withheld this from us? Have we harboured a serpent in our midst?'

'I could say nothing for Rupert's sake,' Elizabeth said, her throat tight. 'I hoped that she would see sense, that she would realize how lucky she was . . .' She took a deep breath. 'I spoke to Caroline this morning. She said that she might talk to Rupert . . . though he did not return until after she had gone home.'

Sir John looked at her sternly. 'It was your duty to inform Lady Saunders, or me, of what you knew. You have not done well by us, Elizabeth.'

'I am sorry if you feel that I am at fault,' Elizabeth said, her cheeks pale. He was blaming her but how could she have spoken earlier? She had not known for certain that her cousin would go. 'I did not know that Sarah intended to run off today. I give you my word. I knew only that she was not happy and that there was someone she had liked before her marriage.'

'If you suspected her of faithlessness you should have told us.'

'No, no, Sir John,' Lady Saunders said and frowned at him. 'This is unfair. You must not blame Elizabeth for what has happened here. How could she accuse her own cousin of base behaviour? To have done so without proof would have been wicked. Rupert would not have believed her – and I should have thought her jealous of her cousin. If she spoke to Caroline this morning I think we must exonerate her of complicity.'

Elizabeth felt the sting of tears. 'I would have spoken long ago,' she said and wiped the tears from her cheeks with the back of her hand. 'I thought only of Rupert's pain and I prayed that my cousin would forget all idea of betraying him. If I have done wrong I beg you to forgive me. I would not have had this happen if I could have prevented it.'

'Where is Rupert?' Sir John asked, transferring his annoyance elsewhere. 'Why can he never be here when he is wanted?' He took a turn about the room. 'What do we do, Lady Saunders? Should we send the servants to look for her or wait for Rupert to return?'

'It would cause a dreadful scandal if we set up a search at this hour,' Lady Saunders replied. 'Elizabeth is not certain that Sarah has gone to a lover. If it should simply be that she and Rupert quarrelled, we should have caused a fuss for nothing. I think we should allow her a little time to reflect. It might be that she will return to us when she is ready. Besides, I think Rupert should be informed before we do anything.' She looked at Elizabeth. 'Is there some further clue you can give us, my dear – the name of this gentleman perhaps?'

'Kester Elbury, though he is known as Kit. He is the son of Lord Elbury.'

'Damn the man!' Sir John growled. 'Well, if there is to be no search tonight I suggest we get on with supper!'

'Yes, my dear,' his wife said calmly. 'I think we shall sleep on it and see what happens tomorrow . . .'

Elizabeth felt that she would rather go to her chamber than sit down to supper, but to do so would cause offence. She did not know whether Lady Saunders had made the right decision or not, but it was out of her hands now. It would be up to Rupert to decide what to do when he came home.

Sarah could not wait for the time to pass. She had spent an uncomfortable night in the hut but even though she was frightened, jumping when an owl hooted or an animal grunted, she would not have returned to the house. At first light, she left her bundle in the hut and crept down to the river to wash her face and drink a little of the water. It tasted brackish but she was thirsty, hungry too, but she thought that she would starve rather than return to her husband. If Kit did not come for her she would . . . but she dared not think of something so awful. Kit had promised to come for her. He must. He must!

The hours dragged by so slowly for she had nothing to do and she was frightened that she might be discovered, because surely they had started a search for her by now. It was with a feeling of wonderful relief that she heard someone approach the hut and then Kit's voice calling to her. She opened the door and rushed out into his arms.

'Thank God you have come,' she said, her voice choked with tears. 'I do not know what I should have done if you had not.'

Kit looked at her, a little surprised at her appearance for her gown was creased where she had lain in it all night, and her hair was beginning to straggle down her back.

'What happened, Sarah?'

'I cannot tell you . . .' She hung her head, feeling distressed by the memory of Rupert's cruelty. 'Please do not ask me. I have left him and I shall never go back there. Never!'

Kit looked at her face and leapt to conclusions in his own mind. 'Damn him to hell!' he said, believing that her husband had forced himself on her. 'He will pay for this one day, Sarah. Believe me, he will pay with his life.'

'No, please,' Sarah said in a choked voice. 'Please take me away before someone comes and finds us.'

'Yes, my dearest, I shall take you now,' Kit promised, for he loved her despite his careless ways and he was shocked and disgusted that any man could treat his wife as Rupert must have Sarah. 'I have a coach waiting for you. My coachman will make good speed. With luck, we shall reach the coast before nightfall and be on our way to France . . .'

* * *

Elizabeth had slept little that night. Several times she had gone down the hall to her cousin's room to knock upon the door, hoping that Sarah might have returned, but now morning had come and she was still not in her room. She thought that there was little doubt that Sarah had gone to Kit, and she dreaded Rupert's return. Would he too think her at fault because she had not warned him?

Rupert felt like death when he left the inn where he had spent the night drinking strong ale and bad wine. He had vomited in the yard and doused himself under the pump with cold water before finding his horse and riding back to the house. His head was drumming with a thousand hammers and he reflected bitterly that he deserved it for his treatment of Sarah the previous afternoon.

His only chance was abject apology. It was unlikely that she would suffer him to touch her again, but at least he could make amends in other ways. But first he must apologize and ask her to forgive him for he was determined that they must make the best of a bad bargain. Sarah could not leave him. She would ruin herself and lose all claim to her reputation if she did.

As he went into the house three people came out into the hall. He stared at their worried faces and an icy chill went through him.

'Sarah? Has something happened to her?'

'She ran away before supper last evening,' his father told him. 'Where the hell have you been, Rupert? We did not know whether to start a search for her – or if she might be with you.'

'I . . . God forgive me,' Rupert said and felt as if his father had thrust a dagger into his heart. He had been drinking when he ought to have been at home, trying to make his peace with Sarah. 'We quarrelled . . . that is why she has run off.' He pushed his fingers tiredly through his hair. 'I must look for her. Has anyone any idea where she might have gone?'

'Elizabeth thinks that she might be with a gentleman called Kit Elbury,' Lady Saunders said. 'We make no accusation, my son. Elizabeth did not wish to voice her fears for she thought to be doubted, but Sarah has taken some clothes and jewels – family heirlooms amongst them . . .'

'Be damned to the jewels,' Rupert said. 'I would give three times their worth to have her back. I shall wash the stink of that inn off me and then I shall try my luck in the village. There are but three roads they could have taken – to London, St Ives or the East. Someone must have seen them.'

'Rupert, I am so sorry,' Elizabeth said as he brushed past them. 'I should have spoken before . . .'

Rupert hardly heard her as he took the stairs two at a time. Sarah had left before supper but she had arranged to meet her lover somewhere nearby. Perhaps he would catch up to them before they had gone too far. He had no idea what he would say to her to persuade her to come back, but he had to try – and if need be he would challenge Kit Elbury to a duel. One of them should be dead before nightfall, and at this moment Rupert hardly cared which of them it might be.

Elizabeth walked up to the manor after Rupert had left in search of his errant wife. She was restless, unable to stay indoors. She knew that Sir John blamed her for this debacle despite all that his wife had said to exonerate her. Rupert might feel that way too when he discovered her part in it, and perhaps she was at fault. If she had only spoken to Caroline sooner! It had been impossible to speak to Rupert or his parents, but Caroline might have believed her and something might have been done to bring Sarah to her senses long ago.

Caroline was sitting in one of the small chambers that led off from the old, medieval hall. The stone walls had been panelled in a hard wood, though not with English oak for the use of oak was frowned on for anything but shipbuilding these days, and foreign woods were being imported to take its place. Softwoods and walnut were much used in furniture now after the Dutch fashion. Caroline was sitting at her needlework but paying it little attention for her nephew was playing with some wooden skittles and a ball, and demanding that she watch him.

'Ah, Elizabeth,' Caroline said, and then, looking at her face, she beckoned to the nurse. 'Go with Ella now, Hal. It is time for your rest and I have a visitor.'

Hal protested that he did not need to rest, but he was taken away by his nurse and Elizabeth invited to sit on the settle beside her hostess.

'You have some news,' Caroline said. 'My mother sent a note earlier but I thought it best to wait here until there was news.'

'Rupert has gone in search of her,' Elizabeth said. 'He said that they had quarrelled. I do not know what happened, Caroline – but I think he already knew about Kit. Her gown had been thrown down and she had taken only a few clothes with her . . .'

'She must have planned to leave,' Caroline said. 'I do not think she would run away without somewhere – or someone – to go to.' For a moment she thought of her cousin Mercy, who had run away because she was carrying a child. Mercy had walked for months, sometimes close to starvation, and died soon after Hal was born, but Sarah was a very different person.

'I think she must have made arrangements to meet him,' Elizabeth said. 'She was so reckless when it came to meeting Kit. I believe that Rupert may have seen them together. When he came back this morning he looked as if he had been up all night, and there was a smell of strong drink about him.'

'God have pity,' Caroline said. 'Sarah was a selfish little thing but Rupert loved her. I knew when they married that she would lead him a merry dance, but I prayed that they would be happy. This is a dreadful day, Elizabeth.'

'I feel that I should have done something,' Elizabeth said pleating the material of her gown with nervous fingers. 'Perhaps if I had spoken out . . .'

'What could you have said?' Caroline asked. 'Rupert would have demanded proof. Sarah had only to deny you and he would have believed her – you would have been thought a troublemaker. It was not your fault, Elizabeth. I know that you care for Rupert and that you were grieved by your cousin's behaviour. You must not blame yourself.'

Elizabeth nodded. Caroline meant to be kind, but the guilt lay heavily on her mind. Perhaps if she'd had the courage to speak to Rupert months ago this might have been prevented.

Sarah refused to stop for food until they had been travelling for an hour or so. Even then she was on thorns, fearing that Rupert might be close behind them, but hunger made her give into Kit's persuasion.

'You must eat, Sarah,' he told her. 'We have some hours of travelling and then a long voyage. You will not wish to eat on board ship, and you will do better with a little food in your stomach.'

She swallowed a portion of the cold meat and bread the inn served them, drinking a little of the red wine Kit insisted on giving her. It was not the kind of food she was used to but she managed to force a few mouthfuls down to please him. She could hardly wait to leave the inn, and urged the coachman to go faster than before.

'We have fresh horses,' she said. 'Let us make all speed . . .'

'Do not fear,' Kit told her with a grim look. 'If your husband should come after us I shall kill him.'

'But you might be wounded,' Sarah said. 'I cannot bear to go back with him. I shall not feel safe until we reach France, for I do not think he will follow us there.'

Kit did not share her optimism, but he was not afraid of her husband's vengeance. Indeed, he relished the prospect of a fight in which he might kill the man who had stolen the woman he considered his own. Yet he knew that Sarah was anxious, and he told the coachman to make all speed. They were bound for a small village on the coast, where he had arranged to meet a French vessel that would carry them safely across the water. He carried papers that would be useful to Cromwell and his cronies if they should capture them. Indeed the sooner they were passed on to the French King the better. There would be time enough for settling with Sarah's husband later . . .

Rupert soon discovered that the fugitives were heading east towards the coast. The coach had been hired at a hostelry in the next village and the ostler was able to tell him that the gentleman who bespoke it had asked for directions that would take him directly to the Suffolk coast.

Rupert thanked the man for his help and paid him some gold coins, then set off in pursuit. A man alone on horseback travelled faster than a coach, and they would need to stop from time to time to change horses or eat. It would be night before they could reach the coast, perhaps they would rest overnight and go on in the morning. If he changed horses but stopped for nothing else, he might manage to catch them before they boarded the ship . . .

'You are tired,' Kit said, looking at Sarah in concern. 'We should stop for the night. Your husband cannot catch up to us. My ship will wait until the morrow. I told them to look for me tonight, but if I did not come to expect me the next night.'

Sarah was bone weary for they had been jolted over country roads that were scarcely better than lanes and had deep ruts. Her head ached and she craved the comfort of a warm bed, but she was still afraid that Rupert might find them, and her fear was as much for Kit as herself. Rupert had sworn that he would kill her lover when they met and she believed him.

'Let us go on a little longer,' she begged. 'I am tired but I—'

The sentence Sarah was about to utter would never be spoken for there was a cry from the coachman and then a dreadful crunching sound and shuddering as he attempted to stop the horses. A fallen tree had blocked the narrow road, which had deep ditches to either side. The coachman fought valiantly to stop the coach crashing into the debris, but because they were travelling at some speed, he was unable to do so and the horses ran into the branches. The noise of their screaming mingled with the snapping sound as a part of the front end of the coach broke in two and it shuddered, rocking for a moment before it turned over on its side and slid into the ditch.

Both Kit and Sarah were flung forward. Kit tried to catch her but was unable to stop himself from falling, and she landed with her head against the door, lying face downwards at a strange angle. Kit was shaken but after a moment he was able to realize what had happened and to pull himself up to a sitting position and look out of the window. The coach was lying in a ditch, the roof submerged in water and the wheels still turning in the air, but at least it would be possible to scramble out of the door once it was opened.

'It is not as bad as it might have been,' he said, turning back to Sarah. 'Are you hurt much?'

Sarah did not answer. Kit felt cold suddenly as he realized that she had not moved since she had landed in that awkward position. He moved gingerly towards her, not wanting to tip the coach further, reaching out to touch her. As the coach lurched slightly her body shifted towards him, her head hanging to one side. Catching sight of her face, Kit gave a cry of anguish. Her eyes were open and staring. He reached out for her, realizing in that moment that her neck was broken. She must have died instantly.

'Are you all right, sir?' The coachman had scrambled down to them and opened the door. 'Do you need a hand with the lady?'

For a moment Kit did not answer, and then he turned his head, the tears upon his face. 'Yes, help me get her out,' he said. 'She is dead but we cannot leave her here.'

'Dead, sir? Oh, my Lord! Forgive me, sir. I did my best to stop but it was impossible at the speed we was going.'

'I do not blame you,' Kit replied, his face cold and angry as he lifted Sarah's lifeless body, inching her up until the coachman and groom could lift her clear. 'There is someone else who will pay for this night's work . . .'

Kit climbed out of the coach as the men laid Sarah's body on the side of the road. He knelt beside her, tears trickling down his cheeks as he bent to kiss her lips. Even in death she was beautiful. He cursed Rupert Saunders who had hurt her so badly that she had been terrified for her life. Had she not begged him, Kit would never have travelled at such speed. He was angry with himself for allowing her to push him into this headlong flight. Better that Sir Rupert had caught up to them. He would have enjoyed taking the life of the man he hated.

All at once the bitterness overcame him and he felt blackness in his mind. He got to his feet and began to walk off. There must be an inn nearby. He would go there and fetch help. He could do nothing for Sarah, but at least he could arrange that she be carried to the inn and buried decently.

His head was aching where he had banged it as he was thrown across the coach, and his mind was becoming hazy. The tears were trickling down his cheeks as he walked, but he was dazed and he had forgotten where he was going . . . forgotten that the woman he loved lay dead on the side of the road.

'Where do you think he be off to?' the coachman asked the groom as they unhitched the horses, one of which was badly injured. 'We'd best shoot this poor beast, 'Arry.' He drew his pistol and placed the muzzle next to the horse's head. The shot reverberated in the darkness and was heard by the traveller some distance back down the narrow track. 'What do you reckon we ought ter do about 'er?' He jerked his head in Sarah's direction. 'He's gone off and left her. Maybe we ought to go and find help – what do yer think?'

'We could put her over one of the horses,' the groom said.

'I don't like leavin' her here, dead or not – but he might come back and look for 'er. 'Sides, if we take her to the inn we might get blamed for doin' 'er in.'

'That's what I was thinkin',' the coachman replied and glanced at Sarah. 'Gives me the creeps to see 'er like that – 'e ought to have stayed with 'er while one of us went for help.'

'I ain't stayin' 'ere alone!'

'Me neither. We'll go and find an inn or a farm, and report an overturned coach. Let someone else come and find 'er.'

'What we goin' ter do then?'

'I ain't goin' back ter the hostelry ter report a wrecked coach and a dead 'orse, ter say nothin' of a dead woman. Gaffer would flay the skin off our backs,' the coachman said with a shudder. 'We ain't that far from the coast, 'Arry. I reckon we should keep goin' and get work on a ship. Someone was after me the other day to join the bleedin' army. I ain't goin' ter get dragged in ter that again. I 'ad enough of that bugger the last time.'

'Yer right,' Harry said and shot another glance at Sarah. 'Come on, we've got three 'orses left out of the four. We'll ride two of them and leave the other here. Someone will find it.'

'I don't know. 'orse stealin' is a hanging offence.'

'So is murder,' the coachman replied. 'I ain't goin' ter 'ang around and let 'em take their pick of what to charge me with!'

'Nah, nor me. Come on, let's get out of 'ere. Someone will find 'er – and I don't want ter be around when they do . . .'

Rupert heard a shot from somewhere ahead of him. It was getting darker but luckily the sky was cloudless and a few stars had appeared to help him see the way. The moon would be up soon, though it was on the wane and would shed little light, but it should be enough. He could after all not be far behind them now, and they were sure to stop somewhere for the night. Sarah would not want to travel much further. She must be exhausted.

He frowned as he reflected how easily he might have missed them for these country roads were little more than cattle tracks and he might have chosen the better road back at the crossroads. Fortunately, a yokel had been driving a herd of cows home for the milking and he'd told Rupert of the coach that had narrowly missed colliding with one of his cows.

'Drivin' like a mad'un he be,' the man said and scratched his head. 'Ain't no mortal need for such haste, master. I reckon he be up to no good.'

'You little know how truthfully you speak,' Rupert said. 'They have stolen my wife and are fleeing retribution.' He put some coins into the man's palm. 'I cannot thank you enough for your help. May God be with you.'

'And with you, sir,' the man said and shook his head. 'I knew there be evil in that'un. Drivin' like the devil was after 'un he be.'

Rupert nodded and set off down the narrow track. It was one of the worst roads he had so far come across and he smiled his satisfaction as he thought of the discomfort it must cause the coach travellers. They would be forced to slow their pace now.

It was at this point that he heard the shot. His nerves tingled for he could think of no explanation other than that vagabonds had attacked the coach. Spurring his horse on, he rode as fast as the rutted track would allow, his heart racing. If the coach was being attacked he would help to drive the ruffians off, but after that . . . His breath caught as he saw that a coach was lying on its side in a deep ditch. As he approached he could see that harness and wreckage was strewn near the ditch, and that a horse was dead. He thought that that might explain the shot. He could see that the cause of the accident was a fallen tree – which might easily have been avoided if the coach had been travelling at a sensible speed. And then his gaze dropped on something lying on the grass at the side of the road. It looked like . . . a woman.

Rupert felt sick as he saw that she was laid out like a dead body, her hands crossed over her breast. He dismounted, his senses already telling him that it was his wife. He knew the gown she was wearing for it was one he had bought for her. Her head was lying at a strange angle, her eyes closed, and as he knelt beside her, he realized that her neck was broken. It must have happened in the accident – but why was she lying here all alone? Why had no one stayed to protect her body until help was brought?

'Sarah – my poor darling,' he whispered as he lifted her in his arms, cradling her to him, his face wet with tears as he rocked back and forth. 'Is this what I have brought you to?' His cruel words, his harsh behaviour and his threats had so terrified her that she had run from him to her death. He was tortured by the knowledge of what he had done. If he had only talked to her kindly instead of making such terrible threats she might still be alive. In his wretchedness he was tempted to put a pistol to his own brain and pull the trigger, but even as he longed for death he knew that he could not abandon her.

Lifting his head he made a howling, moaning sound, like a soul in torment. He felt as if he was being torn in two, his love and remorse tearing at him like the claws of a wild beast.

'Sarah . . .' he moaned, holding her pressed to his heart. 'Sarah, forgive me . . .' But she could not answer. She was dead and he would never see her smile again, nor lie beside her in their bed.

'Oh, Sarah . . . Sarah . . .'

She must not lie here to be torn to pieces by foxes and rats. They should not feed on her flesh, nor must she go to meet her Maker without the blessing of the church. His own feelings, his pain, his emptiness, were the price he must pay for what he had done to her. He would take her home and see her decently buried and then . . . then it would no longer matter what happened to him.

He glanced around for a sight of those who had abandoned her, but nothing remained except the wrecked coach, a dead horse and another, slightly wounded, left to fend for itself.

Rupert approached the horse, catching it and running his hand over its quivering flesh. 'Poor beast,' he murmured. 'Did they leave you to die too? Your hurts are not serious. You shall carry her to the inn I saw a mile or two back on the road and there you shall be cared for.'

He tethered the horse and lifted Sarah in his arms. It was an undignified way to carry her, lying face down across the horse's back, but better than leaving her here while he went for help. He lifted her into position, then caught the reins, which had been cut free of the debris of the coach, and mounted his own horse.

'Forgive me, Sarah,' he said. 'But it is only until we reach the inn . . .'

Rupert rode slowly back down the track he had come. He was numbed, his mind unable to cope with the grief that had descended on him when he found her dead. He knew that he had lost her before her death, for if he had succeeded in snatching her back from her lover she would never have forgiven him.

'Why did you love him and not me?' he asked in his mind. 'Why, Sarah? I gave you everything I had to give. I loved you with my heart and body. I would never have left you to rot by the roadside. So why did you love him and not me?'

There was no answer. Rupert was alone with his grief and his regrets. All he could feel was the burning hatred for the man who had stolen his wife and then killed her by his carelessness . . .

Eight

Kit must have wandered for an hour before his mind cleared sufficiently to realize what had happened and what he had done. Sarah was lying dead on the side of the road, and he had abandoned her! What a heedless wretch he was! She deserved a decent burial at the very least, and he must see to it that she was looked after. He had lost his mind in the bitterness of despair but that was no excuse. He must find help and go back for her.

Looking round, Kit found that he was lost. It was dark now and this accursed countryside was a maze of narrow roads that were hardly better than dirt tracks. He had no idea where the coach had fallen into the ditch or of where he was now. He cursed himself as he became aware that there was nothing he could do that night. He must wait for daylight and then seek help from an inn. And yet he carried important papers and he had already delayed too long. Surely the coachman and groom would have fetched help by now? In truth there was little he could do for Sarah now, and his duty was to the King.

He must find shelter for the night and in the morning he would hire a horse and make for the coast. He crushed his conscience ruthlessly. Sarah was dead. Nothing would bring her back. It mattered little whether her body rotted in a grave or by the side of the road.

Elizabeth was shocked when she saw Rupert's face. She knew that he had brought Sarah's body home earlier that morning, though she had been on an errand for Lady Saunders and had not witnessed his return. The sickness twisted inside her for she sensed his agony of soul and her heart felt as if it would break. He was in such torment and there was nothing she could do to help him.

'I am so sorry,' she said, moving instinctively towards him, wanting to comfort him. 'I wish I could help you.'

'There is nothing anyone can do for me,' Rupert said. His eyes were bleak as he looked at her and she knew that he was looking beyond her, looking into the past as he confronted his grief. 'She ran away because I . . .' His eyes met Elizabeth's and she read the horror and self-disgust in them. 'I threatened to rape her, Elizabeth. She shrank from my touch and I was angry, out of my mind with jealousy because I knew she loved him . . . wanted him to touch her. I threw her down and ripped her gown and told her she would do her duty or I would make her . . . but she shrank from me like a child and . . .' He shook his head for to say that he had withdrawn at the last did not excuse him.

Elizabeth stared at him in distress. Rupert's confession shocked her, turning her cold, and yet still her love for him survived. She realized in that moment that she would never love anyone else, for if she could hear such a terrible confession and still feel this need to hold and comfort him, nothing could change her feelings.

'That is a terrible thing to have done,' she said. 'Yet I think she had driven you beyond bearing. Sarah was foolish. I warned her not to wed you unless she loved you, but she would not listen. Try to forgive her, Rupert. She was a beautiful woman, but she behaved as a spoiled child in her dealings with you. You must remember what was good of her and forget the rest.'

'Forgive her?' Rupert's face twisted with agony. 'Would that I could crawl to her on my knees and beg for *her* forgiveness. I shall never forgive myself for what I did – never!'

Elizabeth watched as he turned and walked away. She would have done anything to ease him, but he was lost in his world of pain and she could not reach him.

* * *

'Rupert hardly lives,' Caroline said to Elizabeth a few days after Sarah's funeral had been held in the local church. 'I worry for him. Nicolas says he takes no interest in anything these days. He tried to talk to him about the way things are going in London, for there is much unrest now – and the feeling against the King grows stronger since these latest uprisings. Rupert will not listen. He seems sunk in despair, as if he no longer wishes to live.'

'I believe he wishes that he might die and be with her,' Elizabeth said. 'I have tried to interest him in Angelica's wellbeing but he will not even look at her. I do not think he can bear to be reminded of Sarah.'

'He did speak to me of his daughter,' Caroline said. 'He asked me if Nicolas and I would stand as parents to her if anything should happen to him.'

'He wants you to take her?' Elizabeth's throat caught. She had prayed that Rupert would think of taking a wife for the sake of his child. If he had done so she believed he might have turned to her. She wanted his love, the kind of burning passionate need that he had had for Sarah, but if he had asked her to be mother to his child she would have taken the chance and hoped that one day he would turn to her in love. 'What does Lady Saunders say to that?'

'She believes it might be for the best. She would care for the child if asked, of course – but in my nursery Angelica will have company. She and my darling Claire are cousins and will learn to play together with Hal. It is surely better than that Angelica should be brought up here. My parents are not young and it might be too much for them as the child grows, especially if she should be wilful.'

'Yes, perhaps that is best for her,' Elizabeth said. She looked down at her lap, hiding the pain she felt inside. Her love for Rupert was hopeless. She would have died for him, but he hardly knew she existed.

Elizabeth was walking in the sunshine. She wanted to gather some wild flowers as a gift for her kind hostess. It was her last day as a guest in Lady Saunder's house. On the morrow Nicolas and Caroline returned to London, and she was to accompany them. Caroline had told her that she would live with them in future.

'You have become dear to me,' Caroline had held out her hands to her affectionately. 'And I know that you care for Angelica. Rupert has told me he is going away, and I shall take his child into my nursery. You will help me in so many ways, my dear – but if you should wish to marry I shall not try to hold you. Indeed, it would please me to see you wed to a good man.'

'I believe Captain Benedict has been in Oxford for some weeks,' Elizabeth said. 'He wrote to me from there a week last Saturday. I think he intends to come here after his visit with Mistress Farringdon.'

'Well, you may write to him and tell him that we intend a visit to London,' Caroline said. 'Have you thought more on whether you will marry him?'

'Sometimes I think I should like to be wed,' Elizabeth said and smothered a sigh. 'But I am not ready yet.' She was waiting for Rupert to notice her but as yet he had shown no sign of doing so. Perhaps he never would. Elizabeth knew that she was not beautiful in the way her cousin had been. Rupert had loved Sarah so much it was possible that he would never love again.

She hesitated before entering the wood for she had not often been there, but it was so warm that she thought it might be pleasant to walk in the cool afforded by the trees for a while. She liked the woody scents and the scents of the flowers, including the wild orchids she found flowering in a sunny glade. She picked a small bunch of them to take home, thinking how pretty they were.

Finding a fallen tree she sat there for some minutes, enjoying the freedom of her last day in the country for some weeks. In town she would not find it so easy to slip away, and sometimes the oppression she had felt because of her cousin's unhappy death made her feel that she needed solitude. If only

Sarah had behaved differently . . . and yet it would all have been so much better if Rupert had loved her instead of her more beautiful cousin.

'Oh, why could you not have loved me . . .?' the question was as always in her mind but unspoken. 'Rupert, I love you so . . .'

As if she had conjured him up from nowhere, she saw him approaching her through the trees. Her heart raced and she stood up, waiting for a moment as he came up to her.

'Elizabeth,' he said and smiled slightly. She saw that he carried a brace of woodcock, which made good eating. 'I have been gathering tomorrow's supper – but I think I have not seen you walking here before?' His eyes were bleak, dark with pain, and she knew that he was in torment.

'No, it is the first time I have come here alone. I usually walk to the Manor or the village – but it was so warm today that I felt I should like to . . .' Something in Elizabeth cried out that she could not bear to see him suffer another moment. And she knew that if she did not speak now it would be too late. 'Oh Rupert,' she said. 'I shall not see you again for some time. We are leaving tomorrow. I have to tell you. I have to speak. I love you. I have always loved you from the first night I found you wounded after the battle at Naseby. I ache for your pain. I would give anything to ease you.'

'I should have loved you, shouldn't I, Elizabeth?' Rupert said, his voice husky. Looking at him, she saw that tears were trickling down his cheeks and she moved towards him impulsively, putting her arms about him, lifting her head towards him, her lips soft and inviting. 'Elizabeth . . .'

Rupert was sobbing as she held him to her. She placed her hands on each side of his head, pulling it down to her, kissing his forehead, then his eyelids, tasting the salt of his tears, and then she kissed his lips. For a moment he made no response, then his arms suddenly tightened about her and he was kissing her, kissing her with hunger and passion the way she had dreamed of, longed for on so many restless nights.

It was as if something had broken inside Rupert, a dam welling up his pain and despair giving way as he held Elizabeth to him, kissing her, stroking her, his passion carrying him with it as he drew her down to the soft dry carpet of undergrowth the wood had shed it seemed just for them. The smell of the earth and bracken was in his nostrils, mingling with the fresh flowery scent of her hair.

'Love me, Rupert,' Elizabeth whispered as she lay in his arms, the passion she had held inside so long flowing out to him, embracing him, pulling him into its warmth and seduction. She was a lovely woman, loving and giving, offering him all that his wife had denied, giving it freely, showing her need for him without shame or restraint. Rupert moaned into the softness of her hair, her pliant body holding him by invisible chains. 'Take me, my dearest, let me know the happiness of being yours if only for this once.'

His lips were at her throat, his tongue seeking out the soft hollow between her breasts as he inhaled the enticing musk of her arousal, felt the urgent need throbbing between them. His hands were gentle, reverent as he touched her, marvelling at the sweet giving of her flesh, the welcoming wetness of her femininity as she opened to him as the bud of a rose, offering her nectar for his plunder. She came to him with all the love and longing that she had struggled to deny, so that he slid into her and she hardly felt the pain of his entry so ready was she for the loving that was all her heart desired.

Their bodies were perfectly matched as they strove to pleasure each other, taking and giving, like a sweetly tuned instrument. Elizabeth cried out, her nails clawing at his shoulder as the passion mounted in her and she writhed beneath him, gasping and panting with the extreme pleasure that swept over her in waves. Rupert moaned as his body shuddered and he spent himself inside her, lying still at last, his face buried in the softness of her breasts. It was some minutes before either of them moved, for they both knew that what had happened between them was something special and neither wished to break the spell.

It was Rupert who spoke at last, as he rolled away from her, lying on his back with his eyes closed for a few moments. 'Thank you,' he said and turned to her, gazing into her eyes as she moved her head to face him. 'I shall never forget the wonderful gift you have given me, Elizabeth. You do not know what you just did. I had come to believe myself a monster, unlovable and incapable of giving pleasure to a woman.'

'You gave me something too,' she said and smiled at him. It was the smile of a sensuous woman, a deeply passionate woman who had much to give. 'I shall not forget, Rupert. Whatever happens now I shall keep this time sacred in my heart.'

He got to his feet and pulled her up with him, and stood gazing down into her face. 'You are the most generous woman I have ever known,' he told her, a kind of reverence in his voice. 'And that makes me a monster for I have taken advantage of you for my own selfish . . .'

'Shush.' Elizabeth placed a finger to his lips and smiled up at him. 'You did nothing I did not want you to do, Rupert. I have thought of being with you like this so many times and now when I lie alone at night I can think of this day, and this happiness.'

'You know that I should ask you to wed me now,' Rupert said. 'I know that it must be, Elizabeth – but please give me a little time. I would marry you at once if there should be a child but . . .'

Elizabeth stared at him. She had believed that his need, his passion during their loving meant that he cared something for her, but now she saw that it had meant little more than fleeting pleasure. He was begging for time before he did his duty. He would wed her but only because he believed he had dishonoured her and his honour as a gentleman meant that he owed her marriage.

'No,' she said and she was shivering with cold now despite the heat of the day. She had given herself to him completely, and he had taken her gift, seemingly with delight, but he still loved Sarah. He would marry Elizabeth out of duty, but he would never love her. Suddenly she was angry, and ashamed of what she had done. She had thrown herself into his arms, begged him to love her. He had pleasured her, taken his pleasure of her, but still he did not love her. 'You do not need to marry me, Rupert. There will be no child . . .'

'Elizabeth!' Rupert called as she broke from him and began to run. 'Please listen to me. I did not mean it to sound that way . . .'

Elizabeth did not stop when she heard him calling to her. Tears were trickling down her cheeks as she ran, praying that he would not follow. It would shame her if he saw her weeping and she simply could not stop the tears. She had never given up hope that one day Rupert would turn to her in love, but even though passion had flared between them, even though he had wanted her, needed her desperately, he did not love her.

Her heart was breaking for she knew that her dream was ended. She could not go on hoping for something that she now saw was impossible. Yes, Rupert would marry her if she asked it of him, but he would see it as a duty. And she could not bear the idea of being an object of duty. Perhaps sometimes when his physical need was great he would come to her and they would lie together, but the wonderful upsurge of love and passion that had flowed between them in the wood would not be there – it would be merely a marriage of convenience and Elizabeth had suddenly realized that it was not enough. She wanted to be loved and she wanted to be able to feel affection if not love for her husband. She thought that if she married Rupert knowing that his heart still belonged to Sarah she might become bitter, and that would ruin any chance of happiness for them both.

It was over. The dream was over. She must put it behind her and think of the future – but it hurt. It hurt so much . . .

Rupert cursed himself for his clumsiness. He had hurt Elizabeth when all he had wanted to do was to reassure her that he would wed her. She had given herself to him so freely, and it had made him feel whole again. He had been sinking under a cloud of despair, but now, at last, there was a light at the end of the dark lane down which he had been travelling. He had been on the verge of taking his own life, though he knew it to be a wicked sin, but he had seen no hope for the future. When Elizabeth told him that she loved him, and that she wanted to lie with him, he had felt something give inside himself. The burden of guilt over Sarah's death had not gone, but it had eased.

He could not yet let it go completely. He felt that he had to atone in some way for treating his wife so disgracefully. It was not that he had wanted only to use Elizabeth for his own physical satisfaction. His affection for her was sincere and of long standing. Her love and kindness towards his daughter had not gone unnoticed. She was a generous woman, and though she behaved modestly there was fire in her. A fire that had helped to cleanse the hatred and disgust he felt for himself.

Elizabeth was everything her cousin had not been. Rupert acknowledged it, even though he could not pretend that his love for Sarah had gone. Despite knowing that she had never loved him, despite her betrayal, her selfishness and her hatred, he still ached for her. She cried out to him from her grave and would not be denied, reaching into his dreams to wake him to remorse and grief. He did not deserve happiness after what he had done. It was because of him, because of his brutality that day that Sarah was dead.

How could he offer marriage to Elizabeth when he was still tied to the past? Rupert knew that it would not be fair to her. It was true that they might both find comfort in the marriage bed, but Elizabeth deserved more. He respected her far too much to offer her the empty sham that was all their marriage would be at this time. He needed more time to rid himself of the nightmares, the regrets and the remorse. Somehow he had to earn the right to be happy with her.

He ought not to have taken what she offered. Rupert blamed himself for destroying her innocence. Perhaps one day he might be able to offer her a heart free of grief. Elizabeth deserved to be loved and he believed that one day he might come to love her, but that day was not yet.

He had been approached by a group of Royalists who were plotting to help the King escape from the castle at Carisbrooke. He had refused them brusquely for he had believed the cause lost, but now he believed that perhaps his salvation lay in joining those who had not given up the struggle. He would take himself off to join the rebels, for what did his life mean to him now?

But before he went he must apologize to Elizabeth. He must tell her that when his grief had abated he would come back and marry her.

Elizabeth told her hostess that she had a headache and would not come down for dinner that evening. Lady Saunders was concerned but accepted her apology. For herself she was sorry that the girl was to leave them, and she had hoped that Rupert might see sense and realize that his daughter needed a mother. Elizabeth would have been an excellent choice, for she adored the child and it was obvious to any with eyes to see that she cared very deeply for Rupert. The look in the girl's eyes indicated to Lady Saunders that some sort of hurt had been inflicted on her, and she was cross with her son for his insensitivity.

When he asked her where Elizabeth was later that evening she gave him a stern look and told him that he was on no account to disturb the girl.

'She has an unpleasant headache, Rupert, and she must be up early. I beg you, do not make life more difficult for her than it already is.'

'I have never wished to hurt Elizabeth,' Rupert said. 'I have always admired her spirit and her generosity.' And yet he had hurt her, inflicting a grievous blow with his careless words. 'If I write a letter to her, will you see that she gets it before she leaves? I shall not be here in the morning, but I owe Elizabeth an explanation.'

'Write your letter,' his mother said, 'and I shall give it to her.'

'Thank you,' Rupert said, a strange expression in his eyes. 'I must hope that she will read it and forgive me.'

Lady Saunders nodded. She left him to write his letter alone and went up to the nursery, for this was the last day she would have her granddaughter under her roof for a while and she would miss her. When she came down she found two letters on the table. One was addressed to Elizabeth, the other to his daughter in the event of his death. She frowned over them and slipped them into a drawer in the great oak buffet that stood at one side of the room. She thought that she would keep the letter for Angelica and give Elizabeth hers in the morning.

However, when she saw Elizabeth's pale face, noticing the dark shadows under her eyes, which were the result of a restless night, she decided that the letter should remain where it was for the moment. She had no great opinion of her son's common sense and felt that she did not wish to see Elizabeth suffer further. She was a pretty girl and in London she might meet a gentleman she could love. Then she would forget this unhappiness and become the loving, gentle woman she was meant to be.

Elizabeth had spent the night trying to forget what had happened between her and Rupert. Their coming together had been so wonderful that she knew she would want to remember it one day, but just for the moment she had to forget or it would tear her apart. His words had shamed her deeply, hurting more than she had thought possible.

She learned from Lady Saunders that Rupert had left at first light. He had important business to attend and knew not when he would be returning. Those words hammered the death knell to Elizabeth's hopes for if Rupert had truly wished to marry her, he would surely have left a message of some kind for her. During the restless hours when she was unable to sleep, she had wondered if she had misunderstood him or whether she ought to have waited for him to make himself clear – but now she knew that she had been right from the start.

Her pride made her walk from the house with her head high, and she did her best to be cheerful when Caroline greeted her into the comfortable travelling coach. Everything had been provided for their needs; rugs, a wicker hamper filled with food for the journey, books and comfits to help wile away the hours. It was a journey of several days and they would need to stop at inns overnight, but they had a full complement of Lord Mortimer's servants with them and would be well protected.

It was true that there was a war of sorts going on in the country, but the fighting was sporadic and seemed uncoordinated. They did not meet with bands of armed militia on the road as had been the case during the early months of the first war, and their journey was fairly uneventful, apart from a few tears from the children. However, they all had their nurses with them and so caused the least discomfort for Caroline and Elizabeth.

It was during the second day of their journey that they came across a band of gypsies. The roaming people had camped at the side of the road and the smoke of their fires drifted on the air. Looking out of the window, Elizabeth saw children and dogs playing, as the women sat making pegs and dolls to sell at the fairs. The men stared sullenly at the small cavalcade of coaches and wagons carrying the wealthy ladies to London, the women barely looking up from their work, but some of the children ran after the coaches holding out their hands to beg for money.

Seeing their thin bodies and dirty faces, Elizabeth was moved to pity. She took some pennies from her purse and leaned out of the window to scatter them for the children. As she did so, one of them, bolder than the rest, ran up to the coach and grinned at her.

'Tell your fortune, pretty lady?' he offered.

Elizabeth's heart caught for she could not fail to notice how like Caroline's nephew he looked, and something made her reach hastily into her purse and bring out a gold coin, which she threw to him. He caught it and bit it, giving a crow of triumph when he found it was made of gold.

'You shouldn't encourage them,' Caroline said with a little shake of her head. She had been reading a book of poetry and had not seen the children approach the coach.

Elizabeth wondered if she should tell Caroline that she'd seen a boy who had looked just like Hal – except that he was taller and very dirty. She decided it might be best to forget it. After all, the gypsy boy could not be anything to do with the Mortimers – could he?

Elizabeth was relieved when their journey ended, even though it had passed without any serious delay. They were taken to the same house at which they had previously stayed, for Lord Mortimer had leased it for a period of five years.

'I have considered buying it, should we wish to spend more time in London,' he told Caroline at supper that night. 'But we must see how things go for I like not the mood of Parliament at the moment.'

'What do you mean, Nicolas?'

'Some of them are calling for His Majesty to be tried as a traitor,' Nicolas said looking serious. 'It is not that I admire the King, but neither do I admire those who are in power at the moment. In truth they seem spiteful and intent on revenge.'

Caroline nodded. Many of those who now held power seemed bent on destroying the old traditions and pleasures of the common folk. They had already begun to ban the usual merriment at Christmas, declaring that it was a Holy time and should be kept for worship. Dancing round the maypole and other simple pleasures were also being denounced as sinful. It seemed that the Puritans' grip on the country was tightening, which was not what Nicolas and many others had fought for.

'I am not sure that I would want to live in London all the time,' Caroline told her husband, 'though if it is your intention to do so I must bend to your wishes, Nicolas. I should not want us to be parted for long periods.'

'Nor I,' he replied and smiled at her. 'I have agreed to remain in London for the moment, Caroline. Cromwell must be with the Army if they are to put down these uprisings. I doubt not that he will dispatch all the troublemakers in a short space of time, for they seem but hotheads to me. The King is still imprisoned and the Prince of Wales is in Holland. Even if it is true that some of the navy has revolted in his favour, I do not believe he has the experience to win this struggle. Charles Stuart was a fool. The General Council of the Army offered him generous terms and he refused them. Had he agreed there would have been no need of this latest struggle. He might have been King again, and these bigoted men who seek to make us all live in misery would have been put in their place.'

'And you wish to do here what you can on Cromwell's behalf? I think it a thankless task, Nicolas, but you must do as you think fit,' Caroline said. 'I dare say Elizabeth and I will be as happy here as at the Manor.'

Nicolas nodded, his serious gaze coming to rest on Elizabeth's face. 'I am sorry that your cousin died so tragically,' he told her. 'But I suspected she would cause Rupert some heartache from the beginning. However, I think I owe you an apology, Elizabeth. I once thought that you had a secret lover, but I now see that you were merely your cousin's dupe.'

'Unwillingly, I assure you,' Elizabeth said. 'I would have spared Rupert the pain she caused if I could – and the distress to your family.' As ever she felt the sharp sting of regret for her shame had eased and once again she was tormented by her love for Rupert, which seemed as if it would not let her be.

'Fortunately, it has not caused a great stir,' Nicolas said. 'Few know that she died running off with her lover. However, I believe Rupert may do something foolish. I have to tell you that I believe he has joined with a group of reckless men who would try to free Charles Stuart from his prison.'

'Rupert could not be so foolish!' Caroline cried and looked distressed. 'He gave his bond that he would not take up arms against Parliament again.'

'I pray that he will come to no harm' Elizabeth said, her face pale. 'Can you do nothing to stop him, sir?'

'If I knew where to find him I would have him arrested rather than let him put his head in the noose,' Nicolas said. 'I suppose neither of you has any idea of where he might be?'

'He went off without a word to me,' Caroline said and looked upset. 'I know he was feeling wretched, but I did not think he was so desperate that he would throw his life away in a useless cause.'

'I believe Rupert's life means little to him,' Elizabeth said. 'It may be that he would rather die for what he believes than going on living . . .' Her heart was breaking at the thought, but she fought against the tears that threatened. All she had left to her was her pride and she must preserve her dignity.

'I had hoped he might have spoken to one of you,' Nicolas said. 'I had believed that he might be allowed to live quietly at his estates, but if he is proven guilty of this offence, it could mean his life.'

Elizabeth looked down at her lap, twisting her hands out of sight. 'If I should hear from him I shall tell you,' she promised, though she did not expect it. 'I would rather you arrested him than that he should hang.'

'I could find a trumpery charge to detain him,' Nicolas said. 'But if he is implicated in this plot – and we know that one or more is afoot – he will be tried as a traitor.'

'Then I pray you find him first,' Caroline said. 'Or that my brother is not foolish enough to become involved in this plot.'

'I think it a poor plan,' Rupert objected as he heard the latest of what he thought foolish ideas to rescue the King. 'You would ask His Majesty to change clothes with a washerwoman? It is outrageous. He would never agree. It is far below his dignity. Do you expect him to shave off his beard?'

'It will be dark and no one will see his face for he will be wearing a hooded cloak,' said Thomas Becker, the gentleman who had proposed this plan. 'Mistress Tucker is prepared to stay behind and face the consequences. It is a brave sacrifice on her part and I think we should try it.'

'It is a foolish notion and doomed to failure,' Rupert replied angrily. 'We should gather as many loyal friends as we can and storm the castle. In that way we retain honour as well as His Majesty's dignity.'

'It is impossible to take the castle by force,' another gentleman said. 'Do you not think we have discussed this many times? It would be foolhardy and men would be killed needlessly. I believe we should smuggle a rope into the King's chamber so that he can escape from the ramparts.'

'And break his neck if he falls?' yet another voice demanded.

'I still think His Majesty should change clothes with the washerwoman,' Thomas Becker said. 'It would be a simple disguise and must have a good chance of success.'

A dozen voices shouted him down, for Rupert was not the only gentleman present to think it beneath His Majesty's dignity. Bored with all the talk that was getting them nowhere, Rupert walked from the room. He went outside, staring up at the sky, which was lit by only a few stars. He had been fired up with new hope when he came here, but common sense told him that these men had no real hope of setting the King free.

The plots they talked about were endless and seemed doomed to failure, as had been His Majesty's own idea of escaping through his window at the castle. Unfortunately, his head had passed through but his body would not and he had found it difficult to struggle free. Rupert thought that most of the plans these men made would have little better success.

Perhaps he would serve the King better by joining one of the rebel factions who were still fighting in other parts of the country. For a moment he considered going to London to talk to Nicolas, whose judgement he respected – but then he knew that he could not unless he was ready to ask Elizabeth to marry him.

His letter had asked her to wait for a few months. This second war as some called it could not last long for there was no one to coordinate the various uprisings, which were as much a popular protest against the way the people were being suppressed as support for the King.

He would not stay here to waste his time in idle speculation, Rupert decided. He had recently received a letter from a friend who was determined to ride north and join the Duke of Hamilton, who was gathering an army to invade and force Parliament to free the King. He would leave in the morning and ride to join his friend, and perhaps there he would see the kind of action that his bruised pride needed, and if he should die in the fight then so much the better. In death he might find the peace that Sarah denied him.

It was a very warm day in July. Elizabeth had decided to walk by the river at the bottom of the garden. Caroline had debated whether to join her, but she had decided to rest because she was feeling a little tired.

'I do not know for certain,' she confided to Elizabeth, 'but I think I may be with child again.'

Elizabeth looked at her doubtfully for it was but a few months since the birth of Claire, and she knew that Caroline had suffered desperately.

'Are you certain?' she asked.

'No, not certain,' Caroline told her. 'I have not yet spoken to Nicolas for I fear to raise hopes. I was fortunate last time in carrying my child full term but I do feel very tired, though I have not yet begun to feel sick in the mornings.'

'Would you like me to send for your physician?'

'No, I am not ill, just tired,' Caroline said. 'Go for your

walk, Elizabeth, but if you intend to leave the garden you should take a maid with you.'

'Yes, of course,' Elizabeth agreed. 'I should not dream of leaving the gardens on my own, but I think I can be quite content walking as far as the river. I shall not stray away so do not be anxious for me.'

Caroline had smiled and gone to her room. Elizabeth had wandered down to the riverbank to watch the swans glide by. The adult birds had reared five cygnets earlier that year and sailed by in stately convoy. She wished that she had begged some scraps of bread from the kitchens to feed them, but had not thought of it until now.

A wave of sadness came over as she wondered where Rupert was and what he was doing. She did not think he had been involved in the latest plot to free the King for Nicolas had told them that some of the plotters had been arrested.

'I am thankful that Rupert was not amongst them,' he had told Caroline and Elizabeth the previous evening. 'We did not take them all, but I am reliably informed that the names are known and Rupert is not on the list of traitors.'

'I thank God for it,' Caroline said. 'At least my poor foolish brother is not hunted as a traitor.'

Elizabeth had said nothing. If Rupert had not been with the plotters, then where was he? She had waited in vain for a letter, and was now convinced that she would never receive one. Rupert had forgotten her – and she must make up her mind to forget him.

She had met several gentlemen since they had returned to London, and more than one had shown an interest in her. She had felt no awakening desire to know any of them more intimately. Indeed, she had made up her mind to it that she would never marry. She knew that she was welcome to make her home with Caroline, and she thought that it was the best she could hope of life.

Turning, she began to stroll back to the house. When she saw the man walking towards her, her heart began to thump.

For a moment she thought it might be the man she had longed for with all her heart, but as they came closer to each other she saw that it was Captain Benedict.

'Ah, Elizabeth,' he said and smiled at her. 'I was told that I might find you in the gardens and it seems that my information was correct.'

'Yes, indeed, sir,' Elizabeth said. 'I have been to the river to watch the swans. It is such a beautiful day that I did not wish to stay indoors.'

She was a modest girl and had no idea of how lovely she looked with her hair hanging loose about her face, tangled by the wind. Her cheeks had a fresh colour to them, and the man's body quickened at the sight of her. He had taken his time to make up his mind, because he was a cautious man, but now he knew that his instincts had been right. Elizabeth had changed in some small subtle way, becoming even more desirable than before.

'Indeed, no,' he agreed. 'It is far too nice a day to be cooped up inside. I should have liked to walk with you, but I think it was your intention to return to the house?'

'Yes, I must return for I have been out nearly an hour and I would not worry Caroline.'

'Then we shall walk back together,' he said, but stood where he was for a moment, hesitating before he began again, 'Elizabeth . . . I have not spoken before because I knew you were not ready, but now I must say what is in my mind. I have a great admiration for you. I would call it love but I think you prefer a more modest tone. Yet I would care for you and do all in my power to make you happy – if you would consent to be my wife?'

Elizabeth was silent for a moment. She knew that if she refused him this time it would be the last time for he would not ask again. He was a proud man and would take rejection hard. Her mind was in great turmoil for she liked him more than any man she knew other than Rupert.

'Captain Benedict,' she said after a moment. 'You do me great honour, sir . . .' She was to get no further for at that moment one of the maids came rushing from the house.

'Mistress Elizabeth . . . Mistress Elizabeth. You must come quickly!'

Elizabeth went towards her. 'What is the matter?' she asked for she knew that something must be terribly wrong.

'Lady Mortimer is in great pain, mistress,' the girl gasped. 'We've sent for the physician but she is asking for you.'

Elizabeth turned to her companion. 'I must go to Caroline,' she said. 'Forgive me. I hope you will call on me again in a few days. I shall give you my answer then.'

'Of course,' he said and looked concerned. 'I shall delay you no longer – but I will return for my answer.'

'Do so,' Elizabeth said. 'And now I must go . . .'

She walked hurriedly back to the house. Her mind was in turmoil for she had been on the verge of rejecting him, though it was not easy to find the words. She had no wish to hurt him, but she was still uncertain how she felt about him, and her heart still cried out to Rupert. If only he would come home or send her some word . . .

Nine

'How are you this morning?' Elizabeth asked as she carried a bowl of sweet smelling roses into Caroline's bedchamber. She was sitting propped up against the pillows looking pale but less tired than she had been since the miscarriage. 'You look a little better, dearest.'

'Yes, I am better,' Caroline replied and attempted to smile. However, the sadness was reflected in her eyes for the doctor had told her that he feared she would not carry another child full term.

'Nicolas thinks you ought to return to the country,' Elizabeth said. 'I am very willing to go with you should you wish it.'

'No, no, my dear,' Caroline said. 'I shall stay here with my husband. If I went home I should pine. It is better that I remain with Nicolas for a while. Besides, did you not tell me that Captain Benedict is to call on you later today? I imagine I know why he comes. Have you decided upon your answer, Elizabeth?'

'I think so,' she replied gravely. It had cost her some sleepless nights but she had come to a decision that differed from the one she would have offered him if they had not been interrupted. 'I do not love Captain Benedict but I do admire and respect him as a person. If he is satisfied with that I think I shall marry him, but I shall tell him the truth and he must decide whether he wishes to withdraw his offer.'

'That is being very direct,' Caroline said. 'Are you certain that that is the best thing? If you feel affection for him could you not just tell him so?'

'I thought it better to be entirely honest.' Elizabeth looked at her thoughtfully. She considered the very least she ought to confess to Captain Benedict was that she did not love him, and she had considered telling him the whole truth concerning her relationship with Rupert. 'Do you not think it would be wrong to allow him to believe something that is false?'

'I cannot tell you what you should do,' Caroline said, 'but a man has his pride, my dear. Have you considered that you may never marry if he withdraws his offer?'

'I had thought never to marry,' Elizabeth confessed. It was in truth her longing for a child that had made her reconsider. She had understood Caroline's suffering at the lost of her babe, and her love for Angelica had made her realize how much she would miss if she were never to have a child of her own. 'Indeed, I had made up my mind to it for you told me I might stay with you for as long as I wished?'

'And that holds true,' Caroline said. 'But there is a greater happiness to be had, Elizabeth. A husband, children, and a home of your own – surely you must hope for them?'

'Yes, I have hoped,' Elizabeth said a little sadly. She had longed for all those things when she lay in bed, remembering the sweetness of Rupert's loving, her body aching for his touch. And she had wished that she was carrying his child, but her monthly flow had come as usual and she had shed tears of disappointment, for she would have borne the shame to have the happiness of bearing his child. 'But I do not think I could lie to Captain Benedict. It would not be just.'

'Then you must do as you wish,' Caroline said and sighed. 'If only my foolish brother had noticed what a treasure he had under his nose, but it seems that he has lost all reason. Nicolas believes he has taken up with the Duke of Hamilton and may be with the invading army. It will fail, as have all the other attempts to vanquish Cromwell's New Model Army – and I fear for Rupert if the defeat is crushing. The Army will show little mercy to those that hold out to the bitter end.'

'I pray that Rupert has not been foolish enough to join

them,' Elizabeth replied. 'This has been a long and bitter struggle, Caroline. I sometimes think of all those young men who began with such high ideals, to fight for their King and what they saw as his divine right to rule. How bitter it must be for them to see all their efforts come to nothing.' How many young men had lost their lives for a lost cause? How many families been torn apart by the bitter contest, their estates ruined or confiscated?

'Cromwell will put an end to their hopes,' Caroline said. 'Nicolas says that James, Duke of Hamilton, is bringing an army south from Scotland and that Cromwell plans to meet them in the North. I fear that the other Royalist strongholds cannot hold out for much longer.'

'Then we must pray that Rupert escapes somehow,' Elizabeth said. 'I have heard that many Royalists have fled to France, and I hope with all my heart that Rupert will do likewise before the end.

'I pray that you are right,' Caroline whispered a silent prayer. 'Better that my foolish brother remain an exile than meet his end at the rope's end.'

'Yes, better that he should live in exile,' Elizabeth agreed. Her heart cried out that she would willingly have followed him to the ends of the earth if he had asked her, but that was something she must bury deep in her heart. If she accepted Captain Benedict, she must never think of Rupert again.

'You know what I have come to ask of you,' Captain Benedict said when they met that afternoon in the small back-parlour that overlooked the gardens, just now in full bloom, the sweet scent of roses and honeysuckle floating in at the open window. The sun threw a dappled light into the room, shaded as it was by the crown of an ancient oak tree. 'I have carried hopes of you these many months, Elizabeth. I waited for I knew that you had no wish to marry and I did not wish to ask too soon, but now I would have an answer.'

'I am very willing to give it,' Elizabeth said. She looked at him steadily, her manner unflinching. 'First I must be honest with you, sir, for it would be wrong to do otherwise. There was another who was close to my heart. My hopes of him were foolish and have been forgotten.' Would that it were truly so! 'I have a warm affection for you, and I admire you very much. You are an honest and good man, and I think that love may come through the years. However, I know that you hoped for more and I absolve you of your offer should you wish to withdraw it.'

'I am not sure what you are saying, Elizabeth. Is it that you will marry me though you do not love me in the way I love you?' He looked at her oddly and she wondered if Caroline had been right. Had she hurt his pride? She was sorry if that were so for she truly liked him, believed that she might have loved him if it were not for Rupert. 'If you will have me, I can and shall accept that you do not feel quite as I do, my dearest. I believe it is often the case, but I see no reason why we should not be happy. I shall do all in my power to make you happy, and that is where true love begins I think?'

Elizabeth's heart jerked, and she wondered if she had been foolish to commit herself to a man she did not truly love. A part of her still cried out for Rupert but she knew that it was hopeless. He did not love her, would never love her. His heart was in the grave with Sarah. Was she to spend her life as an onlooker, watching others? She would never know the fulfilment of bearing children if she cast aside this chance, and yet a little voice at the back of her mind told her that she ought to have told Captain Benedict the whole truth.

It was too late now. His face was glowing with happiness, his eyes giving her a look of such adoration that she found the words choked in her throat and she could not say them. How could she confess that she had lain with a lover? His look would turn to scorn and she could not bear that he should despise her. It might have been best if she had sent him away at the start, but the die was cast. There was no going back now.

'You do me too much honour, sir,' she said and gave him

her hand. 'But I shall try to be a good wife and never give you cause for anger.'

'You could never do that, Elizabeth,' he said and put his arms around her, drawing her close. 'You are everything I have ever dreamed of, the perfect wife – honest, beautiful and generous. What man could ask for more?'

'You praise me too much,' Elizabeth said, smitten with remorse. He was indeed a good man and he did not deserve to be deceived this way – but how could she tell him the truth? It was clear that she could not. She could only pray that he never discovered it for himself. 'I believe I have been more fortunate than I could have guessed, sir.'

Indeed, as he kissed her, his lips soft and gentle, she felt a stirring of something deep inside her and knew that it would not be hard to lie with this man. She wished with all her heart that she need not deceive him, that she could give to him the gift that a woman can give only once. Had she not been foolish she might have gone to him on her wedding night with a clear conscience, but all she could do now was to be faithful and true and spend the rest of her life trying to make amends.

Rupert lay sleepless on the hard ground, his mind reeling with the events of the past few days. The sound of screaming, of the thunder of hooves, and the clash of steel upon steel was whirling in his brain, bringing back the nightmare of defeat, though the battle was over now. He had the stench of blood in his nostrils, the stink of decay clouding his mind.

He had joined with other cavalier officers under the leadership of Sir Marmaduke Langdale, and when the Duke of Hamilton crossed the border with his army of Engagers, they had combined forces. It had seemed then that they stood a good chance of pressing on towards London but the people of Lancashire had given little welcome to the invaders, and on the seventeenth of August 1648 at Ribbelton Moor on the outskirts of Preston, Cromwell had come up with them.

His cavalry had charged down upon them with such force

that they had no time to regroup before the infantry followed with a great push. The Royalists had fought bravely, desperately, for it had been in all their minds that to lose this battle was to lose a dream. Cromwell's army was disciplined and acted decisively on the clear orders given them. Among the Cavaliers there were too many leaders, too many orders and counter-orders, which threw the men into disarray, and they crumbled beneath the concerted onslaught. Rupert guessed that somewhere near a thousand of their men had been killed that day, and many thousands taken prisoner.

Wounded himself in the arm, Rupert owed his escape to the friend who now lay close by on the hard ground, recovering his breath. They had ridden hard and it was two days since they had eaten, but now they were close to a harbour where they believed they might find help.

'I am for France,' Captain Freeman told Rupert when it had been clear that the battle was lost and the Scots were surrendering. 'I am no coward to run from a fight, but I see no point in being caught here like rats in a trap. The cause is lost. What use in fighting on to the bitter end?'

The choice between exile in France or the bitter taste of defeat and surrender was before them. At least if they avoided capture, they could follow the Prince of Wales and offer their swords to him.

'I am with you,' Rupert said. 'Where do you intend to head for?'

'To the coast and a village I know where the fishermen will take gold to carry us over the water,' his friend replied. 'Let those fools who choose surrender taste the sting of humiliation. I'm for France and the pay of any who will hire my sword.'

'Then let us ride with all speed,' Rupert said. 'I'm for freedom. If we are captured we shall be imprisoned or executed, especially those of us who have broken our bonds. You are right, my friend. We'll join those who support the Prince of Wales and bide our time. The people cannot see what they condone in these sour, joyless men who will rule their lives. If they could but see into the future I'll warrant they would demand the King back again.'

'We can only hope,' his friend replied. 'For the time being we must learn to live as best we can in a foreign land, and wait in patience.'

Rupert nodded. For a moment his thoughts strayed to his home and Elizabeth. Had she received his letter? Had she forgiven him for what he had done to her? Sometimes he cursed himself for a fool. These months had been spent in a wasted cause. Had he behaved with more honour he might have been wed to a generous woman and settled in his own home, instead of being brought to this bitter end, when he must sneak away under the cover of darkness to an uncertain life in France.

If only he could go back to that day when she had given herself so sweetly. It should have been Elizabeth he had loved from the start, he absorbed this as he acknowledged that it was too late. He would be a fugitive in exile with nothing to offer her . . .

'Cromwell has routed Hamilton and the Scots,' Nicolas announced when he entered his wife's parlour the morning the news arrived. 'Cromwell sent word of his victory. Four thousand were taken prisoner besides a thousand killed. He believes that the rebels must be finally crushed at last, though some strongholds still hold out.'

'Have you news of Rupert?' she looked at him anxiously. 'We have had no word of him in all this time.'

'The lists of the wounded and prisoners taken have not come through yet, but I shall endeavour to discover if your brother's name was amongst them. I dare say that many escaped and have fled to France – but we do not know that Rupert was with them.'

'No,' she admitted. 'He might be anywhere – at Colchester or even in France.'

'I pray that he is not at Colchester,' Nicolas said and looked grave. 'Fairfax has had that city under siege for some weeks and I fear it goes ill for the inhabitants. I believe the water supply was cut and they have been driven to eating their horses and anything else they can lay hands on.'

Caroline looked shocked. 'Those poor people,' she said. 'It is a terrible thing to starve them like that.'

'Yes, I agree with you,' Nicolas said. 'But they will not surrender and it seems Fairfax has a mind to end this for once and all. Yet I sicken of it, Caroline. I find it hard to stomach all this blood and hatred. It was surely not for this that we began this fight.'

'Nicolas . . .' Caroline saw the weariness in his face. 'My love . . .'

'I wait to hear from Cromwell,' he said. 'I believe there are some moves afoot. After this latest defeat, the King must surely see sense. I hope that we shall at last see a settlement.'

'My dearest,' she said and moved into his arms, feeling the shudder run through him. 'I pray that you are right.' She smiled up at him. 'But we must forget these terrible times and take pleasure in Elizabeth's wedding.'

'Do you think she truly cares for him?' Nicolas asked. 'It would be a shame if she were to regret her marriage.'

'She longs for a home of her own and children,' Caroline said. 'Who can blame her? And Captain Benedict is a good man. I believe she has chosen well . . .'

'You look lovely,' Caroline said as she offered Elizabeth the blue garter for her stocking on the morning of her wedding. 'I believe Captain Benedict will be well pleased with his bride, my dear.'

'I hope so,' Elizabeth said. She had become increasingly nervous as her wedding day approached for she knew that the new found pleasure in her life was based on a lie. What would her husband do if he discovered the truth? Would he hate her for deceiving him? 'I shall try to make him happy.'

'You are too modest, my love,' Caroline said. 'He is lucky to have secured you. Would that my foolish brother had been as fortunate in his choice of a bride.' She frowned. 'Nicolas tells me that Colchester has fallen, but Rupert was not amongst those taken. His name does not appear on the list of those who surrendered. Nor has his name appeared on the list of those who fell at Preston.'

'Is that cause for hope do you think?' Elizabeth asked. 'If he is dead . . .'

'Then we shall hear soon enough,' Caroline replied. 'But I think I should know already in my heart. I do not believe that he was there, Elizabeth. Nicolas says that many Royalists have fled to France or the Low Countries. They will be exiled until the country is settled, and then most will be allowed home, providing they make their vow to take up arms against Parliament no more. It may be that Rupert is amongst them and will sue for peace in good time.'

'Do you believe Rupert will do that?'

'I do not know. I hope he may eventually. I think he needed a period for thought, Elizabeth. When he has faced his demons and conquered them he may return to us.'

'I pray that he will,' Elizabeth replied, her eyes pricking with the tears she could never shed. All hope of Rupert was gone now. She must never think of him again. 'I am ready now, Caroline.'

Caroline looked at her, studying her face, seeing the signs of strain that she could not hide. 'Are you certain that this marriage is what you truly want, dearest?' she asked. 'You may withdraw even now if you have regrets.'

'No, I shall not withdraw,' Elizabeth said, lifting her chin. She had decided never to think of Rupert again. In another hour she would be wed to a man who deserved her respect. It would be wicked of her to indulge in thoughts of another man ever again. 'Captain Benedict is a good man. I am sure I shall be happy with him.'

Caroline nodded. She had encouraged Elizabeth to this marriage, believing it the best thing that could happen to her, but now she had doubts. If the girl was still in love with Rupert . . . but there had been no word from him.

She had only her own instincts to tell her that he was still alive.

If he cared for Elizabeth he would have come back before this. It was his own fault if he lived to regret what he had thrown away.

Elizabeth moved through the wedding ceremony and the reception afterwards as if she were in a dream. She was aware of her groom watching her, of the eager light in his eyes as he kissed her after they were declared man and wife, and knew that he was impatient to be on their way. They were to travel down to his estate in Devon by easy stages for she had declared herself anxious to see her new home and he was pleased to indulge her. Elizabeth had had enough of London for it was a sober place now that all frivolity was frowned upon. At least in the country they would have more freedom to please themselves – at least that was her hope.

She kissed her friends goodbye after the celebrations had proceeded for an hour or so; they would continue to feast after the departure of the bride and groom, but Captain Benedict was anxious to be on his way.

Once they were in the coach, he turned to her with a smile. 'You look so beautiful, Elizabeth,' he told her, leaning forward to kiss her on the lips. For the first time there was passion in his kiss and hunger. She trembled inside, but gazed steadily into his eyes as he let her go. 'I have been wanting to kiss you that way for as long as I can remember. I did not frighten you I hope?'

'No, sir,' she replied and smiled. 'I am your wife and I trust you – why should I fear you?'

'It is so for some ladies,' he told her. 'But it will be proper for you to call me by my name now, Elizabeth. I am Walter – my friends sometimes call me Walt.'

'I think Walter is very nice,' Elizabeth said and smiled at him. 'Pray tell me more about our house, Walter. It was built in the reign of Good Queen Bess I think you said?'

'Aye, and had been in my uncle's family for all that time,' he replied with pride. 'It is a large solid building in the shape of an E and of bricks that have turned to rose with the years. Part of it was in need of repair when it came to me, but I have set that in hand. As for the furnishings, they need a woman's touch, and I shall leave that entirely to you, dearest. You may have a free hand with my purse, within reason of course.'

'You are generous, Walter,' she said, laying her hand in his. 'I am very fortunate to have attracted your affection.'

'It is far more than affection I feel for you,' he replied. 'You are a truly good woman, Elizabeth, and as such I shall honour you all my life.'

Her hand trembled a little in his as he spoke for she was suddenly very afraid. She had not thought his passion for her so intense and she wondered at his reaction if he should guess that she was not a virgin bride. It would wound his pride, but it must also hurt him. She had witnessed Rupert's anger and despair when he realized that Sarah had betrayed him. The last thing she had wanted was to cause so much distress for the man she had married.

Elizabeth dismissed her maid. She was wearing a demure night chemise that tied at the neck and hid her body, though the sweet curves of her breasts were clearly visible beneath. She had allowed the maid to brush her hair until it shone, hanging on her shoulders in a shining mass of dark waves. Now she drew back the covers of the great bed and climbed in, pulling the covers up around her as she waited for Walter to come to her.

He did not keep her long. He was wearing a nightshirt of fine lawn, his hair brushed about his face in the short fashion that prevailed these days, for he had adopted a policy of non-confrontation, outwardly conforming. As he had told Elizabeth on their journey, 'We must do our best to live with our new masters, my dear. I am not a Puritan by nature, but I find some good in the new order. I would welcome His Majesty back if it were possible, but since it is not I shall abide by the new order for the sake of peace.'

Elizabeth thought she had preferred him with the longer locks he had adopted when she first knew him, but it was a small thing. Although some years her senior, he was a handsome man, well-built and fit, his body strongly muscled. Stemming the waves of panic that had begun to flow over her, she welcomed him to her bed with a smile, going to him if not eagerly, then with pleasure as he drew her close.

'My lovely wife,' he murmured against her ear as she allowed him to kiss and caress her. She did not feel the same rush of hot desire she had experienced when Rupert made love to her, but still felt a warm readiness to be loved by him. 'You are so sweet . . . exactly as I knew you would be.'

Elizabeth stiffened as she felt the heat of his manhood seeking entry, wondering if it would hurt but she found it easy enough to accommodate him, and there was no pain at all. She gave a little whimper of pleasure as his passion mounted and she found that it was good. She did not come to the wonderful climax she had experienced in Rupert's arms, but experienced a quiet contentment as she lay close to him.

Walter was breathing hard as he lay beside her. She waited for some sign that he was pleased with their loving, but he moved away from her without speaking, and then in a moment he left the bed and went through the connecting door to his own chamber. The warm glow faded as Elizabeth lay tense and disappointed. She had looked forward to talking as they lay together in bed, hoped for a bonding of their minds as well as their bodies.

Had she done something to displease him? He had not accused her of it, nor had he dragged her from the bed and threatened her, and yet she sensed that he knew she was not virgin pure. How could he have guessed? Had she been too willing to respond to his loving? Perhaps she would have done better to shrink from him and pretend to a pain she did not feel? But she had wanted to please him, to show him that she welcomed his loving. She had not thought that he would know, but somehow he did and she knew that she had wronged him. She ought to have found the courage to tell him when he proposed marriage. Now he had found her out. She might have expected anger or accusations, but he had simply left her to sleep alone.

Elizabeth did not know what to think. Why had he not vented his anger upon her? She thought she might have preferred it to his silence. Was this to be the pattern of their married life – or would Walter speak his mind when he had had time to think things over?

She lay sleepless for some hours, her remorse torturing her as she accepted that she had not been fair to him. She had cheated him almost as badly as Sarah had cheated Rupert and she was not proud of herself.

Where was Rupert now? Her thoughts turned to him despite her determination to forget him. Was he well? Did he think of her? Would she see him again?

They continued their journey the next day. Elizabeth was a little nervous of meeting her husband the next morning, but he greeted her with cool politeness when she went down to the private chamber he had secured for them.

'I trust you slept well, Elizabeth?'

'Yes, thank you, Walter,' she lied for she had tossed restlessly in the bed once he had left it. She longed to ask him where he had spent the night, but she was afraid to say anything that might lead to a quarrel between them.

After they had broken their fast, they continued the journey. However, Walter chose to ride beside the coach, leaving Elizabeth to spend some hours in lonely contemplation of her folly. She ought never to have married him without first telling him the truth, she thought now.

Yet what could she do about it? They were married and she could see no way out of this predicament. It was too late for she could change nothing. She looked at the countryside they passed, finding no pleasure in its beauty. Gradually, the thought came to her that she must find some way to bridge the gap that had opened between them – but how? Should she pretend ignorance and ask why he was angry with her? It would be a false position and she felt that she had already deceived him. She might do better to beg his pardon for offending him.

When they reached their destination for the night, he told her that they would be occupying separate rooms. It was on the tip of her tongue to beg him to stay with her, but she could not find the words. Perhaps he would forgive her in time, and in the meantime she could only wait.

They were five days on the road, and in all that time Walter hardly spoke to her other than to tell her the things it was necessary for her to know. She could see by his face that he was controlling his emotions, and she sensed that he was angry – or perhaps hurt by her betrayal.

Elizabeth wished sincerely that she had behaved differently. Her conscience had told her from the start that she ought to confess the whole to him but she had not found the courage to do so. As the days passed she realized that she could not go on with this silence between them, and she made up her mind that she would speak once they had reached Walter's estate.

On the morning of the sixth day they at last reached their destination. The estate was partly wooded, partly pasture on which were grazing the sheep that had made Walter's uncle a wealthy man. Their golden fleeces were much prized and fetched high prices so although it was not as large an estate as Thornberry it was prosperous. The house itself was solid and built of red brick in the Elizabethan fashion, the thatched roof sloping low over small windows with panes of dull grey glass.

Inside, it was comfortable enough, though it lacked many of the things that a busy woman could supply with her needle. The furniture was oak and plain, country made but adequate for their needs, and in the bedchamber to which she was shown by a serving wench, it was clear that some effort had been made to supply the comforts she would need.

She asked the maids to leave her alone for a while. Gazing out of the window, she saw that the view was pleasant and looked out on rolling green meadows and a stream. The woods cut off all sight of the small village that lay beyond them, giving the house a feeling of solitude, though it was just possible to see the church spire. It appeared that they had no near neighbours and Elizabeth realized that she would miss the company of other women. She had been used to her cousin's company, and then Caroline and Lady Saunders had become her friends. It would seem odd to be alone here with just the servants and her husband.

Hearing a sound behind her, she turned to see Walter watching her as she ran her hand over the surface of a smooth oak coffer.

'I trust the house meets with your approval, Elizabeth?'

'It is comfortable and will be more so when I have my own things about me,' Elizabeth said with her usual honesty. 'It is a good house, Walter, and I like the view from this window.'

'Then you will be content here as its mistress?'

'Yes, of course. I shall make some changes of course – with your permission?' He inclined his head. 'I cannot wait to begin. It will be pleasant to have the order of my own house, Walter, for I have always lived in other people's homes. My uncle relied on me to help him care for his household for Sarah had no interest – though Mistress Furnley was a great help to us.'

'Mistress Furnley? I do not think I have heard you speak of her?'

'She was Sarah's companion.' Elizabeth frowned. 'I often think of her for she was doubtful that she would find another place to suit her.'

'You liked her?'

'Yes, very much.'

'Perhaps you would like to invite her to be your companion now you have your own home,' he said. 'We have no neighbours near enough to pass the time of day, though you will meet them when we attend church on Sundays. It is fitting that my wife should have a companion for I am a busy man and may be away sometimes. You have my permission to invite her if you wish it.'

'Thank you, Walter. I shall think about it,' Elizabeth said. 'It is generous of you to offer me this kindness.' He shrugged and turned away, but she moved towards him, catching his arm. 'Please do not leave yet. I would speak with you . . .'

He hesitated, his gaze narrowed, hard. 'Yes, I suppose we must speak, Elizabeth. I have held my tongue for I did not wish to say things that could not be taken back. I am disappointed and hurt. You know of what I speak of course?'

'Yes, I know,' she said, raising her head so that she looked into his eyes. She would not flinch though it was hard to look into his eyes and see the disappointment there. 'I know it is not an easy thing to forgive. I should have told you everything. It was wrong of me to deceive you.'

'You have angered me, Elizabeth. Had I given rein to my temper I might have harmed you. I held my hand for I am not a violent man – but you have disappointed me. I shall find it difficult to forgive your deceit.'

'Would you rather I went away?'

'Where could you go?' He studied her face and saw that she had no true answer. 'You think that Caroline might take you in? Yes, perhaps she would – but I do not care for her or anyone else to know that you are a whore, Elizabeth. It would shame me – and there is no need for it. I have decided that you must stay.'

Her cheeks were stinging with the hot colour that had rushed into them at his harsh words. 'You wrong me, sir. What I did was once and out of love – to comfort someone who . . .'

'Rupert Saunders I suppose,' he said, his gaze narrowed and angry. 'You always wanted him. I saw it in your face when he married your cousin. He used you when she made a fool of him. Then if you are not a whore you are a fool, madam. Either way, I prefer that you remain here and do your duty as my wife.'

Elizabeth swallowed her hurt for she had perhaps deserved this. 'I shall try to make you happy, Walter. If you could find it in your heart to forgive me this . . .'

'Forgive you? I am not sure that I can forgive, Elizabeth – but I may overcome my anger and my distaste. You see I do not care to be made a fool of – and I still find you desirable. You are a lovely woman. I have decided that we shall continue as man and wife. I believe I can find it in my heart to see that you have all the comforts that are your right as my wife. We shall be comfortable enough for few marriages are based on love. In time I dare say we shall learn to accept our lot.'

Elizabeth felt the coldness flow over her. She had not bargained for such a marriage. Yet she had only herself to blame. What he was suggesting was a bleak prospect, but it seemed that she had no choice but to accept his terms.

'I must thank you for your forbearance, sir,' she said. 'I shall do my best to be a good wife and I hope that one day you may feel some of the warmth you once felt towards me.'

'I doubt it, Elizabeth,' he said and the icy look in his eyes crushed all hope within her. 'I may find you useful at times, and we must do our best to make the world think us content with our marriage – but you have killed any love I had for you. I shall come to your bed tonight, but once you have done your duty I shall leave you to sleep alone . . .'

Elizabeth stood as if turned to stone as he walked from the room. She felt as if he had punched her hard in the stomach. Indeed, she wished that he had used his fists on her. Anything would have been better than this cold indifference.

For a moment she considered running away, but then she realized that she must stay and do her duty. She had made her bed and she must lie on it no matter how hard it might be . . .

Ten

'I have been asked if I will be one of the commissioners to attend on His Majesty at Newport in the Isle of Wight,' Nicolas told Caroline when he returned one evening at the end of August. 'We are to speak directly to the King for one last attempt to negotiate a settlement.'

'Nicolas,' Caroline said, looking at him in surprise and some dismay. 'Shall you go? I know you have been uneasy in your mind for some weeks at the way things stand.'

'It is for that reason that I must take this chance,' he told her with a frown. 'You know my opinion, Caroline. I like not the way some would rule this country with a rod of iron. There are those within the Levellers who prate that all should be equal and no man allowed to rise above another – and I tell you I fear for the madness that stalks amongst us now. No man's property would be safe from them.'

'Do you mean they wish to confiscate the property of Royalists?'

'Oh, they will do that,' Nicolas said, 'but they talk of everything being shared amongst the common man. One of their ideas is that all men should be allowed to vote, regardless of whether they be property owners. I know that Ireton and Cromwell are against it as are most men of sense, for they think that it would lead to the abolition of private property. I tell you, it makes me shiver when I think what could happen if men of that ilk came to power. For that reason I shall accept the commission offered me. I would have the King brought back to a limited power if it were possible.

Charles Stuart was in my opinion a bad king – but these men are more ruthless than he ever was.'

Caroline shivered as he spoke. She felt that a dark shadow hovered, not only at her shoulder but also over the whole of England.

'Then you must go to Newport,' she said. 'And I shall pray that your mission will be successful.'

'Yes, I think I must go,' he said. 'But it means that I may be some days – or weeks away from you.'

'Do not fear for me, my love,' she said. 'I have my children, the servants and a few good friends.'

'You will miss Elizabeth I think?'

'Yes, I shall miss her,' Caroline said with a smile, 'but I like to think of her settling in her new home. It is time that she found some happiness.'

'Yes, you are right,' he said. 'I have wished that she was still with us – but perhaps we shall find a companion for you, my love. We should look for a woman of a suitable age to keep you company.'

'I am content enough as I am,' Caroline said. 'But do not stay away from me longer than need be, Nicolas, for it is you I need.'

'I shall return as soon as I may,' he promised and took her into his arms, kissing her softly on her mouth. 'I worry for you, my love – after your last illness.'

'Then you should not,' she replied. 'All I ask is that you come back safely.'

'I shall return soon and then perhaps we may think of the future . . .'

Elizabeth had begun an inspection of the linen and household accoutrements the day after she arrived. She found the house well stocked with most things, though she could see much that needed to be done to make it a comfortable home. The previous owner had been a widower for some years and the tasks that rightly fell to a wife had been neglected. She was glad of it for it gave her something to occupy her mind.

'I shall need cloth to make new drapes for the windows and the beds,' she told her husband at supper that evening. 'Do I have your permission to order it, Walter?'

'I told you that I should leave all such things to you, Elizabeth. Make up your list and I shall have it delivered to the merchants in town. I am aware that the house is in need of some refurbishment and I would expect you to order things as you wish. I intend that we shall entertain some of the local gentry in good time, and I would have everything as it ought to be.'

'Thank you,' she said. 'I shall make my list when I have finished an inventory of the linen and plate.'

'Very well,' Walter said. 'Tomorrow is Sunday. You will accompany me to church, Elizabeth. I wish to begin the way we mean to go on.'

'Yes, of course, husband. I have always attended church regularly and would wish to continue.'

'I understand that the Reverend Medford is of the Puritan persuasion,' Walter told her. 'It was not my habit to worship in that way, but it is the new order and we must abide by it. You will dress very plainly for church, Elizabeth. Do you have a black dress and hat?'

'Yes, Walter. I had them for my cousin's funeral.'

'Then you will wear them tomorrow and whenever we go to church. I prefer to see you in colours, though nothing too bright – but in future you will choose gowns of a sober hue. I would not offend our neighbours.'

'As you wish, husband,' Elizabeth said. She kept her gaze on the tablecloth, not wanting him to see the flash of defiance in her eyes. Was this his punishment for what she had done?

'I shall come to your bed this evening,' he said. 'I shall stay only as long as need be.'

'That is your choice, Walter.'

'Yes, my choice,' he said and his voice was icy. 'I hope that we shall have children. It is a wife's duty to bear her husband's children – and to keep his home. Please me in these things, Elizabeth, and I shall be generous enough.'

'Thank you, you are very kind.'

His coldness made her want to weep, but she held back the tears. He believed that she had deliberately deceived and tricked him, and this was his way of punishing her.

Sunday was fine though cold. Elizabeth and her husband walked to church through narrow lanes, which were thankfully dry underfoot. A single bell was summoning the faithful to church, and the congregation was quite large for a small village. It looked as if almost all the villagers had answered the call to prayer.

Elizabeth discovered the reason for so many worshippers when she heard the Reverend Medford's sermon. He delivered a fiery speech, thundering down on the sinners in his congregation and threatening hellfire and damnation to all those who did not lead a godly life.

A girl who had been accused of lewd behaviour with a married man was denounced from the pulpit and forced to stand before them in a white shift to accept her punishment, which was to be pelted with rotten vegetables in the marketplace the next day. Tears trickled down her cheeks as she was pointed out as a wicked woman and told that she would go to hell. She could not have been much more than seventeen, and yet it was she who bore the blame, the man not having been named.

Elizabeth found the sermon harsh and hated the bare look of the church, which had been stripped of anything that might have made it beautiful. It was as austere as the sermon given by the Reverend Medford and she missed the lovely chapel at Thornberry Manor where she had gone to worship with Caroline and her family sometimes.

She missed her friend deeply, and had wished herself back with Caroline a thousand times. Why had she not given her answer that first day? Better perhaps that she should have died unwed than live the kind of life she saw before her now. However, she had made her choice and knew that she must accept the future whatever it held for her.

When she was introduced to the Reverend Medford after

the service, he smiled on her approvingly and she was glad that Walter had thought to tell her to dress in a suitable gown.

'You are very welcome, Mistress Benedict,' he said. 'And Captain Benedict. It is an honour to have you both in our congregation.'

'It was a fine sermon, sir,' Walter replied. 'I am glad to see that you care for the souls of your stray sheep. I hope you will continue to hand out righteous justice to those who transgress.'

'A man after my own heart,' the reverend said and smiled. 'They are but children, sir. We must guide them in the right way – a sharp reprimand to one deters others from the same sin.'

Elizabeth thought that it had been a harsh judgement, but she held her tongue. It was not for her to interfere. She knew that anything she had to say would be scorned, and therefore it was best to say nothing.

'Yes, I believe we think much alike,' Walter replied. 'You will honour us by dining with us soon, sir? My wife is busy putting the house to rights but next month we should be ready to receive visitors – and I hope you will be a regular guest.'

'I thank you for your invitation, and I believe we shall do well together,' the reverend said. 'The local magistrate – Sir James Pellingham – does not always see eye to eye with me. I may ask for your assistance with some of the measures that we need to introduce in the district. A few judicial words from you, sir, might help me a great deal.'

'We shall talk,' Walter promised. 'Excuse us, we must move on . . .'

As Walter led her away to talk to their neighbours, Elizabeth reflected on the thought that she had married a man she did not know. She had thought him a Royalist, but it seemed that he was fast becoming a Puritan.

It was the middle of the next week. Elizabeth had been to the village to buy meat from the market, and it was as she made her way home that she chanced to meet Reverend

Medford. He doffed his tall steeple hat to her, remarked on the cool breeze and moved on, but something in his manner made her shiver. She did not know what it was she disliked about him, but the way he had looked at her had made her uncomfortable.

She hurried on, feeling that she would be glad to be inside her house. She was feeling chilled and it was not just because there was a hint of autumn in the air.

Like others of the commissioners who had come to treat with the King, Nicolas was shocked when he saw the changes in Charles. He had allowed his hair to grow, refusing to have it trimmed in his usual manner, and it was no longer kept as immaculately as it had been. His clothes were clean but his dress more careless than it would once have been. It seemed that he no longer cared for his appearance as he once had.

'This change disturbs me,' Nicolas murmured to one of the men standing near. 'What occasions it? I understood he was being treated well here?'

'It has been this way since he was no longer allowed to have his own people about him. It was thought that he might escape and the need for a stricter routine was thought necessary.'

'And is his health good?'

'Yes, it would appear so – and he is more cheerful than we would have expected in such circumstances.'

'I like not to see any man so changed,' Nicolas said. 'Let us hope that he will see reason and we may come to some agreement.'

'I doubt he will listen to you. He believes in his divine right and will not bend. The man is a fool to himself.'

'But surely he must know that this is his last chance?'

'From what I hear he believes it a sign of weakness that this commission has come to him, and I think it may be so. We won the war. Why should we come cap in hand to him?'

Nicolas shook his head. He knew that negotiations were not going well, and he was sorry for it. He had not been given a chance to speak to the King privately, and he feared that those who did were clumsy fools who put their case badly. If he could but make the King see what the alternative was . . . but he was merely an observer. Others of more importance to Parliament were leading the mission, and it seemed the negotiations would grind on forever.

Elizabeth had worked hard to make the house presentable in time for the first guests her husband had invited, and as she looked around her table that evening she felt justly proud. The table had been polished until the maids could see their faces in the surface, the silver and pewter burnished, the linen clean and sweet. It was a cool evening and a fire burned in the large hearth, spreading its warm glow over them as the wine flowed. Everyone seemed to be enjoying themselves, she thought, for the food was excellent as was the wine and sack Walter had provided.

Twelve of her new neighbours had been invited, the chief amongst them Sir James and Lady Pellingham. Sir James was stout and of a high colour, his wife thin with a long face and sharp eyes, but they were friendly enough. Some of the gentlemen were widowers and had come alone, but there were three other ladies present, all of them much older than Elizabeth.

She had met no one as yet who she thought might become a close friend, and thought wistfully of her life with Caroline. Yet she was finding a certain content in being mistress of her own home, for she enjoyed seeing to the small tasks that made a house comfortable, and she believed that Walter was pleased with her. She glanced at him and received a nod of approval, giving him a smile in return.

Her gaze moved down the table to where the Reverend Medford was sitting. He was not looking at her, but seemed to be watching one of the serving wenches. Elizabeth frowned, for something in the way he watched the girl was disturbing. However, the next moment she had forgotten it as Lady Pellingham spoke to her.

'How do you find your new home, Mistress Benedict?'

'It is a fine house,' she replied. 'There are still some changes I would make, but already I have been able to make some improvements.'

'It was neglected for some years,' the lady said and gave her a nod of approval, 'but I am sure you will set it all to rights, my dear. You must visit me one day. I shall be pleased to welcome you to Pellingham Hall.'

Elizabeth thanked her. Of all her neighbours she liked the Pellinghams best. Sir James seemed an honest man, and his wife was kind despite her looks.

'I should enjoy that,' Elizabeth said. 'You are very good, my lady.'

She turned her head to find that Walter's eyes were upon her, and she knew that he would visit her bed that night.

'Oh, Nicolas, you are back,' Caroline said and jumped up to embrace her husband as he entered the parlour one day early in November. 'Tell me, my love – what news?'

'None good that I can see,' he replied. 'Charles refused to listen or agree to our terms. An agreement of sorts has been reached but I do not think it will serve. He has not said positively nay nor yet a definite agreement. And he will not yield on the matter of the Bishops for he supports their divine right, and therefore his own, and will not see them abolished.'

'Then your mission failed for the Army will not agree to those terms.' She shook her head over it, for since the fall of Basing House the King's cause was well and truly lost – and the manner of its fall and the aftermath were shaming to a nation that prided itself on justice and mercy. 'They are drunk on their power and success, and this obstinate stand from the King will not please.'

'Indeed it will not,' Nicolas agreed grimly. 'I believe that moves are afoot for a very different solution, and I like it not.' His expression was severe as he looked at her. 'There was a change in the King, Caroline. No matter his faults, he is a noble man and should be treated in accordance with his station.'

A little smile touched her mouth as she saw that he was sorely tried by what he had seen and heard. 'You began as a parliamentarian, Nicolas, and now I think you have become a Royalist.'

'Nay, I am no Royalist,' Nicolas said and sighed. 'Charles was a bad king and I fought for justice. I am still on the side of justice, Caroline, and I see very little of it these days on either side.'

Caroline nodded, looking at him sadly. Nicolas had carried such high ideals throughout the war and it was a sorrow to see that the folly, greed and injustice of his fellow men had brought them so low.

'I do not like to see you thus, husband. It is not like you to be so low in spirits.'

'It is the future of this country and its people that weighs on me, Caroline. What did we fight for if it was not freedom and justice for all? And is Charles Stuart not a man as much as any other?'

'But if he persists in being stubborn he brings his fate upon himself.'

'You are right,' Nicolas said. 'But I would that it were otherwise.'

'You can do no more than you have done,' she said. 'We must just pray that all will be well in time . . .'

Caroline gave a little cry of distress as Nicolas entered the parlour where she was sitting some two weeks later. From the bruises to his face, and the cut on his lip, she could see that he must have suffered some kind of violence.

'You are hurt,' she said rising to go to him. 'What happened my dearest? Were you attacked?'

'It is nothing,' he said as he saw the anxiety in her face. 'Do not distress yourself, Caroline. The doctor told you that you must rest and not become over excited. You have been ill, my love.'

'I am much better now,' she said and smiled at him lovingly. 'Besides, I shall worry more if you do not tell me what happened to you.'

'I was jostled as I was leaving Westminster,' he told her. 'There was a crowd gathered outside the hall and the mood was ugly. I believe there is trouble brewing and I am not sure what Cromwell means to do about it.'

'What kind of trouble?'

'Parliament will soon be purged of all those who would support the King,' Nicolas said, his expression grim. 'They talk openly now of his trial and I fear the worst. I think they will have his head if they can. Indeed, I spoke out in his cause, and this injury was the result of it.'

'Oh no,' Caroline cried, a chill trickling down her spine. 'I think it would be an evil day for England if that were to happen, Nicolas.'

'I agree with you,' he replied. 'I have stayed in London while there seemed some hope of a settlement, Caroline. I believe Cromwell hoped that it would happen, but the Army is become very powerful. Since the fall of Colchester and Basing House there is none to oppose them. We fought for a just peace, but I think that may be impossible. These men who would rule us now are beyond reason. Cromwell asked if I would take my place in the House, which I am entitled to by reason of my birth – but I do not think I care to be a part of this Parliament. I believe I shall return home very soon.'

'Are you sure that is your true wish?' Caroline asked. 'You do not make excuses for my sake?'

'I must confess that I think you would be better in the country,' Nicolas told her with a smile. 'And I am sure the air is better for the children. The air in London is foul and there have been more cases of the plague in the city. We are safe enough here I think, but we should be better at home.'

'Will you be content to be simply a country gentleman?'

Nicolas gave her a wry grin. 'Indeed, my love, I would that I had been nothing more these past years. The war hath been overlong and I am heartily sick of it. I want no more of life than to live in peace with you and our children.'

Caroline's face shadowed with grief. 'I would that I had given you a son, Nicolas.'

'We have Claire, and Rupert's daughter, and it may yet be that God will see fit to grant us another child. But if that does not happen we have an heir in Hal.'

'Yes, we have Hal,' Caroline agreed and sighed for she longed to give him his own son. 'Have you ever wondered about Rowena's son, Nicolas? I told you that I saw him at St Ives that day, and I am certain he is Harry's son – his eldest son.'

Nicolas frowned. 'What are you saying, Caroline? Hal is Mercy's son and we know that she loved Harry and was faithful to him. But Rowena Greenslade was a whore. She warmed the bed of more than one officer in Oxford during those first months of the war. We could never be sure that her child was my brother's. Besides, I would not set him in Hal's place for he has been as my own son.'

'I suppose not.' Caroline felt as if a dark shadow hovered at her shoulder. 'It is just that I have thought of him so often. His life must be hard and I would not have a child of your brother's live in such a way.'

'Are you asking me to try and find Rowena and her son – to discover the truth?'

'Would you consider it?' Caroline asked. 'I could not ask before for you have had much on your mind, but if we are to go home . . .'

Nicolas frowned. 'I make no promises, Caroline, for I am not certain it would be a good thing if he were found. I doubt his mother would give him up – and if she claims to be Harry's wife it could cause problems for all of us.'

'It is just a silly lie,' Caroline said. 'We both know that your brother would never have married her. He loved Mercy but he could not marry her because he needed money to pay his debts. Yet despite Rowena's spite and her threats, I do not like to think of the boy living such a hard life. We could do something for him, Nicolas – could we not?'

'You have a soft heart and a generous nature, my love,' her husband said. 'To please you, I shall see if the boy can be found, but do not set your hopes on it. If Rowena has chosen to live with the gypsies it may be that she does not wish to be found. Do not forget that the villagers would have stoned her as a witch. She was accused of murder and memories are long amongst the village folk.'

'Yes, I know,' Caroline admitted. 'It may all be folly on my part but I feel . . .' She was interrupted by the arrival of a servant with a letter, which she took with some pleasure. 'It is from Elizabeth. I had begun to think that something must be wrong for it is more than two months since she was married and this is the first letter I have had from her.'

'I dare say she has been busy getting to know her husband and her new home,' Nicolas said. He smiled at her as she broke the wax seal on her letter. 'I shall leave you to enjoy yourself, Caroline. You may write back to her and say that we shall be at Thornberry Manor for Christmas. She and Captain Benedict will be more than welcome to join us should they wish it.'

'It would be a fair journey for them,' Caroline said, 'but I shall give them the invitation, though I do not think they will accept . . .' She held her letter in her lap as she looked up at him. 'Where are you going, Nicolas?'

'There is a meeting I must attend this evening, Caroline, and then I shall speak to Cromwell, tell him that I have decided to go home. I fought for what I believed was justice for the common man, but I have no taste for politics.'

'Then I shall tell the servants to begin packing,' Caroline said. 'My mother wrote asking for news of Rupert but I had none to give her. I suppose you have heard nothing of him?'

'I believe he got away to France,' Nicolas said. 'I would

have thought he might write either to his parents or to you – but perhaps he will do so when he is settled. He was foolish to throw in his lot with the insurgents. I helped him once, Caroline, but I think it will be a long time before those who held out to the last will be forgiven. The mood of the country is against them.'

'I wish he had never gone off the way he did.' Caroline sighed. 'If only he had never fallen in love with Sarah. Elizabeth would have made him a much better wife and I know that she loved him . . .'

'Elizabeth has married another,' Nicolas said. 'She made her choice and that is an end to it, Caroline.'

'Yes, I know.' She glanced down at her letter. 'I was merely thinking how much nicer everything would have been if Rupert had married her instead of Sarah. It is hard to think that he is condemned to a life of exile . . .'

'I fear that Rupert was always headstrong,' Nicolas said. 'He has made his bed and he must lie in it.'

Elizabeth found the girl crying when she entered her bedchamber with an armful of linen she had been mending. Lisa wiped her face hastily on her apron when she saw her mistress, but her red eyes gave her away.

'What troubles you, child?' Elizabeth asked for Lisa could be no more than sixteen years of age. 'Are you ill?'

'No, ma'am,' Lisa said hanging her head. 'At least . . . I don't know . . .'

Elizabeth saw the fear in her eyes and her intuition led her to a sad conclusion, for there would be no mercy in this parish if her suspicions were true.

'Are you in trouble, Lisa?'

'I – I don't know,' Lisa confessed, tears trickling down her cheeks. 'Oh, ma'am, it wasn't my fault. I resisted him, I swear I did – but he made me.'

'Who was it? Your sweetheart?'

'I have no sweetheart,' Lisa said. 'It was . . . No, ma'am, I dare not tell you for you would not believe me.'

'I would give you a fair hearing, child,' Elizabeth said. 'Tell me the truth for otherwise I cannot help you.'

'You will call me a liar,' Lisa said, hanging her head. 'You will say I blacken the name of a godly man.'

'You do not speak of my husband?'

'Oh no, ma'am, the captain be a good man – but the other hath two faces. He showeth one in the pulpit on a Sunday and another when the lust is on him . . .' Lisa gave a cry of fear as she realized that her tongue had led her astray. 'I do not lie, ma'am. 'Tis true that he lay with me and forced me to it. I do not like him, though he be fair of face and tongue – but it be a sin what he hath done to me, Mistress Benedict, and that be true or God strike me down as I stand here.'

Elizabeth went cold all over. She was shocked by the girl's revelations, which she found difficult to believe. How could a man of God – a man who stood in the pulpit every Sunday and denounced sin in others – do such a thing to a girl young enough to be his own daughter? And yet had she not seen something in his eyes when he looked at her the day she passed him on her way home from the village? Something about him then had chilled her.

'If this is true he should be driven from the parish,' Elizabeth said. 'I shall speak to my husband about this for it cannot be hidden, Lisa. You will soon begin to show your condition and then you will be shamed in church before us all. Unless that man can be brought to do his duty by you.'

'Oh no, Mistress Benedict,' Lisa said. 'I would rather die than be wed to him. Please do not speak to Captain Benedict for he will send me away in disgrace and I have nowhere to go. My parents will disown me and I shall be driven from the parish.'

Seeing the terror in the girl's face, Elizabeth hesitated. She knew that her husband might well denounce Lisa as a whore and dismiss her. His mood seemed to improve of late for he had not been harsh to her for some weeks now, and he visited her bed often, sometimes staying with her for most of the night.

'Very well, I shall wait for the moment,' Elizabeth told her. 'But the time will come when something must be done.'

'Yes, ma'am, I know,' Lisa said, 'But perhaps I can find some way to recover from my shame.'

'You mean that there is a man who might marry you?'

Lisa nodded. 'He be older than me but he be kind and he might take me, child and all.'

'Then I advise you to speak with him sooner than later,' Elizabeth said. 'But mind you tell him the truth or he may disown you afterwards.'

Lisa curtsied and left the room. Elizabeth went over to the window, looking out. She felt sorry for the serving wench for she knew that most would not believe her story, though she herself was inclined to think it true. Had Walter been a different man she would have told him the whole and relied on his judgement – but she feared for the girl if her husband decided against her. Had she been married to Rupert she knew he would have treated the girl kindly, and, had the parson been guilty, driven him from the parish. Walter liked the Reverend Medford and she doubted that he would believe a word Lisa said against him.

Despite her determination not to think of Rupert, Elizabeth found her thoughts turning to him once more. She wondered where he was and what he was doing – whether he ever thought of her . . .

Rupert's lip curled in disdain as he watched the men drinking and gambling. The inn was filled with English gentlemen, but they behaved as if they were as base as the worst scum of society. He understood the feeling of desperation that possessed them, for these were men who ought to have been sitting in their own houses, secure in possession of their land and fortunes. They had in many cases given their all for the King; silver plate sold to buy arms, land and houses either sold to pay debts or now at the mercy of the men who had become rulers in the King's stead. Some estates would be given to men loyal to Parliament, others would be sold and the money confiscated or taken as fines. It was little wonder then that these men spent their nights and often their days in drinking, whoring and gambling.

Rupert was not sure what he had expected when he fled to France. His friend had taken to the life, living on the money he won at the dice or the cards. Rupert had no real taste for either gambling or whoring. He had been trying to find work for his sword since he arrived, but it seemed that there were already too many Englishmen in exile looking for work and few takers.

'Come and join us,' Freeman called to him. Already three parts drunk, he had a pretty wench on his knee, his hand moving beneath her skirt as he threw the dice and won the pot. 'Come, Rupert. I'll stake you – and Lucille will share her favours between us. I dare say she has an appetite for all of us let alone one.'

Rupert smiled for it would be churlish to refuse, though he had no need for the wench and the dice would be merely a way of passing the hours. Yet as he moved forward he noticed that someone was staring at him from across the room and he stood still, looking into the other's face. A man he had seen but once before. He was dark-haired and handsome, his eyes bold and . . . angry. Yes, angry. He was looking at Rupert as if he wished to kill him. Now he was striding towards Rupert and the expression on his face was one of hatred.

Coldness trickled slowly down Rupert's spine as he realized who the other was, and understood the look in his eyes. He was Kit Elbury and it was clear that his feelings for Rupert were as bitter and fierce as Rupert's for him. There was unsettled business between them.

'So, we meet at last,' he said as the other man came up to him. 'You stole my wife and owe me satisfaction.'

'Willingly,' Kit replied, his voice harsh with hatred. 'But she was mine first and you took her from me.'

'She came willingly,' Rupert said, his anger as cold and hard as frosted iron on a winter's morning. 'She was my wife. You dishonoured her and then you killed her, left her by the side of the road to rot had I not found her.'

For a moment Kit's face worked with grief. 'I was dazed by the accident. I left others with her . . .'

'You deserted her and I took her back,' Rupert said harshly. 'She is buried with my ancestors now where she belongs – and I will have justice of you for her death.'

'Where and when?' Kit said. 'I am at your disposal, sir.'

John Freeman had seen something was going on. Although inebriated, he recognized that a challenge had been issued. 'I'll stand second to you, Rupert,' he said. 'Not this night for I would see double of him – but tomorrow before dusk on the common ground behind this inn.'

'Name your seconds,' Rupert said, his expression hard as he faced Kit. 'Will you have swords or pistols?'

'We'll use a gentleman's weapon,' Kit replied. 'I want to teach you a lesson, Saunders. I mean to make you pay for Sarah's grief. She told me what you did to her and I vowed that I would kill you for it.'

'Swords it is,' Rupert said. 'You are her murderer, Elbury. I loved her and I hurt her – but it was because of you.' And how he had regretted the angry words that had driven Sarah to flee from him to her death! Even more than the bitterness of knowing she had never loved him was the pain of his own guilt.

'Come away now,' John Freeman said, pulling at the sleeve of his coat. 'It will be done in the right way. No use in trading insults, my friend. Let your sword do the talking.'

Rupert allowed himself to be drawn away. 'Perhaps I shall join you in a game of cards,' he said, but his friend shook his head.

'What I need is a bucket of water over me,' he muttered, 'and then some sleep. A duel is a deadly business, Rupert. Elbury is known for his skill and will give no quarter.'

'None is wanted,' Rupert said for the taste was bitter in his mouth and he cared not whether he lived or died.

* * *

It was a fine, still day, the sun shining though the wind had a bite to it. A perfect day for what was to be done. Rupert was still of the same mind as previously when he and his seconds, John Freeman and James Tewkesbury, attended the meeting place the next afternoon. His most urgent desire was to kill the man who had stolen his wife and exact retribution.

He had spent the afternoon writing to his sister and enclosing a letter for his daughter, which was to be given to her when she was sixteen. They would be sent only if he was fatally wounded. He had considered writing to Elizabeth but decided against it for there was little he could say. She had probably forgotten him by now and found someone else to care for.

Kit Elbury arrived a few moments after Rupert, his seconds gentlemen of good repute though unknown to Rupert. The proper procedure was followed and the duel began. It was clear from the first moment of clashing swords that this was going to be a fight to the death and not a mere ritual of honour.

Kit came at him fiercely, driving him back with a flurry of savage blows that took Rupert's breath. Time and again he had to give way to the other man, twice losing his footing as he stumbled on the uneven ground. Kit was a master swordsman and his sword arm was strong, his movements lightning fast, as he lunged and parried.

For the first few minutes Rupert thought himself outclassed and it was all he could do to hold off his opponent, but then he began to realize that Kit was allowing his anger to cloud his judgement and sometimes extended too far. Keeping a cool head, Rupert watched for his opportunity before making a riposte that took Elbury off centre and made him falter for perhaps the first time. Rupert extended his thrust without lunging and succeeded in drawing the first blood as the tip of his foil slashed the other's sleeve, inflicting a minor flesh wound.

Elbury came at him again; lunge, parry, thrust, driving

Rupert back once more, but then, as he realized he had gained the higher ground, Rupert whirled to one side and made Elbury miss his footing. They disengaged for a moment, both breathing deeply, and then began once more. Their foils touched in a salute, Rupert the first to thrust this time. Now Elbury was retreating and Rupert pressed home his advantage, only for Kit to take it back again.

Rupert stumbled and felt the sting as Elbury's sword pierced his upper arm, drawing blood. He staggered back, but then found his appetite for the fight had suddenly become stronger. Now it was as it had been on the battlefield when the issue was life or death, and his hunger for life had somehow reasserted itself as he began to attack; thrust, parry, lunge.

Elbury was tiring. Rupert guessed that as one of the King's equerries he had seen little actual fighting on the field of battle. He was a pretty swordsman, and skilled, but he lacked stamina. He was tiring sooner than Rupert, who had learned that a man must keep on his feet at all costs if he wanted to live at the end of the day. Now he was winning more often than he lost, driving Elbury back and back again. Suddenly, he saw his opportunity and with a twist of his right arm, sent the other's blade flying. Elbury could not reach his sword and he stood before him, defenceless.

Rupert looked into his eyes and saw the same pain, the same grief as he felt and realized that he no longer wished to kill him. Sarah was not worth it. She had been a selfish, thoughtless woman and her death had come about through her own folly. She was not worth the cost of a man's life.

'No,' he said and lowered his sword arm. 'No, I shall not grant you an easy death, Elbury. Live on and consider what you have done . . .'

As Rupert turned away, Elbury drew a dagger from inside his doublet and made to stab at Rupert's back. A warning shout was not in time and he felt the blade enter his flesh. He turned on the instant, driving his sword forward and piercing Elbury's chest. For a moment Elbury hung there, smiling, and then he crumpled to his knees and fell forward onto his face.

Rupert swayed, for blood was oozing from the wound to his shoulder and the ground seemed to be coming up to meet him. He was aware of his seconds rushing to his side and then the blackness descended.

Eleven

'You seem quiet, my love,' Nicolas said as he entered the small back parlour at Thornberry and found his wife sitting there alone. She had some sewing beside her but she was not working on it, merely staring into space, her eyes seeming to indicate that her mind was far away. 'Is something wrong?'

'I think Rupert is in trouble,' Caroline said. 'I felt it – a sudden coldness all over. He has been wounded or lies close to death.' She shivered, and her face was pale with anxiety.

'You cannot know that, Caroline.'

'I feel it,' she said. 'I have never spoken of these feelings, Nicolas, but they come to me sometimes. A gypsy once told me that I have the gift of second sight, but I thought her merely seeking to please me – though she warned me that it was not always a good thing. I knew when Rupert was wounded the first time, and I knew that you would come safely back to me at the end of the war. I cannot see all things, but only some.'

Nicolas was thoughtful, dubious of this gift of which Caroline had never before spoken. 'And you believe that Rupert is ill?'

'I felt pain in my shoulder,' she said. 'It was fleeting but I believe he was wounded and is now close to death.'

'You wish me to make inquiries for you?'

'We do not know where he went,' Caroline said. 'My mother has been worried for months, but he has sent no word. It may be that we shall hear if he dies . . .' Her voice broke on a sob. 'God save that he does not!'

Nicolas hardly knew how to answer her for he had no faith in such powers, and had it been any but Caroline he would have denounced it at once, but her anxiety moved him. He could only pray that she was wrong.

'I had some news for you,' he said, 'but perhaps now is not the time . . .'

'Yes, please tell me,' Caroline begged. 'Does your news concern Harry's other son – Rowena's child?'

'Yes,' Nicolas frowned. How had she known that? 'It seems that she was seen in Huntingdon a month ago, and she had a boy with her – a boy much as you described him, Caroline.'

'Do you know where she is now?' Nicolas shook his head. 'But your agent will continue to make inquiries?'

'Yes, of course. As you said, the boy may be Harry's son, though illegitimate. I have caused a search to be made in Oxford, but there is no record of a marriage between Harry and Rowena Greenslade. I am certain that she was never his wife, for he would have married Mercy if he had not been pressed for money. Even so, I am prepared to do something for my brother's son.'

'Then we must continue to search for him,' Caroline said. She smiled at him. 'And now, my love, I have news for you. I am carrying your child once more.'

'Caroline – are you sure?' Nicolas was torn between his natural desire for a son and fear for her. 'I had hoped we had been careful enough that you would have longer before you conceived again.'

'Do not be concerned for me,' Caroline begged for she had seen the anxiety in his face. 'I am well enough and with luck I shall carry this child the full nine months.'

'I pray it will be so,' he said feeling apprehensive. 'Like you I long for a son, Caroline – but an heir would be as nothing to me if I lost you.'

'Yes, I know,' she said. 'And we have our darling Hal – but still I would give you a son if I am able.'

'Then you must take great care of yourself and cease to worry over Rupert for you cannot know that he is ill.'

'I dare say it was just a foolish notion,' Caroline said to please him, but in her heart she knew that Rupert had been wounded and that he was very ill. But since it troubled Nicolas she would not mention her fears again.

Elizabeth looked with pride at the rows of preserved fruits and herbs on her shelves. They represented a great deal of work on her part and she felt pleased that they would now have sufficient to last through the winter months. As well as the preserves, she had seen to the salting of beef and pork, and several barrels were stored in the cellar where they would keep well.

Ale and wines were also kept there. She had not been able to make much wine this year but she had a few jars of Blackberry and Elder wine, which she hoped might be ready to drink in the spring or summer. Next year she would make many more varieties, and she would be able to bottle more soft fruit, for the gardens were well stocked.

She wiped her hands on her white apron and left the still-room, intending to visit the kitchens. They were to have pigeon and capon that evening together with a remove of sweetbreads cooked in wine and cream, and she wanted to make sure that the cook had forgotten nothing.

As she passed through the hall, she saw that a letter had come for her from Caroline, and she slipped it into her bodice, intending to read it later

Rupert was aware of the soft hands stroking his hair back from his face. He had been aware of her often as he hovered between life and death. Elbury's dagger had struck a deep blow and the wound had taken harm, bringing a severe fever. It was the fever that had laid him low, for the wound itself was now healing well.

He opened his eyes to look into the face of the woman bending over him. She was familiar to him, though for a moment he could not recall her, and then he realized it was the whore from the tavern.

'Thank you,' he said in a weak, whispery voice. 'You have been kind to me, mistress.'

'I did not wish such a handsome man to die,' Lucille replied, smiling at him. Her full red lips were ripe and luscious as was her body. She was dressed in a white tunic over a red skirt, and a drawstring of ribbon pulled the neckline low over her breasts so that Rupert could see the rosy peaks of her nipples as she bent over him, bathing his forehead. 'Besides, your friend asked me to nurse you, and I was happy to oblige him.'

'Is Freeman still here at these lodgings?' Rupert asked, frowning as he tried to count the lost days. 'How long have I lain here?'

'For almost a week,' Lucille told him. 'At first we thought you might die, but the physician came and lanced your wound and now you are recovering.'

'Did you send for the physician or was it Freeman?'

'It was me!' His friend's voice hailed from the door. He entered and stood gazing down at him, a look of satisfaction in his eyes. 'You owe your life more to Lucille than anyone, Rupert. She has scarcely left your side since you were wounded.'

'I thank you, lady,' Rupert said. 'When I earn some money I shall make you a present.'

'I have no need of presents,' Lucille denied. 'You are a fine brave man, sir, and I would do as much for any man in your position.'

'You may be able to reward Lucille sooner than you think,' Freeman said and tossed a leather pouch onto the bed. 'I think they belong to you. Apparently Elbury asked that in the event of his death they be returned to you.'

Rupert pulled at the strings of the pouch, which opened and spilled the jewels Sarah had taken with her when she fled onto the bed covers. It was a small fortune, and though he would hesitate to sell some of the pieces, which were family heirlooms, there was enough to tide him over until he could find work. He sought amongst the pieces and found a ruby ring that he had given Sarah. Selecting it, he offered it to Lucille.

'It is a small token, lady, but it would please me if you were to accept it.'

Lucille was aware that it was a valuable ring, but she took it from him with a smile and placed it inside her bodice. 'I thank you for your gift, sir,' she told him. 'And now I shall leave you gentlemen to talk – but do not attempt to rise yet, sir. I shall bring you food and wine in a little while.'

'So Elbury returned the jewels Sarah gave him for safe-keeping,' Rupert said. 'She has done damage enough and I must return some of these to my father for they rightly belong to him. Those that I gave her I shall sell and they will fund me for a few months, at least until I find some work.'

'You are in no state to work for a while yet,' Freeman told him. 'I have been advised to seek a position in the Low Countries, and I have thought of leaving soon. To be honest I have grown weary of the life here, Rupert. It sickens me – the waste of time, the drinking and the gambling. If I thought I could gain a pardon I would go home, but that requires money of which I have precious little. So I am forced to offer my sword to a foreign prince and hope that I may survive until I may go home again.'

'I thought it pleased you to spend your time gambling and drinking?'

'At first, but these pleasures pall in time and I need some new adventure to keep me from falling into despair.'

'Perhaps I shall join you when I am fit,' Rupert said. 'Let me know where you go and I may follow.'

'I waited only to be certain you were on the mend,' John Freeman told him. 'There is nothing to keep me here – Lucille would rather warm your bed than mine, and I need to seek my fortune elsewhere.'

'Then go with God,' Rupert said and his eyelids flickered for he was weary. 'I would fain sleep, John. Thank you for your care of me.'

'Take care of what I gave you,' John said. 'Lucille would

not steal from you, but others are not so nice in their ways. If we do not meet again in this life, I wish you a merry one.'

Rupert nodded, his eyes closing as he felt the weakness steal over him. The jewels lay beside him on the bed, and when Lucille came to feed him later, she pushed them under his pillow. There were things she would have of this cavalier should he smile on her, but his family jewels were not what she craved. He was as gentle and generous as he was handsome and she had a mind for a new lover.

'Elizabeth,' Walter called to his wife as he saw her busy in her stillroom. She was often to be found there of a morning for she was an industrious woman. 'I would have words with you, my dear.'

'Yes, Walter.' She went to him at once for it was not often that he called her from her work in the middle of the day. 'What is it that you need, husband?'

'It has come to my notice that one of the serving wenches has got herself with child, Elizabeth. Did you know of this?'

'Yes, I knew.'

He frowned. 'And you did not choose to tell me? Is the culprit willing to wed her?'

'I think not,' Elizabeth said. 'He is a man who should know better, Walter, but I fear there is little we can do to compel him. Lisa says that he would deny all knowledge of her. She had hopes that someone else might offer her marriage, but I believe it has come to naught.'

'Did she tell you who had carnal knowledge of her?'

'Yes, Walter – but if I tell you, you will say she lies.'

'Tell me. I would hear her side of the matter before I judge her.'

'She swears it was the Reverend Medford. She says that he forced her to it and that she never wanted to lie with him.'

'And you believe her?' His brows rose in disbelief. 'Surely you cannot have been so deceived? I know you have a generous heart, Elizabeth – but the girl deserves to be punished for her wickedness. To accuse a man of God of such evil is beyond anything. Had she named a local lad I might have been able to do something for her – but Medford is above reproach.'

'Is he?' Elizabeth looked at him steadily. 'Why is he to be believed above her? She has always been a good girl. She works hard and does not behave in a lewd manner. Why will you take his word above hers?'

'I know the man and like him,' Walter said and frowned. 'Trust my judgement in this, Elizabeth. I shall speak to the girl and ask for her story – but I do not doubt that I shall find her out.'

Elizabeth hesitated. Her instincts told her to beg for mercy on behalf of the unfortunate girl, but she knew that it would not avail either of them. Walter would be angry with her if she seemed to question his judgement and then Lisa would suffer more.

'Even if she has lied she is young and afraid,' she said. 'For my sake be gentle with her, Walter. Do not turn her off without a penny.'

'She shall have her wages for the month,' he said and hesitated. 'And for your sake she shall have two shillings more – but she may not remain in this house for her shame is known and I cannot have it reflect on us. In the name of decency and respectability, she must go, Elizabeth.'

Elizabeth was silent. She would have preferred mercy to respectability but she kept her silence. At least Lisa would be given some money and that was all she could hope for in the circumstances. She prayed that the girl would leave the village before she was shamed in church and driven away by the goodwives with stones.

'You must do as you wish, Walter,' she said, 'but remember that she is barely more than sixteen years.' She turned away and went back to her work with a heavy heart. How could she expect mercy for a serving wench when her husband had precious little for her?

She thought of Rupert and his gentleness, for thus he had been until Sarah betrayed him. Surely he would not have turned the girl off when it meant she would be forced to walk from village to village, begging for her bread? Or were all righteous men the same?

If what Lisa had done was a sin, then the man who had lain with her was equally guilty but it appeared that he would be allowed to escape without punishment.

Rupert walked about the gardens of the inn where he had lain in his sickbed for some weeks. He was feeling better at last, the draining weakness almost gone. He had recovered his appetite and with it had come something he had thought lost forever. He had discovered he could laugh again, and that he found joy in living. The sun was quite warm that morning, and it made him feel that it was good to be alive. His grief and shame had somehow left him while he was ill and he could remember Sarah with fondness but without the hurt.

He smiled as he recalled the first time he had seen her. She was so beautiful, such a naughty minx. She had sat on his bed and flirted with him while he lay looking up at her and imagining her in his arms. Yet there had been an innocence and a sweetness about her that made him think he wanted to protect her from harm.

He ought to have known that such a quicksilver girl was not for him; he was too ordinary, too dependable for Sarah. She had needed someone like Kit Elbury – had loved him even then. He was sad that she had not stayed true to her love, for if she had never made him fall in love with her he might have married Elizabeth.

It was Elizabeth who had taken him in when he was wandering in her garden, dazed and ill, and it was she and Sarah's companion who had cared for him, binding his wound. Sarah had done little but pout and laugh, and look pretty. It was Elizabeth he ought to have loved from the start, Rupert thought ruefully. She had grown into a beautiful, passionate woman while Sarah had remained a child.

He thought of the day Elizabeth had given herself to him

so sweetly, and the way he had left her so abruptly. Surely she must hate him now? He had left her a letter, asking her to wait for him, but since then he had made no attempt to contact her. It would be foolish to imagine that she could still care for him. She would have grown tired of waiting and found someone else to love.

'Ah, there you are,' Lucille's voice called to him. She walked towards him, her hips swaying enticingly, her lips red and sensuous as she smiled at him in the way he knew meant she was ready to lie with him should he indicate a desire for her. 'Are you better today, sir?'

'Much better, thank you, Lucille. I think I must soon leave you, though I shall never forget your kindness.'

'I wish that you would stay,' she said. 'I have heard of a French Marquis who needs a secretary. Your understanding of French is excellent. Could you not take the position?'

'It might have served had I no other plans,' Rupert said. 'But I have been thinking. It is my duty to return to my home and give my father the jewels that belong to him. And there is something else I must do . . .'

Lucille looked into his eyes and knew that she must lose hope of him. She had given him chances enough these past weeks but he had not been tempted, and she believed she knew the reason.

'There is a lady, isn't there? Someone you care for back there?'

'Perhaps . . . Yes, I do care for Elizabeth,' he said, apprehending he felt much more than he had understood until this minute. 'I do not know whether she has forgot me – but I must see her.'

'She will not have forgotten you,' Lucille said. 'Women do not forget a man they have loved – and she has loved you, has she not?'

'Yes, I believe Elizabeth loved me truly,' Rupert said. 'I hurt her but it may be that she will forgive me.'

'If she does not you may return to me,' Lucille said and suddenly pressed herself against him, her lips to his as she invited one last time. Rupert laughed, slapped her backside and kissed her gently but without passion. 'Go then to your lady,' she said and moved away. 'But remember me if you should need someone to warm a cold bed of nights.'

'I would accept no other,' Rupert said, smiling at her. But already he was thinking of home and Elizabeth . . .

'Oh, Mistress Benedict,' the woman cried as she entered the kitchen that morning to find her mistress there, making a hot posset for a servant who had taken a terrible chill. 'I was about to come and tell you – it's poor Lisa. She jumped into the river from the bridge and was drowned last Sunday. I did but just hear it from the lad who brought letters from the receiving station at the inn.'

'Lisa was drowned?' Elizabeth felt sickness turn in her stomach and for a moment she felt faint. She knew that her husband had turned the girl off after lecturing her on the sins of lying and lust, and she had seen Lisa run away from the house in tears. She had gone to the door to call after her, but the girl had not stayed to listen. 'Oh, the poor child. She was so young.'

'And innocent,' Clara said, nodding her three chins and looking angry. She pounded the dough she had left to prove by the fire with new vengeance. 'She told me what happened to her, ma'am, and I believed her, for she was a good girl, not given to flirting. It was not she who should have been punished but someone else – someone who ought to know better.'

'Yes, I agree with you,' Elizabeth said. She felt the anger rise up inside her and knew what she must do. 'Do you know if my husband has returned from his business earlier?'

'Yes, Mistress Benedict. He is in his library.'

'Thank you. I shall see him there.'

Elizabeth was so angry that she did not stop to think of consequences. If Walter had listened to her he would have given the girl another chance. Perhaps one of the village lads might have been induced to wed her if a dowry had been paid. If Elizabeth had money of her own she would have done it herself, but she had nothing save what her husband gave her for housekeeping.

Walter was sitting at his table, his writing-box before him, reading a letter when she went in without knocking. He looked at her with surprise for she usually waited for his permission before entering when he was at his accounts. Indeed, she scarcely ever ventured into this room for it was dark, its walls of grey stone and sometimes damp despite the fire that was kept burning at all times. She wondered that he cared to sit here for hours at a time, but when she questioned him on the wisdom of it he had ignored her.

'Did you want something, my dear?'

'Yes, Walter. I thought you should know that Lisa is dead. She took her own life on Sunday.'

'Dead?' His face went white and he looked at her oddly. In that moment she knew that he had believed the girl's story, even though he had sent her away. 'How did that happen? I gave her the money I promised you and a little more.' He had in fact given her six months' wages, though he knew that it was not justice, for the girl had been innocent of any crime. But he had not been able to bring himself to admit that she was not to blame.

'She killed herself, Walter,' Elizabeth said, and her anger was plain to see. It was the first time she had shown anger since they wed, and it shocked him. 'She was so desperate that she jumped off the bridge into the river and drowned herself.'

'God have mercy!' Walter drew the sign of the cross over his breast and stood up. His hand trembled as he gripped the letter he had been reading. 'I had this today and I believe it is not the first time that Medford has behaved thus to a young girl. I had meant to speak to Sir James tomorrow, for it is not fitting that such a man should lead us in prayer. I have been grossly deceived in him, Elizabeth.'

'Why would you not believe me when I told you Lisa was innocent?' Elizabeth cried for she had lost all caution, her anger justly roused so that she no longer feared his censure. 'I know that you were disappointed in me, Walter, but I have tried to make up for what I did by being all that you want in a wife. Despite your harshness to me, I care for you and I respect you. I think you mostly a just man – but that was not justice. You treated that girl ill and she is dead because of it.'

'Yes, you are right to accuse me,' Walter said. He cleared his throat, for all her accusations were just and he knew himself at fault. 'I have not treated the girl fairly for I knew that she was innocent, and I had begun to suspect that Medford was not as he ought to be in all things. I wrote to the parish where he was last a preacher and have this day had my answer – they dismissed him for just such an incident, but kept it quiet for the sake of others. Had Sir James known this I feel certain that he would never have employed the man for he does not care for him.'

'It is too late for apologies, Walter,' she said, her anger a little abated since he had taken the trouble to inquire. 'That poor child is dead and you turned her away when you knew she had nowhere else to go.'

'You are right, Elizabeth,' he said looking distressed, for at heart he was a just man. 'I wish I might turn back the hours but I know it is too late. Yet had the girl not taken her own life I would have done something to help her, arranged that she be wed . . .'

'She could not know that, Walter. Sometimes when you leave someone no hope you kill the wish to live in them . . .' She choked on a sob for now she was thinking of herself as well as the girl. 'There have been times when I have contemplated the path she took . . .'

'Elizabeth . . .' It was a cry from the heart for he was genuinely shocked and suddenly afraid that he might lose her. 'Forgive me . . . I was angry, hurt . . . but I did not mean to . . .'

He moved towards her, then stopped, gave another cry, this time of pain and clutched at his chest. For a moment he swayed on his feet and then seemed to crumple before her eyes; he sank to his knees with a groan and then fell forward onto his face.

'Walter!' Elizabeth cried. She ran to him, bending over him to see what ailed him. His eyelids flickered and he moaned, but when she spoke to him he could not answer though his face worked strangely. 'Walter, please do not worry. It was not all your fault. I shall call for help.' She ran to the door and called for her servants in a loud voice, which had the effect of bringing several of them running. 'Your master has been taken ill. We must carry him to his room and one of you must go for the physician. Tell him he must come to us urgently.'

Her orders were obeyed without hesitation for Elizabeth was a good mistress. Her servants respected her and knew that she behaved justly towards her husband, whom they thought a fool for his stern manner towards her. Elizabeth followed as he was carried upstairs to his own chamber, and then, keeping only one of the girls to help her, she removed his clothes, pulling a clean night-shirt over his head and settling him comfortably in a warm bed.

'Elizabeth . . .' he moaned, his eyelids flickering. 'Forgive me . . . do not leave me . . .'

'I am here with you, Walter,' she told him, laying a cool hand on his brow. 'I shall not leave you. The doctor will be here soon and then we may discover what ails you, my dear.'

He made no answer and she feared he had lost the power to speak or understand for the moment, for a trickle of saliva ran from the corner of his mouth and down his chin. She wiped it away with her kerchief and smoothed his dark hair back from his forehead.

'Oh, Mistress Benedict,' the girl said to her fearfully. 'I do mind my father taking a fit like this and dying before he were forty. 'Tis a seizure that's what it be.'

'Yes, perhaps you are right,' Elizabeth said, because it was what she feared herself, 'but we must wait until the doctor has seen him – and we should pray. He may yet recover for I believe that it is often so.'

The girl nodded but looked doubtful, as was Elizabeth in truth. It had been so sudden that she was shocked for she had not thought her husband ailing. He had seemed such a strong man, giving no sign of illness.

'You be young to be a widow, ma'am.'

'Do not say such a thing,' Elizabeth remonstrated. 'I would not see my husband die, May. He is a strong man and I believe he will recover.'

The girl nodded obediently, but Elizabeth knew that she did not believe it. Impatient with such pessimism, she sent her away, sitting by Walter's bed alone. She reached out and stroked his forehead.

'I am sorry for upsetting you,' she said. 'You were wrong, Walter, and you have been unkind – but I would not see you die.'

He could not answer her. She was not sure that he heard her or that he even knew she was there, but she hoped that her presence would ease him. It was all that she could do for the moment . . .

'Caroline, dearest,' Nicolas said, coming into her parlour. He was smiling, though there was also anxiety there for he worried that she would not be strong enough to bear her child the full term. Already the physician had told them that she must take great care. 'Do not be alarmed or too excited – but there is someone to see you.'

Caroline saw the concern in his face and knew at once. 'It is Rupert, isn't it? I have felt that he was better and that he was thinking of us. Please ask him to come in, Nicolas. It will not upset me.'

'Caro, dearest,' Rupert said and came striding into the room, his face alight with pleasure. 'No, no, do not get up. Nicolas tells me that you have not been feeling well. I hope I do not disturb you?'

'How could you disturb me?' Caroline asked, lifting her face for his kiss but not rising from her chair. It was true that she had been feeling unwell and she was trying to obey her doctor and do as little as possible. 'Are you better now, Rupert? I was very anxious for a while.'

'You knew that I was ill? Did someone write and tell you?'

'No. I felt it,' she said. 'But then I knew that you were recovering. What happened to you? Were you wounded?'

'It is not important,' Rupert said. 'It is over now – it is all over now, Caroline. Thanks be to God! I have forgiven Sarah and myself.'

'I thank God for it,' she said and took his hand as he sat on the settle beside her. 'I hope that you will spend this Christmastide with us?'

'Yes, I had planned to stay two days with Mother,' he said and then the light died from his face. 'She tells me that Elizabeth has married Captain Benedict?'

'Yes, she married a few months ago,' Caroline said and was saddened as she saw the disappointment in his face. 'I think she despaired of hearing from you, my dear.'

'Did she not have the letter I left for her with mother?'

'I do not know. She did not mention it and I think not. Elizabeth loved you, Rupert. I do not know what occurred before you left the last time, but she was greatly distressed. She looked for a letter for some months but when she did not receive one . . . this offer was perhaps her last chance for a home and marriage. I believe she wanted to have children above anything. She loved Angelica and often sends her a small gift even now.'

Rupert smothered a groan for he had known it, and he had known where his duty lay. 'I would have married her had she waited. It was . . . too soon. I meant to marry her when I returned.'

Caroline shook her head at him. 'How could she know that? None of us heard anything of you. We thought you might be at Colchester or with the Duke of Hamilton?'

'I spent some time on the Isle of Wight,' Rupert said, 'but the plans to rescue His Majesty were wild and foolish, so I rode north to join with Hamilton, but I escaped when it became certain that we were doomed to fail and took ship for France. It was there that . . . I met with my accident.'

'Was it Kit Elbury?' Rupert nodded and Caroline understood. He did not wish to speak of what had happened. She would not force him to speak of it until he was ready. 'Why did you never write, Rupert? If Elizabeth had been given hope I believe she would have waited.' Indeed, she knew that Elizabeth had been in two minds even on her wedding day.

'It was my fault,' he said. 'I cannot blame her for taking another in my stead.'

'Nor would I if I thought her happy,' Caroline said. 'I think she has found her marriage less than she had hoped, Rupert – but it is done now.'

'Yes, I suppose . . .' Rupert looked away from his sister's gaze. When he had first heard of Elizabeth's marriage he had thought all hope lost, but now . . . perhaps she might wish to be free of her bargain. It could not hurt to at least ask her. 'But if she is unhappy . . .'

'Rupert,' Caroline warned. 'Do nothing that might harm her I beg you.'

'Of course not,' he replied, but was relieved by the interruption caused by the arrival of her nephew Hal, who came bouncing into the room full of his doings and ended any chance of private talk between them. 'I would never harm her – and I believe I have a gift for this young rascal . . .'

After that he was given no peace until he produced the beautiful harness he had bought for the child's pony as a Christmas gift. Hal went into raptures over the fine leather and silver mountings, and told his uncle that he must come and watch him ride his pony immediately. Faced with more questions from his sister or a child's eager excitement he chose the easier and let Hal hurry him out to the stables.

'Is Rupert not aware that we are supposed to forgo such indulgences at Christmastide?' Nicolas asked of his wife with a smile. He was mocking her for he had no intention of neglecting to give his wife and children gifts no matter the new doctrine that forbade all the old customs and commanded that they keep the day Holy and spend it in prayer. 'But he has been absent for a long time. I dare say he does not know what we have come to in his absence.'

'Providing we do not break the laws openly I daresay we shall escape retribution,' Caroline said, smiling because she knew her husband had no intention of obeying such stringent strictures. He had been forced to remove brass and silver from the church and to replace it with plain wooden items, but as yet he had refused steadfastly to do the same in their private chapel.

'Well, I still have some influence here for the moment,' Nicolas said. 'If our firebrand of a preacher goes too far I may suggest that he is wasted here. I am sure there are others in the city that stand in more need of his guidance than us, my love.'

'Yes, perhaps,' Caroline said, a wicked gleam in her eyes. Sometimes Nicolas had a stern manner that had come upon him as a mantle during the war, but at other times he became the merry lad she had known when they were children. She hoped that in time he would lose much of the worry that had weighed him down these past years. His estate was prospering, and like others in the war he had been rewarded for his loyalty to Parliament. 'I shall hope that he does not try your patience too far, my love. Mr Willingham is a good man though sometimes over zealous in the pulpit – but at least he does not do as some others do and inflict severe punishment on those who transgress. I believe he is moved to sorrow more than anger.'

'As I said, I have some influence,' Nicolas said. 'I will have no stocks erected in Thornberry, nor shall I permit a wanton woman to be stoned. I think there are punishments more fitting, and Mr Willingham has been brought to see my point of view.'

'By way of a new roof for his vicarage I dare say,' Caroline said and laughed. She did not care how her husband chose to wield his power for she knew that he was a just man, and that she was fortunate to be his wife.

For a moment she thought about her friend Elizabeth. Elizabeth had never told her that Captain Benedict was harsh to her, but somehow Caroline had sensed it. Elizabeth's letters lacked spirit and that told her much, but her latest letter had been to tell of her husband's illness.

'I should like to see Elizabeth one day,' Caroline told her husband. 'She says that Walter has recovered from the worst of his seizure, but he is confined to bed and for the moment he has lost the use of his left arm and his right leg. He has told her that she ought to have a woman to help her run the house, and she has invited Sarah's former companion, Mistress Furnley, to join them at their home.'

'I am glad she is to have a companion, but sorry that her husband is ill. It is most unfortunate when they have been married such a short time,' Nicolas said. 'Clearly she cannot come to us – but perhaps we may visit her. It cannot be until after the birth of course . . .'

'No. I should be unwise to travel until the child is born,' Caroline agreed. 'But perhaps we may visit her one day?'

'You know that I would do anything to please you,' Nicolas said and bent to kiss her. 'And now my love, I shall rescue your brother from our beloved Hal. I wish to speak to him.'

'Yes, of course. You may tell him that I wish to see him again before he leaves, if you will.'

Nicolas smiled, nodded and left her. Caroline bent over her needlework. It was good to know that Rupert was safe, but she hoped he would not try to see Elizabeth, for that might cause trouble for her and she had trouble enough.

'I fear that they will bring His Majesty to trial soon,' Nicolas told his brother-in-law when they had sent Hal scurrying to his nurse. 'It means that there is little sympathy for Royalists at the moment. I have not told Caroline yet, but I plan to go to London after Christmas and speak with Cromwell. I shall speak on your behalf if the opportunity occurs but I cannot say what his answer may be.'

'I would not have you risk yourself for my sake. I had thought of seeking employment in the Low Countries. My father would wish me to stay in England if a pardon could be had, but I have reneged on my promise to lay down my arms once and I fear they will not think a fine sufficient this time.'

'Nevertheless, I shall do what I can,' Nicolas told him. 'And if I do not succeed this time I shall not give up until you are pardoned.'

'I shall not say you nay,' Rupert said. 'And I thank you for your good offices, though I think you waste your time. I have little to keep me here – though there is someone I must see.'

'Do you mean Mistress Benedict?' Nicolas frowned for he could not approve of Rupert's intention. The marriage vows were sacred and he would not see them broken. 'I believe her husband is ill.'

'I owe her an explanation,' Rupert said. 'I expect nothing from her – nor should I – but I must and shall see her.'

'Then say nothing to your sister for it would upset her,' Nicolas said. 'She has not been well and I fear that she will miscarry again.'

'I am sorry for it,' Rupert said. 'It must be a disappointment to you.'

'To us both,' Nicolas agreed, 'but for myself I am more concerned for Caroline. If she does not carry the babe this time I shall make certain that we have no more disappointments. I have consulted with physicians who know more of this condition and I believe I know how it may be done.'

'Then I shall pray for you both and the child,' Rupert said. 'And now I must return to my mother for she was loath to part with me and I must leave her as soon as Christmastide is over.'

'You will say goodbye to Caroline, for she wishes to see you before you leave.'

'Yes, of course, though I may only stay a few moments.'

* * *

Elizabeth had been reading to her husband for the best part of an hour, but now she saw that he had fallen asleep. She got to her feet, walking softly from the room so as not to wake him. She knew that he was restless for much of the time and it was good that he had found some peace at last.

Walter was worried about the future for at the moment he was unable to rise from his bed and needed constant nursing. He had told her to leave his ablutions to the servants, but she would not be satisfied until she had done all she could to make him comfortable.

'You are my husband,' she told him when he said that she must not tire herself in his service. 'How else should I spend my time when you are ill?'

'I do not deserve your goodness. I have not been as kind as I might have been since our wedding night.'

'You have not been violent,' Elizabeth replied.

'I could never beat you,' he said. 'I despise myself for having taken out my spite on you, Elizabeth. I was angry and jealous and I said things that would have been better had they never been spoken. I must ask you to forgive me if you can.'

Elizabeth was touched with pity as she saw how abject he was. A dribble of saliva was trickling down his chin, and one side of his face had twisted a little so that he squinted from his right eye. Even so, the doctor had told them that his seizure had not been as severe as it might have been, and that another might kill him.

'I have forgiven you, Walter,' she said and touched his hand. 'Please do not continue to berate yourself. I was at fault for I should have told you the whole truth before we wed.'

'Yes, you should – but I ought to have understood your reticence and been more forgiving.'

'Can you forgive me now?'

'I have forgiven,' he replied. 'I may never be able to forget – but I have forgiven.'

'Then we may start again,' Elizabeth said and smiled. 'We

are husband and wife, Walter, and I would have us live in peace and comfort for the rest of our lives.'

'It may be that I have only a short time, Elizabeth.'

'No! God could not be so cruel,' Elizabeth said. 'Had he meant you to die you would have died when you had the seizure. I pray that this paralysis that troubles you will pass. I am told that it should in time, though it may leave your limbs a little weakened.'

'If I am to be an invalid it would be better I had died. I do not wish to see you waste your life tied to a man who cannot leave his bed without help.'

'My life will not be wasted if you are kind to me, Walter. My prayers are for your recovery, not your death.'

'Is that truly so, Elizabeth? You would be free and your widow's jointure is a considerable one, for Lord Mortimer would have it so in the marriage contract.'

'Believe me, Walter. I am your wife and would not be a widow.'

He stared at her a moment longer and a tear trickled from the corner of his eye. 'Thank you, my dear. I shall remember your goodness and hope that we may be happy together – whatever the future brings.'

'Tomorrow brings the arrival of Mistress Furnley,' Elizabeth reminded him. 'She was very glad to take the position I offered her and I am looking forward to having her with us.'

'It will be good for you to have a companion,' Walter said and smiled at her. 'I am a little tired, my dear. Would you read to me? For I find that the sound of your voice helps me to sleep.'

'Would you prefer poetry or a passage from the Bible?'

'Something gentle today,' he said. 'For I think I may rest now that we have had this talk.'

She had read some of John Donne's poetry to him, and now he was sleeping peacefully, the first real sleep he had had in some days. Elizabeth felt a weight lift from her heart. She was glad that they had made up their quarrel for she had been terribly lonely and afraid for the future. Perhaps now she might look forward to a kind of happiness, and at least she would have a companion, for Mistress Furnley would soon be with them.

She sighed a little for her dearest wish had been to have a child. She had loved Rupert's child, and when she held Angelica after her birth it had almost seemed that the babe was hers. She thought that if she could have a babe she would be content enough with her life, though she would never forget Rupert.

She had tried to put all thought of him from her mind, but sometimes in the night she could not help remembering the sweetness of their loving, for it had given her the greatest happiness of her life.

Yet she believed that a child would bring her a sweet content and give her something to live for. She was not sure that Walter would ever be well enough to father a child, but she prayed for it, as she prayed for his recovery.

Twelve

'You cannot know how delighted I am to be here,' Mistress Furnley told her when she arrived the next morning. 'I do not speak of the journey, though that was hard enough for the roads were nothing but mud in some places and I thought we should never pass them. Yet that is as nothing compared to the noise and chaos of my sister's house. She has had two more babes since I went to her and I thought I should never know peace again!'

Elizabeth laughed and kissed her cheek. 'You cannot be more glad than I, Mistress Furnley. I have more than enough to do with the house and my husband's illness, and you will lift some of that burden from me. The servants are very good, but there are tasks that I cannot leave to them that I know I may entrust to you.'

'I hope you will let me make myself useful with needlework and the stillroom, Elizabeth? I am never happier than when I am busy with such tasks.'

'I remembered that you made an excellent tisane that helped to bring ease when sleep seems impossible. Walter sleeps very little these days and I would make use of your skills to help him.'

'I have had some experience of his illness for my father suffered three seizures,' Mistress Furnley said. 'It is not good for him to lie in bed too long. We must try to get him up and help him recover the use of his limbs.'

'That is what he hopes for,' Elizabeth said, 'though he fears he will be an invalid for the rest of his life.'

'We must see how he goes on,' her companion said, 'but

the tisane is not the only remedy I make that may help him.'

'I see that you will be a great help to us,' Elizabeth said and felt that a weight had lifted from her shoulders. 'I am thankful that you could come.'

'You look tired, my dear,' Mistress Furnley said, looking at her in concern. 'You must rest. Now that I am here I can do many of the things that have taxed your strength.'

'I have not been out of the house for more than three weeks . . .'

'The fresh air would do you good. Why do you not go for a little walk? It is cold but bright, a little frosty underfoot – but if you wrap up well you will not feel the cold.'

'I think that is what I should like of all things,' Elizabeth said. 'I have always liked to walk and I have missed the freedom to do so these past weeks.'

'Then you should go now while the fine weather lasts, for it may snow soon enough . . .'

Elizabeth breathed deeply of the fresh air. She had been feeling weary after being tied to the sick room for so long and it was good to walk briskly for the ground was hard and crunched beneath her feet. She looked up at the sky. A pale sun had lit the day when her friend arrived, but it had become much darker since she came out and she believed it might snow when night fell.

She walked as far as the lane, which led to the church and the village, but halted there. She did not want to be away from the house for too long even though she knew that Mistress Furnley could be trusted to see that Walter was being cared for properly. Yet for a moment she stood where she was, staring at the church and thinking of the man who preached there each Sunday. As yet Walter had been able to do nothing about having him dismissed and Elizabeth felt angry that such a man should be able to continue with his preaching when he was not worthy of respect.

She thought of Lisa who had been treated so unfairly and who had taken her life in desperation. Why was it that life was so unfair? Lisa's only sin was that she had yielded to a man who had treated her ill.

Elizabeth was lost in her thoughts and at first took no notice of the horse and rider coming towards her. It was beginning to get darker and she suddenly realized that she ought to go home. Walter would worry if she was away too long. As she turned, she became aware that the man had got down from his horse and was staring at her intently.

'Elizabeth?' His voice sent shivers down her spine and, as she looked at him again, she suddenly knew him. He was dressed very plainly in clothes that were not his usual attire and she had been misled into thinking him one of her neighbours. 'It is you, Elizabeth?'

She was wearing a hooded cloak pulled forward over her face to protect her from the cold and she knew that he was as uncertain as she had been. She threw her hood back and went towards him, her heart racing with excitement.

'Rupert . . .' She felt the sting of tears on her cheeks and her throat was tight as she choked on the words. 'Oh, Rupert . . . you are alive! You are alive! I feared that you must have been killed and that we should never know . . .'

'Elizabeth!' He moved towards her, catching her in his arms, pulling her close to him. In the delight of seeing him, she made no attempt to resist. She looked up at him, unable to breathe or speak as he bent his head and kissed her lips with such passion that she near swooned in his arms. 'Elizabeth, my love . . . forgive me. What I did was unforgivable but I beg that you will find it in your heart to forgive me.'

'Oh, Rupert . . .' she drew a sobbing breath. 'There is nothing to forgive . . . other than that you went away and left me. What happened that day . . .' She shook her head knowing that she could not tell him because it would be a betrayal of her marriage. 'It does not matter. I have forgotten it.' She had remembered that she was married, and she tried to pull away from him, but he held her fast.

'No, you do not mean that,' Rupert said, his grip tightening on her arms. 'Look at me and tell me that you don't love me, Elizabeth.' She shook her head, turning her face from him. 'You cannot tell me because it is not true. You still love me. I know that you love me – as I love you.'

'No, Rupert!' She wrenched herself from his embrace as the enormity of what she was doing became clear to her. She must not do this! It was wrong, despicable to be with him when her husband lay in his sick bed. 'You don't love me. You would not have left me with no word for so long if you had loved me. I waited and waited for some word but you did not write . . .'

'I left a letter for you, begging for your pardon and your patience,' Rupert said. 'My mother thought you had been hurt enough and did not give it to you – but I asked you to wait until . . .'

'No!' Elizabeth cried, her face going white as she realized what he was saying. If she had waited he would have come back for her – he had come back for her – but it was too late. 'You must not say these things to me, Rupert. It is too late for us. I am married. Walter is a good man and I cannot betray him. He knew that we had lain together . . . and he has forgiven me. If I betray him now I am no better than a whore.'

'Elizabeth,' Rupert gave her a little shake. 'You could never be that – I will not hear such foolishness from you. You still love me. Deny it if you will but I know . . .'

'No, I do not deny it,' she said, and her eyes were bright with tears. He could not know how desperately she longed to throw all caution to the wind, to lie with him, to go with him wherever he would take her – but he must never know! 'I do love you, Rupert. Perhaps I always shall, but I cannot betray Walter. He is my husband.'

'Leave him and come to France with me!'

'You have no right to ask me that,' Elizabeth said. 'Would you have me do to my husband what Sarah did to you?' She saw that she had inflicted pain and it echoed in her own heart. 'No, Rupert. We could never be happy knowing that we had broken the laws of God and Man. I should feel guilty and you would resent my guilt. I cannot live with the sin of adultery in my heart. I will not leave my husband.'

Rupert looked at her, torn between anger at her stubbornness and admiration for her strength of purpose. 'You prefer to hurt both yourself and me?'

'I wish that I might turn back the clock,' Elizabeth answered him, her face reflecting her passion and her pain though she knew it not. 'I wish it with all my heart – but it cannot be done, Rupert. I am wed and I will not shame my husband or myself.'

'So you will send me away to a life of loneliness and despair without you?'

'You will find someone else . . .'

'No!' His hands gripped her arms, shaking her, his eyes wild with passion as he looked down at her. 'There will be no one else for me. I beg you, Elizabeth. I beg you to come with me now for all our sakes!'

'I cannot,' she whispered, feeling as if she were being torn in two. For how much longer could she remain strong, for how long could she resist what was in her heart? 'It is too late, Rupert, much too late. I am having my husband's child . . .' As his grip went slack, his face reflecting the pain she had inflicted, she took the opportunity to evade him and stepped back. 'I shall always love you, but I can never come to you, Rupert. Goodbye, my darling.'

She turned and fled, running towards the house while he stood watching her. She heard him call her name once but she did not look back. Perhaps one day he would know that she had lied and he would hate her. Perhaps it might be better if he did . . .

Elizabeth sat by the window looking out at the moon. It was a bitterly cold night, though the snow had not yet begun to fall. She was sure it would cover the ground by morning and she hoped that Rupert had reached an inn safely, where he might stay for the night.

She had not asked him where he had been or what he had

been doing these many months. There were so many things that she wished she had said to him, but she had been afraid for she knew that she was weak where he was concerned. If she had let him persuade her . . . but she must not let her thoughts stray to what might have been. She had made her choice, the only choice a woman of conscience could make in the circumstances.

Yet the regrets were strong. A part of her rebelled against her life. She was tied to a man she did not love, a man who might never be a proper husband to her again. She might never have a child, though she had lied to Rupert for she had known it was the only thing that would convince him to let her go.

'Oh, Rupert,' she whispered to the night. 'Why did you go away that day? Why did you not ask me to wait?'

He had left her a letter, which she had never received – but if he had but spoken to her in the woods how different their lives could have been. She would have gone with him to France or anywhere he wished if only he had asked her to wait.

But it was too late now: much too late. She had sent him away because her conscience would not allow her to do anything else, but she knew that she would never be able to forget. Tears trickled silently down her cheeks, but she wiped them away with the back of her hand. She would not weep for something that could never be. She had given her word to Walter that she would be a good wife to him, and she had meant it when she spoke – Rupert's declaration meant nothing.

If he had loved her he would never have gone away for so long. A few lines to tell her where he was would have been enough. She stood up, her face pale but determined. The past was gone. She must put away her memories and her regrets. It was over. She would make what she could of the future. She loved Rupert. She thought that she would always love him, but she was Walter Benedict's wife.

Rupert looked from the window of the inn watching the snow, which had driven him to seek shelter; it was falling thick and fast over the landscape, covering it in a heavy white blanket. He felt the isolation of utter despair as he looked back at his life and finally understood the depth of his foolishness. How was it that he had not seen Elizabeth's worth at the beginning?

Yet he had been lost from the moment Sarah had sat on the edge of his bed, pouting at him flirtatiously, her smiles making his blood race with an urgent need to lie with her. He had found her totally fascinating with her little girl frowns and her flirtatious eyes, but she had been shallow and selfish, loving only herself. He regretted that he had not chosen more wisely for Elizabeth had shown her integrity in refusing to abandon her husband, and in doing so had brought home his own shallow folly. Caroline had warned him not to try and see her, but he had ignored his sister and must now pay the price, for if his need had been great before he saw Elizabeth it was greater now.

His thoughts turned to his sister for a while. He had said goodbye to her as she lay recovering from her latest miscarriage, and he had seen the grief she had tried so hard to hide. Caroline had longed so desperately to give her husband a child, but their hopes were almost certainly at an end, for her physician had told her there would be no more babies. She had suffered too cruelly and Nicolas was determined to see that she did not suffer this again.

The bitterness of regret turned in Rupert as he watched the snow settle. He doubted that he would see Caroline or his home for a long time. He had agreed to meet Nicolas in London, but after that he would leave England. He was not sure what he meant to do with the rest of his life. Indeed, there were moments when he felt that he would welcome its end, and yet somewhere deep within him flickered the will to survive.

It seemed that the snow had stopped falling at last. He would sup at the inn and leave first thing in the morning. Once the thaw came it would make the roads almost impossible.

* * *

'I do not like to leave you like this,' Nicolas told his wife. Caroline was sitting up in bed, some needlework and her books to hand, a jug of restorative tisane at her side. 'Perhaps I should simply send word to Cromwell that I am detained at home.'

'No, you should go,' Caroline said holding out her hand to him. She smiled as he sat beside her on the bed, his fingers entwining with hers. 'The doctor told you that the danger was past, Nicolas. I am feeling much better, just a little tired. I have the children and my mother will come to sit with me. I should feel badly if I kept you from your duty.'

She felt saddened by the condition of the King, for he had been brought from Carisbrooke, where he had been well treated, to Hurst Castle, which was a bleak position, being as it was extended even into the sea on a narrow strip of sand and beleaguered on all sides by the winds and tide.

'Cromwell has never pushed for the King's trial,' Nicolas said, 'but now it is to be he will do what he sees as his duty. It is by the will of this scandalous parliament that they call the Rump. It hath been purged of any that might cast in favour of His Majesty and is therefore in itself unjust. Cromwell knows this, though he must treat with them. He asks me to be present so that I may see that right was done.'

'Can it ever be right?' Caroline asked, her expression anxious. 'Do they have the right to try him at all?'

'It is a matter of contention,' he replied. 'I think that is why Cromwell wants me there, because there are deep divisions amongst both the Army and Parliament. Yet now that it has been agreed he will prosecute it with all the determination he hath applied to the war.'

'Then you must go,' she said. 'Do not worry for my sake, my love. I shall be well enough here.'

'I intend to see what may be done about a pardon for Rupert,' Nicolas told her. 'He says that he will go abroad until it is safe to return, but I know that your parents would wish him to stay here, as would you, my love.'

'I fear that he will try to see Elizabeth,' Caroline said. 'I pray he does not for I know her answer. She will not leave her husband even if she has not found the happiness she hoped for when she wed.'

'I warned Rupert against it as did you,' Nicolas said, 'but he was ever a headstrong lad and has not changed in all these years. I fear he must discover the truth for himself, my love.'

'If he had but wed her instead of Sarah,' Caroline said and sighed. 'Poor Rupert. It minds me of a phrase from a poem I once read ". . . and love lies bleeding." I think that Rupert's heart must bleed for his lost innocence.'

'Rupert's is not the only heart to bleed,' Nicolas said. 'This war hath been a blight upon a fair land, and perhaps with the King's trial we shall see an end to it.'

'I pray that you are right, my love.' Caroline smiled at him. 'And now you must go for it is your duty.'

'How can it be that such a small body of men can declare themselves the supreme authority in the country?' Nicolas asked of Cromwell when they met in London, to which city the King had been brought as a prisoner to prepare for his trial. 'If such be the case then why did we fight? I thought it was so that all men might be more equal and to restrict a King who believed he had a divine right to rule. If men like these can take the power unto themselves and dismiss any that do not agree with them where is the difference? At least the King had the right of his ancestors.'

'Charles Stuart hath been given every chance to negotiate with us,' Cromwell said heavily. He was a man of conscience and had wrestled with this problem mightily. 'Had we set out to depose the King, to disinherit him of his proper place in life, then we should be traitors and rebels and have no justice. But this hath come upon us by the Providence of God and we must submit to His Will for His is the divine power.'

Cromwell had spoken similar words in the House, though he had not yet been brought to speak publicly of his private feelings on the case.

Nicolas felt a surge of impatience for though he was himself a man of faith he did not believe that the men who had taken this upon themselves in the name of God truly acted upon a divine intervention. It was men who had grown tired of war and trying to talk to a King who would have none of them – who clung to his beliefs in the face of adversity and refused to answer their charges – that had brought about this sorry state.

'You will attend the trial?' Cromwell said. He looked strained, tired and anxious, for what they were about to do was of such serious import that any man would tremble at the doing. 'I wish you to see that he is given his chance, Nicolas. I do not know what history will say of us, though I fear we may be misunderstood.'

'Yes, I shall attend,' Nicolas said. He was not one of those chosen to judge Charles Stuart and he thanked God for it. 'Have you thought more on what I mentioned to you of my brother-in-law?'

'He must present himself to Parliament. If he does so he will be judged and accorded whatever punishment is thought fit for a man who reneged on his promise not to take up arms against us again.'

'And that is your judgement?'

Cromwell's eyes were flinty. 'As God is my judge I shall treat with all those I am called upon to try with the same strict fairness. I may not always enjoy my duty, Nicolas, but I shall do it.'

A chill trickled down Nicolas's spine for he knew that his one-time friend had made up his mind. Charles Stuart would be found guilty and there was but one punishment for treachery . . .

'You are a little stronger today, Walter.' Elizabeth entered his room to see that he was sitting in the chair by the bed and held a book of poetry that she had left with him in his hands. 'I am happy to see you out of bed at last.'

Walter looked at her and smiled. 'Very much better thanks to the care you and Mistress Furnley have taken for me, Elizabeth. I have recovered the use of my arm, and I think that my leg improves. Perhaps by the spring I shall be able to go out again.'

'I pray for that every night, Walter.'

He nodded, his gaze emotional and deeply moved. 'I know that I have you to thank for my life for there was a time I might have died if you had not fought for me.'

'I would not have you die, husband.'

'Then I shall live,' he told her. 'And one day I shall be a proper husband to you, Elizabeth.'

'Nothing would please me more, Walter.' She handed him a letter that had come for her earlier. 'This is from Caroline. She says that Nicolas has gone to London and will witness the King's trial.'

'God protect and keep His Majesty,' Walter said. 'For I fear he will receive little justice . . .'

One hundred and thirty-five men had been called to be commissioners at the trial of their king, but some would not answer the call. Some came though in fear and trembling, knowing that to refuse put their own lives at risk, but some like Sir Thomas Fairfax, one of the greatest generals of the war, excused himself from the court.

For as he said, 'I did positively oppose Cromwell, Bradshaw and others who would have the trial go on the reasons that . . . the king could not be tried by that court.' When it was said to him that legal or not they would have the King's head, Fairfax told them that he could not stop them but would have no part of it.

Nicolas was one of the onlookers as the trial began that day, the twentieth of January 1649. Some of the commissioners looked sick, their faces waxen as they huddled in the gallery and watched Charles Stuart brought out. Voices in the crowd called out, some calling for the traitor to die, others – notably a woman – cried out that they should let His Majesty go and called for the blessing of God upon him. Her husband prodded her to silence, but others echoed the feeling she had voiced in a low murmuring.

Nicolas felt compelled to watch the King. His face was white but he had dressed immaculately and looked every inch the noble man, a king in truth as well as heritage. His dignity was such that Nicolas felt a stirring of anger that this should be happening. He had fought against bad laws, in the hope that Charles would be brought to a new understanding with his parliament and that there might be fairness for all.

What had they now? A body of vengeful, bigoted men that would rule as they saw fit and brook no opposition of their will.

The president had begun the proceedings, 'In that Charles Stuart, King of England, the commons of England assembled in Parliament being deeply sensible of the calamities that have been brought upon this nation . . .'

Nicolas listened as the charge droned on. It was true that the King bore a heavy responsibility for loss of life and bloodshed, but his was not the only hand to bear the stain.

A whisper went through the court as Charles touched Mr John Cook, solicitor for the Commonwealth, on his shoulder. The silver head of his cane fell to the floor and no one retrieved it, forcing Charles to do it himself. It could not be anything but an ominous sign, for if any of his judges had thought he might escape this trial they would not have allowed such a slight.

It was clear to Nicolas and to the King's friends that judgement had already been passed. A silence fell as the King began to speak.

'Now I would know by what authority, I mean lawful . . .' His Majesty's voice rang with its own authority, sending a chill through many that listened. 'I was brought hence and carried from place to place . . .' His eyes moved round the court and then continued, 'When I know what lawful authority I should answer. Remember I am your King, your lawful King, and what sins you bring upon your heads, and the judgement of God upon this land . . .' Was there any that could deny him in all justice? Nicolas thought not, but the King continued, 'In the meantime, I shall not betray my trust. I have a trust committed to me by God, by old and lawful descent; I will not betray it, to answer you a new unlawful authority, therefore resolve me that, and you shall hear more of me.'

Bradshaw valiantly defended the court's authority, but he was clearly nervous, his eyes looking from one side to another as if he were afraid of what he did. Men murmured and moved uneasily in their seats for the trial was clearly not lawful.

Attempts to make the King plead were made but he would not answer them unless they could show him how they were lawful when clearly they were not; they had taken the task upon themselves with no precedent and as such could be no more than tyrants bent on vengeance.

In the end, Bradshaw was unable to get a plea from the King and adjourned the court for a day.

Nicolas felt sickened as he left the court. What he had witnessed was a travesty of justice. These men had manipulated the commissioners so that they were bound to win the day whatever was said, and they would carry out their vile intent whether it was lawful or not.

'Can nothing be done to end this travesty?' Rupert asked when they dined that evening in the inn at which they had arranged to meet. 'Surely anyone can see that it is not justice?'

'They have a stranglehold on Parliament; besides, Ireton and Cromwell believe that what they are doing is the only way to end this – and perhaps in that they are right, though I would not have it so. I did not pledge my sword to this parliament, Rupert.'

'Would that we had fought harder when we had the chance,' Rupert said. 'We were full of such hope at the start, Nicolas. We failed him and the sin of this is upon us all.'

'You fought as best you could,' Nicolas said. 'I fought against you, but we have remained friends. What will you do now, my friend?'

'I shall go abroad,' Rupert said. 'I shall wait for the outcome of the trial, though my heart tells me that it will be an evil judgement – nevertheless I shall wait.'

'Then take good care not to be caught,' Nicolas warned him. 'I do not think you would receive much justice in that case – for my opinion is that there is none left in this land.'

His voice was bitter, as cold as the night, which had settled about them.

When the trial recommenced, the King argued that by trying him unlawfully they denied the proper course of law to the people of England, for if they could take such arbitrary action against their King there would be little justice for the common man.

Nicolas felt himself more in agreement with the King at this time than he had ever been, and his sense of anger and injustice grew as the trial continued.

It was a matter of law that was being discussed and the King's arguments so rattled his prosecutor that he looked to the gallery for help. Charles was an able orator and it was clear that he had good argument against the authority of the court, for in law they had none. Driven to desperation the Lord President refused the King permission to deliver an eloquent speech he had prepared on his theological and legal objections; he was refused permission to speak on such matters and the court proceeded to examine witnesses. When the answers required by his judges were given without chance for cross-examination, forty-five commissioners retired to deliberate on their verdict and the inevitable sentence.

On the twenty-seventh of that month Nicolas was back at Westminster Hall to hear the judgement, and when it was given the King asked that he might be allowed to speak.

'You are not to be heard after the sentence.'

'No, sir?' asked the King in disbelief.

'No, sir, by your favour, sir. Guard withdraw your prisoner.'

'I may speak after sentence. By your favour, sir, I may speak after sentence, ever. By your favour – hold. The sentence, sir – I say, sir – I am not suffered to speak. Expect what justice other people will have.'

Nicolas heard the denial of justice in horror. To what depths had these people sunk in their desperation to be rid of their king? He watched as the King was hustled from the court, still demanding to be heard.

Nicolas followed, feeling compelled to watch as His Majesty was taken through the streets where hostile crowds had gathered to jeer at him. The thing that struck him most was the King's manner, which was serene and that of a wronged martyr.

What did these fools imagine they were doing? Nicolas found it incomprehensible, for to execute the King without justice being seen to be done would be to make him a martyr, and as such he would live in the minds of men forever.

The execution warrant was signed though not all the commissioners could be brought to put their names to such a document. Nicolas spent the night before the planned execution with Rupert. They spoke little, drinking more than was their wont, numbed by the awful feeling of helplessness that had overtaken them. It seemed impossible even now that such a vile act could come to pass.

'I never thought they would do it,' Rupert said. 'I believed that at the last they would draw back.'

'You know not the kind of men who rule us now,' Nicolas said. 'I have lost all faith in their justice.'

'I would not know them if I might,' Rupert replied, a little drunk. He stood unsteadily. 'I am for my bed for I would not miss the morrow. I shall be present to see murder done.'

Nicolas nodded but said nothing. Rupert had spoken truly, for without a just trial it was nothing but murder. The commissioners had determined to kill a king, and nothing would have stopped their intent.

The morning was fiercely cold. Nicolas wrapped warmly in a heavy coat and his cloak over, for he knew that he might be standing for some time if he were to be near enough to witness the execution. He was determined to watch it so that he might bear witness to the evil deed if it were ever asked of him.

It was past the middle of the day, perhaps something after half past one in the afternoon when the King made his last journey from the Palace of St James along Whitehall to Banqueting House, which had seen happier days for him. Guards lined the way, but behind them the press of both men and women was heavy, for it seemed that like Nicolas they were compelled to watch the most unhappy sight that their country had ever witnessed.

On all sides voices called to His Majesty, calling for God's blessing upon him, and weeping. It was clear that the King heard them but he gave no sign, seeming cheerful and unafraid. Some noticed that he wore only his shirt under his cloak, but did not shiver despite the cold. The crowd was respectful and even his guards seemed to be suffering under the task that had been put upon them.

When the King stepped out onto his scaffold there was a gasp that seemed to come from every throat, as if it was unbearable to see such a noble man brought so low. Women could be heard weeping, men whispering prayers as though they feared that God might take his vengeance on them for merely standing by.

Nicolas took in the scene, which seemed imprinted into his mind. The scaffold was hung round with black, and the axe and block lay in the middle of the square. Foot soldiers and cavalry officers were packed about the scaffold as if they feared that an attempt to rescue the King would be made even now. People pressed closer and Nicolas thought that if enough of them broke through the barriers he would be amongst those who sought to snatch the King, but despite the growing horror amongst those who watched, the surge did not come.

The executioners had hidden their faces for fear of retribution, but others stood boldly, cloaked only in their self-righteous certainty. And then at last, Charles was allowed to speak.

It was difficult to hear his words, for no one was allowed near enough but Nicolas was able to pick out some passages of his speech. He blamed Parliament for the troubles that had fallen on their nation.

'I think it my duty to God first, and to my country, for to clear myself both as an honest man, a good king and a good Christian. I shall begin first with my innocence . . .'

His speech went on for some while and after he asked that the two houses of parliament should be exonerated of guilt for ill instruments between them had been the chief cause of misunderstanding. After this he came to accept that he too had been at fault, most shamefully by acceding to the execution of the Earl of Strafford.

He asserted that the health and prosperity of his subjects had been his chief concern as their King and went on to state his commitment to the Protestant religion and the Church of England.

'In truth, sirs, my conscience in religion, I think is very well known to the world and therefore I declare before you all, that I die a Christian according to the profession of the Church of England as I found it left to me by my father and this honest man I think will witness it.'

His speech finished, His Majesty spoke to the executioner. His nightcap was brought so that he might tuck his hair inside it. Bishop Juxon spoke to him but Nicolas was unable to catch the words. However, he heard the King's answer clearly.

'I go from a corruptible to an incorruptible Crown where no disturbance can be.'

The Bishop replied, 'You are exchanged from a temporal to an eternal Crown, a good exchange.'

The King took off his cloak and his Garter insignia, giving this to Bishop Juxon with some words that Nicolas could not quite hear about the prince, meaning his eldest son. After this the King knelt and laid his head on the block, and after a short prayer stretched out his hands. The executioner brought down his axe and with a skilful blow severed his head from his body.

Nicolas had been prepared for it but it made him recoil and a bitter sickness rise in his throat. A sigh issued from every throat but afterwards the crowd was silent as if they could not believe what they had witnessed. For some minutes they stood in uneasy silence before they began to drift away, and from the stunned looks on almost every face, Nicolas knew that they felt as he did – that a terrible crime had been done that day in their name.

He turned to look at Rupert standing by his side and saw that tears were on his face, and feeling the cold on his cheeks he put up his hand to discover that he too was crying.

'I never liked Charles Stuart as well as this day,' he said to Rupert. 'I shall not forget how bravely he went to his death.'

'He was a noble man,' Rupert said. 'In God's truth I know this to be a cursed land and what its people suffer now is judgement upon them.'

Nicolas did not answer.

'Farewell, my friend,' Nicolas said as they stood on the harbour. The wind was biting cold and it was night. The French ship would leave with the tide. 'This has been a bitter day and one we shall not easily forget – but I wish you well for the future and hope that you may find some happiness in life.'

'I wish you health and happiness,' Rupert replied. 'Give my love to Caroline, and tell her not to worry for my sake. I shall find my way and perhaps one day I may return.'

'We shall pray for it, Rupert.'

'I know that you will care for my daughter. I leave her with an easy heart for I know she could not be in safer hands and my life would not be suitable for a child. I dare say I shall be often on the move. Tell Caroline not to expect a letter from me, though I may send a present sometimes for Angelica.'

'Write if you can,' Nicolas urged. 'For your parents as well as Caroline's sake.'

'If I can,' Rupert replied and offered his hand. 'I am glad I was there, Nicolas. I think the story of this day will be told and told again, but I am glad to have witnessed it for myself.'

'And I,' Nicolas said. 'Already the whispers start but we know the truth.'

'They think they have bought peace by the blood they shed,' Rupert said. 'But they forget he has a son – and one day that son will take back his father's crown.'

'Perhaps.' Nicolas clasped his hand. 'God be with you. The bell tolls. I think it is time you went on board.'

'God be with you and yours.'

Nicolas watched until Rupert was safely on board the ship, and then he turned away. It was time that he went home to Caroline.

Thirteen

It was spring at last. The winter had seemed long and cheerless, a shadow hanging over their lives. Nicolas had worn it as a cloak when he returned from London, and she knew that he had wrestled with his conscience, wondering where it had all gone so badly wrong.

Caroline felt the warmth of the sun, welcoming it with all her heart, though she regretted the traditions lost. There would be no maypole this year, nor would the young folk go a-maying for it was considered a sinful practice that might lead to wantonness. All the old country traditions were being suppressed, which led to murmuring and discontent amongst the people.

She was sorry for the new order that seemed intent on taking the joy from people's lives, though in truth most of the new laws did not affect her greatly. She had been happy to have her husband home safely and to learn that her brother had got safely away to France.

'I do not intend to visit London for some time,' Nicolas had told her when they were talking before their parlour fire that first night. 'What I witnessed sickened me, Caroline. It was not a trial for there was no justice in it. They intended his death no matter what, though I think in the end few took joy in it. I would not lie in their beds for their consciences must torment them.'

'But you must not let it torment you,' Caroline said. 'You fought for your beliefs which were honest and true – and you do not share the blame of Charles Stuart's murderers.'

'You must not speak so freely to any but me,' Nicolas

warned her. 'We live beneath an iron hand, Caroline, and we must go carefully. If they dealt with a king so arbitrarily what think you they would do to the likes of us?'

Caroline knew that he was right, and she was careful never to let anyone hear her speak of these things, but despite the strictures placed upon their lives, she had found that she was happy. Her body had healed and with it her spirit. She had come to accept that she would have no more children.

At first she had felt like weeping, but then she began to realize how lucky she was. She had a husband she adored and three wonderful children; they were not all of her body, but she loved them equally.

Claire was a sweet loving child who caused her little trouble. She was content to sit on her mother's lap and laughed when Hal teased her, as he did endlessly. Caroline seldom found it necessary to reprimand him for he loved his sister.

One day they would have to explain to Hal that Claire was his cousin and not his sister, but there was time enough in the future. Angelica was often quiet. She sat and watched the others playing, her big blue eyes wide with wonder as she watched Hal at his play. Caroline thought that she looked very like her mother, but she was not wilful and seemed to accept her place in the hierarchy. Hal came first of course, then Claire and then Angelica.

It was not deliberate on Caroline's part, for she often nursed both the girls together, and they both had their nurses, but it seemed to happen that Hal's boldness and charm placed him first, and that the two little girls tagged after him, toddling unsteadily in his wake as they began to walk. Angelica's first word was Hal, though Claire said Mumma and Dadda, graduating to Hal only as she added more words to her vocabulary.

Now that the warmer weather had come they spent more time out of doors for Caroline believed that the fresh air did them good. She liked to spend time with them, watching them play, guiding them as they learned to negotiate their way about the gardens.

It was on a particularly warm day in May that Nicolas came home from visiting a tenant and found his wife and the children sitting on rugs on the grass close to the rose garden. Her green gown spread out like a silken bell about her, her hair free of the cap she often wore and nestling upon her shoulders.

He stood watching for a while unbeknown to her, hearing her laughter and the laughter of the children, and the ice melted from about his heart. Finally, he could put the shame he had experienced that day at Whitehall behind him and accept that there was nothing he could have done to change the course of history; he was just an ordinary man who was extraordinarily fortunate to have such a wife and family.

'Nicolas?' Caroline had turned and seen him. She held out her hand to him, beckoning to him to join them. He went to her and squatted on the rug beside her, watching as Hal patiently threw a ball to Claire. The little girl dropped it more often than she caught it, but when she did her laughter was so beautiful that everyone smiled.

'He is so patient with her,' Caroline said. 'He loves to tease her, but he is never careless or hurtful to her . . .' She broke off as Hal threw the ball at Angelica and knocked her down. 'Careful, Hal, she is only a little girl.'

'She doesn't know how to catch,' Hal said and came running. 'Come and play with us, Father. Angelica is silly and Claire has had enough of playing catch.'

'I shall play with you in a moment,' Nicolas said. 'I want to talk to your mother for a while.' He turned to her, smiling as she lifted her face to the sun, clearly enjoying its warmth. 'Do you know how beautiful you are?'

'Flatterer,' Caroline said, a naughty light in her eyes. 'We have been married too many years for you to court me, Nicolas.'

'My love only grows stronger with the years,' he told her. 'You are better now, Caroline – and happy I think?'

'Of course I am happy. I am always happy when I have

you and the children, Nicolas. And we have been blessed. We have three lovely children to love and care for.'

'Yes,' he said. 'We have our own Claire, Angelica – and Hal. He may not be of our making but I love him as I would my own son. He shall be our heir, Caroline. I have asked my lawyer to come to Thornberry so that I may make my wishes known. It must be set down properly. I shall adopt him for otherwise he would not be safe. I have distant cousins who might claim the title if I neglected to do what is necessary.'

'Yes, you must do it, Nicolas,' Caroline said. 'I have accepted that I shall not have another child. We must make Hal safe for the future . . .' Her gaze narrowed as she looked at him. 'I suppose you have heard nothing of Rowena's child?'

'A fair will come to St Ives next month,' Nicolas said. 'It is my intention to make inquiries amongst the gypsies then. Perhaps we may learn something – though I wonder if it would be wiser to let things lie.'

'I know you doubt the wisdom of finding the boy,' Caroline said. 'But I feel that it would be wrong to ignore his existence. We owe it to Harry to do what we can for the boy, even if it is only to give him some property that he may inherit when he is older. Sometimes I have foreboding for the future and it concerns that lad.'

'I have given you my word,' Nicolas said. 'I shall do what I can – but if Rowena is determined not to be found my search may fail.'

'Yes, I understand.' They sat in silence for a moment, and then, 'I had a letter from Elizabeth today,' Caroline said. 'She has invited us to visit them this summer. She says that Walter is much better. He can walk a little now, but is not yet well enough to travel long distances. What would you have me answer her?'

'You must do as you wish,' Nicolas said. 'I dare say you would like to see her. Write and make arrangements if you will – and now I must go and play ball with our son for he is becoming a little too boisterous for the girls . . .'

* * *

Elizabeth watched as Walter negotiated the stairs, taking them very carefully, leaning on Mistress Furnley, who was guiding and encouraging him. She had done wonders with him, for he responded to her far more than he would have done to Elizabeth. He respected her for her knowledge and the healing cures she had made for him, which had brought him thus far. And now he was beginning to regain the proper use of his arm and legs.

He gave Elizabeth a smile of triumph when he reached the hall and found her waiting for him. 'There, it is done, though I am not certain I can climb back up again.'

'You will if you take your time,' Elizabeth told him. 'I am happy to see you so much better, Walter. In a few days you may be able to take a turn about the gardens with me.'

'When I can ride my estate and see what neglect has occurred I shall be better pleased,' he told her with a frown. 'But I have taken the first step towards becoming a man again, Elizabeth. I pray God it will not be the last.'

'I am sure it will not,' she said for she understood what he meant. He had hinted once or twice recently that he would like to share her bed again, and she knew that it would happen soon. 'And now I have some news that I think will please you, my love.'

'Sir James has found us a new Vicar I hope?'

'I believe he expects the next incumbent to arrive shortly,' Elizabeth said. 'But that was not my news. Caroline and Nicolas are to come and visit us next week and they will bring the children with them.'

'You will be pleased to see your friend again, and your cousin's child?'

'Yes, I shall be pleased to see all of them, Walter. Caroline was very good to me when Sarah died, and of course I shall enjoy having the children here – all of them.'

'You would like children of your own I dare say?'

'If God sees fit to bless us,' Elizabeth said and smiled at him. She held her hand out to him. 'Come and sit with me, dearest. And do not look so uncertain – of course I shall welcome you to my bed when you feel able to seek it. And I very much hope that we shall have children in time.'

'So you really have forgiven me?'

'I think the question is whether you have been able to forgive me, Walter.'

'I have already told you it is so.'

'Then we shall not speak of this again. We are fortunate that you have made such a good recovery.'

'We owe much to Mistress Furnley. It was a fortunate thing that she could come to us, Elizabeth. She has helped me in many ways.'

'Yes, she has.' Elizabeth reflected that a stranger seeing them together might almost think them man and wife, but she knew that Walter saw the older woman only as his nurse. She could not doubt his love for her, because he had shown it in many ways since his illness, and in truth she had become fond of him. There were moments when her spirit rebelled from this quiet existence and she longed to be with Rupert, to travel and laugh and take delight in loving, but she controlled them beneath a demure manner. And when she was restless she went for long walks until her spirit eased. 'We owe her much, Walter.'

'Will you read to me, Elizabeth?' he asked. 'No one reads as you do, my dear. To hear your voice refreshes me and it would please me if you would choose something from that book of poetry you had the other day.'

'Poetry, Walter?' She was a little surprised for his usual choice was the Bible.

'Yes, Elizabeth, poetry. I have not forgot all the pleasures of life, even though I abide by the doctrine that is given us by our new masters. I fought for King Charles and loved him well – but he was a stubborn man and would not bend. God rest his soul.'

'I told you that Nicolas was there, didn't I? Caroline said he was haunted by it for some months after he returned home, but she believes that he is feeling better at last.'

'It is well that they are to visit us,' Walter said. 'It will do us good to mix with friends again, my love – and now, please read me one of your poems . . .'

'You look well, Elizabeth,' Caroline said as they sat together in the gardens. The roses were in full bloom and the scent was wonderful, borne on a refreshing breeze that made the heat bearable. 'Are you happy, my dear?'

'Happy?' Elizabeth thought for a moment, and then, 'I believe that happiness for me would be a child, Caroline. Walter loves me and though our marriage was . . . difficult at first, it is much better now. I care for him but to be truly happy I would be a mother.'

'Walter is stronger now, isn't he? There is a chance that you may resume . . . that you will be given the happiness you seek?'

'Yes, I believe so in time,' Elizabeth told her with a smile. It had not happened yet but she believed it would not be long, and she knew that she would welcome the change. She had made up her mind to take what pleasure she could of her marriage, and being a passionate woman it would be no hardship to accept her husband's attentions. 'But that is in God's hands for it is not given to all of us to have all that we would desire.'

'No, indeed; I hoped to give Nicolas a son but I know now that it is impossible.'

'Oh, Caroline,' Elizabeth cried and blushed. 'How thoughtless of me! I did not think what I said . . . forgive me. I did not mean to hurt you.'

'There is nothing to forgive,' Caroline assured her. 'It was painful for a while but I have accepted it now. Besides, I have been blessed. I have Claire and Angelica for the time being, though she must go to Rupert if and when he returns, and of course Hal is Nicolas's heir. We have adopted him to be certain that he cannot lose the title or the estate to a distant cousin.'

'That was well done of Nicolas,' Elizabeth said and frowned. 'Do you think Rupert will ever come home?'

'There is little chance of it at the moment for the mood

of the people is against it,' Caroline told her, 'but we hope that things will change one day. Nicolas still has influence if he chooses to use it, though for the moment he prefers not to have anything to do with men he once called friends.'

'He is still angry about the King's trial and execution?'

'I do not think he will ever forget or forgive what he sees as a travesty of justice. Nicolas fought for justice and equality, for the liberty of every man to live as he chooses within a fair and just law. He believes that the world has turned upside down since the King's execution, and that his ideals have been forgotten. He feels justly angry.'

'But is it not so that Cromwell himself hath turned against the Levellers? He crushed their mutiny and imprisoned their leader, did he not?'

'Yes, that is true, and Nicolas received a letter from him; it was written at length explaining his views. I think it went some way to reconciling them, and I believe that Cromwell may have begun to realize what a monster they have created – but for the moment there is little we can do but abide by the laws they have made for us.'

Hal's voice called to them and they saw him running towards them, his face alight with excitement. He had been exploring and a rather ragged looking dog followed at his heels.

'Where did that creature come from?' Caroline asked feeling horrified. Its coat was filthy and matted and she suspected that it would have fleas. 'It is a mangy beast. Send it away at once.'

'It is hungry and lonely,' Hal said giving her a wheedling look that had worked wonders in the past. 'He needs a bath and his coat brushing. But most of all he needs feeding – someone to look after him. If I send him away he may die.'

'Hal . . .' Caroline said, but she was not proof against the longing in his face. She laughed for he would have his way as ever. 'Very well, take it to the stables and ask one of your father's grooms to give it a bath, and you may beg some scraps from Elizabeth's kitchen if she permits?'

'Yes, of course,' Elizabeth said, for the child was beautiful and pulled at her heartstrings. 'Run along then, Hal, and tell my cook that I said she should give you the mutton bone that was left from last night's supper.'

'Thank you, Mama – thank you, Mistress Benedict.' Hal bestowed a smile of such sweetness upon them that they laughed together as he ran off.

'Sometimes I do not know whether he be angel or devil,' Caroline admitted. 'I swear he could charm the birds from the trees, Elizabeth – but I do not see badness in him. He is not selfish like his father, though at times a little thoughtless.'

'He is but a child, Caroline,' Elizabeth said. 'I dare say you spoil him but I know Nicolas keeps him in line. Given discipline I imagine he will grow to be a true man and learn by your example.'

'Harry was thoughtless and selfish,' Caroline told her. 'He seduced my cousin Mercy Harris with promises of marriage. I am sure she would never have given herself to him otherwise, and when he left her alone and with child she was so ashamed that she ran away from us. She returned only when her child was due and begged me to care for him.'

'Which you have done as if he were your own child,' Elizabeth said and frowned. 'You said that Harry was careless and thoughtless – is it possible that he had another child?'

Caroline stared at her. 'Why do you ask that?'

'I once saw a gypsy boy that looked much like Hal . . .'

'Where? Nicolas has searched for him everywhere but so far no one seems to have heard of or seen him. When the fair came to St Ives last month Nicolas's agent made inquiries but there was no news of him.'

'I dare say the gypsies might be afraid to speak, they are secretive people I understand,' Elizabeth said. 'It was when we were going to London once and a child ran alongside of the coach. I gave him a gold sovereign and I thought how like Hal he was . . .'

'You did not tell me, Elizabeth.'

'You told me not to waste my money,' Elizabeth said. 'And I thought it all my imagination – but do you think he was your brother-in-law's child?'

'I have thought it,' Caroline admitted. 'It worries me, Elizabeth. I like not to think of a child of Harry's being brought up in such ways. If we could have found him I would have begged Nicolas to do something for him – perhaps give him property or put him with foster parents who would raise him properly.'

'You would not have adopted him as you have Hal?'

'I do not think it would be possible now.' Caroline frowned for she felt cold of a sudden as if an icy wind had blown over her. 'Hal is Nicolas's heir and yet Rowena's child is the elder.'

'Yes, I see,' Elizabeth said. 'That is difficult for they are both illegitimate and if the gypsy boy is the elder . . .'

Caroline nodded. 'Nicolas has accepted Hal because he was my cousin's son, and he believes that Harry might have married her if he had lived – but Rowena was . . . well, she was not of good birth nor was Harry her only lover. Nicolas would never put her son in Hal's place, but if we could find him I could persuade him to do something for the boy.'

'I wish that I had told you that day,' Elizabeth said, 'but it did not seem important.'

'How could you know?' Caroline said and smiled at her. 'Besides, it may be that I was mistaken – perhaps the child merely looked like Harry . . .'

Yet in her mind she knew that the boy existed and something made her fear for the future. The pictures in her mind came only at night as dreams and were vague, and yet they worried her.

She looked up as Nicolas and Captain Benedict walked towards them across the smooth lawns. 'Ah, here comes your husband and mine, Elizabeth. I believe they have finished their business, whatever it might have been, and are ready to join us at last.'

* * *

Hal was nine years and a few months old that spring morning when he walked into the woods at Thornberry in search of wild flowers to pick for his mother. He was feeling very happy for his father had given him a magnificent sword the previous day. It had belonged to Harry, his father's brother, who had once been Lord Mortimer.

His father had tried to explain to him that he was not Claire's brother but her cousin, and that though he was now his father's son he had once been the son of Harry. It was all rather strange, but Hal had accepted it because his mother and father had told him that they loved him and that he was the heir to Thornberry.

Hal did not mind if Claire was his cousin rather than his sister for it meant that he could marry her when they were old enough. He loved Claire with a fierce protective love that had manifested itself when she was born and his father was often away from home. His mother had told him he must love and protect his sister, who was now his cousin, and he had from that first moment.

He liked Angelica but she was silly, and she stared at him with her big eyes when he pushed her or said something unkind, and then he felt awful because he knew that he had hurt her. His mother said that he must be kind to his cousin, but he did not always want to be kind to her. Something about her irritated him and he did not love her as he loved Claire.

At his heels trotted the dog he called Rags. He was still an unattractive creature, always ravenously hungry, but devoted to Hal and the other children. Hal had told Claire that she might pet him when she wished, but Angelica was only allowed to do so when Hal was in a sunny mood, which was most of the time but not always. He was becoming aware of a temper inside him that could flare suddenly and might come out as harsh words or perhaps a hard push, especially when it was directed at Angelica. She was such an irritating girl and she followed him around all the time. No matter how fast he walked she kept following and that annoyed him. She had followed him when he came out this morning, but he hoped that he had managed to shake her off when he entered the woods. Angelica was afraid of the woods – but then, she was afraid of a lot of things. Silly girl!

Why could she not be more like Claire? Claire never sought his attention, though she was always delighted when he played with her, which was why he thought that he would marry her one day.

Hal halted as he caught the scent of wood smoke. Someone had lit a fire in the woods. His father had forbidden the villagers to light fires here because they could do damage unless they were properly controlled.

As he came into the clearing, he saw that a gypsy caravan had camped there. A horse was tethered a little way from the van and dogs were tied to the wheels; a woman sitting before the fire was stirring a large black pot from which issued a delicious smell.

'What are you doing here?'

Hal was startled by the voice, which came from behind him. He swung round to see a boy of much his own age perched in the branches of a tree, looking down at him.

'These are my father's woods,' Hal replied, annoyed by the other's impudent tone. Anyone might think he was the lord's son rather than a gypsy trespasser! 'I might ask what you are doing here. And you are not supposed to have a fire – it could cause damage.'

'Do you think we are fools?' The boy jumped down. He was several inches taller than Hal and broader in the shoulder. His eyes were blue, very like Hal's own, though that thought did not occur to him, but his hair was tousled and dull with grease and dirt. His hands and face were dirty too. 'We know how to live in the woods and we shall not damage them – especially these woods.'

'Why these woods in particular?' Hal stared at him. 'Who are you?'

'My name is Jared,' the other boy said and smiled oddly. 'I know who you are. Your name is Hal Mortimer and you live at the house back there.' He jerked his head in the direction Hal had come.

'My father owns the house and all the land around here,' Hal said grandly. 'One day it will all belong to me.'

'It is not yours or his,' Jared said and his eyes narrowed. His fists clenched at his sides as if he would challenge Hal to a fight, and he looked angry. 'It belonged to . . .'

'Jared, what are you doing?' The woman sitting by the fire got up and came towards them. She stared at Hal, her eyes narrowed and angry. 'Come away,' she ordered the boy. 'Now is not the time.'

'Why not?' Jared demanded, looking at her fiercely. 'Why should I not tell him now?'

'Because I said so,' the woman said and aimed a blow at his head. Jared ducked and avoided her but she moved towards him, managing to hit him this time and he gave a howl of pain, then ran off towards the caravan. The woman looked at Hal, reached out and grabbed his arm, her fingers digging deep into his arm. Rags growled, his bristles raised, teeth bared. 'Go away from here,' the woman said. 'And call that creature off before I kill it.'

'Rags would kill you,' Hal said, afraid of her but not willing to show it. 'Leave go of me, woman. My father is Lord Mortimer and he will have you put in chains if you attack me or my dog.'

'I'll curse the brute and you,' Rowena muttered. 'Take it away now and don't come back here if you care for it.'

Hal caught the dog by the scruff of its neck as he backed away from her. Her eyes were strange and she frightened him, but he stuck to his ground, refusing to show fear in the face of her threats.

'You are dirty and you smell nasty,' he told her. 'You have no right to be here and I shall tell my father. He will send you away.'

She muttered something under her breath, but Hal continued to face her until she turned away and went back to her cooking pot.

He walked back the way he had come until the clearing was left behind and then he began to run. He ran all the way home and was out of breath when he went into the house. His mother was in her parlour, sitting with his Aunt Elizabeth, who had come to stay and brought her tiny daughter with her. They were both at their sewing and he remembered that he had gone to pick flowers for his mother, but it did not matter because she smiled as she saw him and beckoned him to come to her.

'Have you been running?'

'Yes.' It was on the tip of Hal's tongue to tell her about the boy and the strange woman in the woods, but then he changed his mind. The woman had frightened him and he could not forget that she had threatened to curse both him and Rags. 'I ran all the way home to you because I thought you might be worried about me.'

'I should have been if you had been much longer,' Caroline said and ruffled his hair. 'I know you fear nothing, Hal, but it is always best to take one of the grooms with you when you go into the woods. Sometimes, gypsies camp there. Most of them are harmless enough, but they take your father's game and if they are caught in the act they might turn nasty. So until you are old enough to protect yourself, it might be better if you took one of the grooms with you, my dearest.'

'I shall take my sword,' Hal said. 'Then no one will dare to attack me. I shall protect you and Claire, Mama. No one will be allowed to harm you.'

Caroline laughed. 'You left Angelica behind, Hal. She came back crying because she dare not follow you deep into the woods.'

'She is a baby,' Hal said scornfully. 'She doesn't know how to play proper games and she cannot run or climb trees as Claire does.

'Yes, perhaps she is a little nervous,' Caroline said. 'But you will remember what I said about being kind to her, dearest?'

'Yes, Mama, of course I shall,' Hal said.

As he left his mother to seek his cousin and Claire, who had been his sister but was now his cousin, he was thinking that he would return to the woods the next day with a groom. He would order the impudent boy and the woman from his lands, and show them who was in charge here. It gave him a glow of pride to think that he could order them as he wished, but the next moment he was regretting that he had not had more time to talk to the boy. All his cousins were girls and he longed for a boy of his own age to run and play with sometimes. He was excited at the thought of seeing the gypsy again.

However, when he returned to the woods the next morning, all that was left was a small burned patch on the ground where the fire had been. He had a feeling of disappointment, because though the woman had frightened him, he had secretly liked the boy. It would have been nice to have a friend he could meet in the woods.

He picked a large bunch of bluebells for his mother as he returned home, and he wondered who the boy was and what he had been going to tell him before the woman came to stop him.

Perhaps they would return to the woods one day. It would be best if the boy came alone, Hal thought, for he had not liked the woman. Her black eyes had frightened him.

However, he forgot them as he took the flowers to his mother and she gave him some of her sweetmeats in return. It did not really matter about the boy or the strange woman. He knew that he belonged here and that one day all that his father owned would be his. Then he would marry Claire and be lord of the manor. He smiled at the thought. Everything was just as it ought to be.